HORSE DREAMS

BOOK ONE

Memories

of a

dirt road

town

Other Books by Stephen Bly

Fortunes of the Black Hills series

Book #1: *Beneath a Dakota Cross*
Book #2: *Shadow of Legends*
Book #3: *The Long Trail Home*
Book #4: *Friends and Enemies*
Book #5: *Last of the Texas Camp*
Book #6: *The Next Roundup*

Contemporary Novel

Paperback Writer

For information on other books by this author, write:
Stephen Bly
Winchester, Idaho 83555
or check out his Web site at
www.blybook.com

Stephen Bly

AWARD WINNING AUTHOR OF

THE FORTUNES OF THE BLACK HILLS SERIES

HORSE DREAMS
BOOK ONE

Memories

of a

dirt road

town

BROADMAN
& HOLMAN
PUBLISHERS

NASHVILLE, TENNESSEE

Published by Broadman & Holman Publishers
Nashville, Tennessee

ISBN-10: 0-8054-3171-3
ISBN-13: 978-0-8054-3171-1

Dewey Decimal Classification: F
Subject Heading: FORGIVENESS—FICTION

1 2 3 4 5 6 7 8   10 09 08 07 06 05

DEDICATION

for the girl
with the
awesome smile
who
sat behind me
in my freshman
English class
Redwood High School
1958

1

You dripped orange Popsicle all over your shirt, Devy-girl." The boy in the short-sleeve blue gingham shirt sat straight up in the saddle, his crisp straw cowboy hat pulled almost down to his eyes.

"I prefer to think of it as a modern-art field of poppies." Develyn kicked the flanks of her horse. He began to trot. "Besides, Brownie doesn't mind."

The boy raced up alongside her. "He's a horse. He's color-blind."

Develyn stuck out her narrow, pointed tongue at her twin brother. "Who cares?" She studied the rolling prairie ahead of them. "Are you sure it's OK to ride north? I think we're lost."

"Mr. Homer said we could ride any direction, as long as we don't leave a gate open or cross a blacktop road. We haven't seen either of those in weeks. We are not lost. All we have to do is turn around and follow our trail back." He serpentined his horse around the gray sagebrush.

"Even if we are lost, Brownie can lead us home. He's the smartest horse in North America." Develyn paused. "Dewayne, I don't want to go home. Do you?"

"Yeah. I haven't played baseball in two weeks."

"Well, I'm coming back," she insisted as she caught up with him.

He turned and rested his hand on the back of the saddle. "When?"

She held her upturned nose even higher. "Next summer."

"Yeah, right. Next summer we're goin' to visit Grandma and Grandpa in Wisconsin."

"Then the summer after that. I'm coming back, Dewa . . . I really am."

"I believe you, Sis. You're as stubborn as . . ."

"Mama?"

"Maybe not that stubborn. I'll race you to that stand of trees down there. One . . . two . . . three . . ."

The crack of the lightning bolt came as if on cue. They galloped toward the small stand of cottonwoods. Thunder rolled all the way to the trees.

"I won!" Develyn shouted.

"I let you," Dewayne declared.

"You did not!"

"A boy is supposed to let the girl win."

"Why?"

"I don't know. It's the rules."

"But I won fair and square."

"Your field of modern-art poppies is getting wet. It's going to rain really hard."

"It better not."

Dewayne brushed drops of water from his dusty face. "What are you goin' to do about it?"

She shook her fist at the sky. "Don't you dare rain on me! Do you hear me, clouds? I've had enough of this. You stop it right now!"

The clouds ripped open, and a Noahian deluge collapsed on top of them.

      ● ● ●

Warm water blasted Develyn's face. She cupped it in her hands and washed her eyes, then turned off the shower. She reached past the cream-colored plastic curtain and grabbed an oversized cream-colored fluffy bath towel.

She was dry when she heard a car pull up in the gravel driveway, and almost dressed when a voice rang out from the adjoining bedroom. "Latte delivery service."

"Yes! You are a lifesaver, Lily. I'll be right out."

"Take your time, Dev, I had them make it extra hot. Say, I do believe your alarm clock's broken."

Develyn Worrell poked her petite blonde head out of the walk-in closet and eyed the woman standing next to the queen-sized bed. "Yes. I'm afraid it's permanently stuck on twenty-one minutes after midnight."

The shorter woman with black and gray wavy hair studied the cracked glass of the round brass alarm clock. "Why do you keep it?"

Develyn padded over and retrieved a beverage in a tall green cup that steamed on the dresser. "Lily, it's the only thing I saved from the bedroom at my old house." She meandered back into the walk-in closet.

The woman wearing black jeans and a pale green blouse tossed the clock into the open duffle bag. "Dev, explain this to me: the clock doesn't work, yet you take it with you?"

Barefoot, Develyn Worrell scooted out into the bedroom, her shoulder draped by a blue dress on a hanger. "It's a reminder of what I want to forget."

Lily Martin pulled her silver-framed glasses down on her nose and peered over the lenses. "Ms. Worrell, that doesn't make any sense."

"Mentally unstable women don't need to make any sense. It's one of the privileges of our lot." Develyn flopped the dress on the bed and spun back toward the closet. As she walked, she tugged at the back of her blue jeans that rode low on her narrow hips.

Lily followed her to the doorway that led to the master bath, as well as the walk-in closet. "Dev Worrell, you are not mentally unstable."

4

Develyn jabbed her hand into the crammed rack of clothes. "How does this pink blouse look? Is it too youthful?"

Lily Martin surveyed the pink, short-sleeve, scooped necked T-shirt with lavender outlined stars trailed across it. "A size six anything looks darling on you, Dev. In over twenty years, I have never seen you look anything but cute and classy."

"Ms. Martin, you always make me feel good."

"And you, Ms. Worrell, always make me feel old and dumpy."

"You are only a few years older than me."

"That might be, but on more than one occasion I've been mistaken for your mother."

"Then, I'm your unstable, coming-apart-at-the-seams daughter."

"That's nonsense, Dev. You just might be the most together woman in Montgomery County. Unknown to most in the community, you've almost singlehandedly held together Riverbend Elementary School for over twenty years. Your incredible stability and strength of character have survived six principals and four superintendents, several of which would have pushed anyone else over the edge."

Develyn shoved a curling iron and a tall fuchsia bottle of shampoo at Lily. "Toss these in for me." Her gray-green eyes bounced around the nearly bare walls of the off-white bedroom. "Five superintendents, if you count Frederick LaClaire."

Lily chuckled. "I had forgotten about good ol' Frederick. I suppose that any man who shows up drunk and makes a pass at Miss Chambers before school starts on his first day at work is not easily remembered as a superintendent of schools."

Develyn exited the bathroom, with an olive green and brown plaid towel and solid brown washcloth. "Betty Chambers certainly remembers him."

Lily rearranged six ruffled floral pillows at the head of the bed. "Dev, you are the finest fifth-grade teacher I have ever worked with."

"Thank you, dear Lily, now tell that to mother." Develyn circled the bed to pull the floor-length curtains on the large window, blocking out most of the early June sunlight.

Lily studied a medium-sized black cat with white paws as it perched in the doorway to the living room and yawned. "Your mother said you were unstable?"

Dev plucked up a small blue glass heart-shaped bottle from the huge oak dresser and opened the lid. "From the first day three years ago, when I said I was divorcing Spencer, I have been a failure in her eyes. 'A family embarrassment,' I believe were her words." She sniffed the perfume, then held it over to Lily. "If I only take one fragrance, should this be the one?"

"Anything called *Melancholy Moments* must be right for you," the older woman shrugged.

"It's not the name but the fragrance that matters." Dev put the blue bottle down.

Lily studied the top of the dresser, then plucked up a white frosted, opaque bottle with a brass lid. "In that case, take this one." She shoved it toward Develyn's hand.

Dev refused to take it. "I will not go on a trip with a perfume called *Wander Lust.*"

"It's not the name but the fragrance," Lily mimicked as she sniffed the perfume. "It smells very nice."

Develyn yanked the perfume out of Lily's hand and tossed in into the forest green duffel bag. "There, are you satisfied?"

Lily wiggled her nose, causing the glasses to creep back up her small nose. "Yes, I am. Thank you," she grinned.

"What am I forgetting?" Dev rubbed her narrow, pointed chin and studied the bed.

"Common sense comes to mind." Lily brushed her hair back over her ears. "You didn't tell me why your mother thinks you're mentally unstable. You did tell her all the circumstances of your leaving Spencer, didn't you?"

"No. There are some things so awful you can't even tell your mother. I have never told anyone that scene, except you. I explained that Spencer was unfaithful and I couldn't live with that."

"Did you tell her you're going on this trip?"

Dev folded the rest of the blouses on the bed, then stacked them inside the duffel. "No."

"Are you just going to drive off into the sunset without telling your own mother?" Lily scooped up the cat with her left hand and began to scratch its head.

Develyn sighed. "She's tied up this week with the garden club bazaar. And, I might add, she's very disappointed that I'm not helping her this year. Lily, I just don't want to have to explain this. It will only make me feel like a failure in her eyes again. I'm forty-five years old. I am what I am. She needs to accept that. She and I are so different."

"I was just thinking how much you are the same."

"You mean, stubborn and opinionated?"

"Yes . . . and gracious and kindhearted."

When Develyn paused, her shoulders slumped. "Mother does have her good moments. I'll send her and David a post-card. They will be in Austria most of the summer anyway."

"Austria?" Lily continued to stroll the room, cat in hand. "Is that her idea or David's?"

"It's Mother's plan. She has it in her mind to do a cultural tour of Vienna and Austria. Dear, sweet David adores her and will do whatever she asks."

"She's quite a lady to find two jewels to marry. David is very much like your father."

"Yes, I don't know what I would do without David around. After father died, mother was at such a loss. Then David drove up in his gold Chrysler and charming attentions. He's perfect for her. And dear mother has reminded me of the fact that there are good men available, but I just don't seem to have the dis-cernment to find one."

"She said that?"

"That's what she implied."

"Ms. Worrell, that makes two of us with no discernment."

"You know, the strange thing is that mother thinks you did the absolute right thing with Donald. It was very justifiable in her eyes."

"When your husband of twenty-five years moves in with another woman three blocks away, you don't have a lot of choices," Lily replied.

Develyn opened the top drawer of the oak dresser and sorted through satin nighties. "I guess that's the difference. I left Spencer, so it must be all my fault." She held up a royal blue nightgown with thin spaghetti straps. "What do you think of this for my one nightgown?"

"It depends on who is going to be seeing it."

"No one is going to be seeing it," Dev snapped.

"Then, it really doesn't matter, does it?" Lily smiled. "So you just drive off without telling your mother a word? You can't be serious."

"I'm very serious, Ms. Martin." Dev tossed the blue gown back in the dresser and shoved the drawer shut. "I'm going to wear sweats for jammies. You are right, no one will see me anyway." She transferred the alarm clock from the center to the side pocket of the duffel bag. "Now, will you feed Josephine and Smoky until Trevor and his family get back from Florida? He'll take care of them and the yard work for the rest of the summer."

Lily stroked the black cat that hung like a pelt from her arm. "I'll feed the cats and your neighbor boy and do the yard. But, gone all summer? The first I heard of this trip was two hours ago."

"Think of it as furthering my education. It will be advanced teacher training. I told you I just need to get away." Develyn toted the duffel bag out of the bedroom and into the entryway, then slapped it down on the white tile beside the front door. She scurried back into the bedroom.

"You only taking one suitcase?" Lily called out.

Develyn waltzed out with a brown leather bag over her shoulder, then dropped it over the duffel. "And a garment bag with one dress and a blanket-lined denim jacket."

"You need more than that when we go for a weekend in Indy." Lily put the cat down on the cream-colored carpet.

Dev buzzed into the adjoining room. "Yes, but I'm not going to Indy."

"And just where are you going?" Lily followed her into the immaculate kitchen.

"I'm surprised you waited that long to ask me." Develyn dug a tray of ice out of the freezer. "I'm going west."

"I was waiting for you to volunteer the information, but it was sort of like waiting for a room mother to materialize before the sixth-grade fall social. I gave up on it happening. Now, how far west are you going?" Lily pressed. "Iowa? Nebraska?"

Dev pulled a tall, blue plastic glass from the oak cupboard. "Somewhere in Wyoming." She plopped in a half-dozen ice cubes.

Lily refilled the ice tray and shoved it back in the freezer. "I hear there's nothing but wind and sagebrush in Wyoming."

"Yes, it sounds wonderful, doesn't it? So peaceful."

"If you're an antelope or a jackrabbit."

"Lily, you are my very best friend in the world." Develyn filled the glass with tap water, then took a sip. She rubbed her upturned nose with the palm of her hand, then sighed. "We've taught side by side for twenty-three years, you with the sixth grade, me with the fifth. You were there for me when Spencer had to be in New York and I was alone when Delaney was born. You held my hand through two miscarriages. You and I drove to Lafayette day after day, summer after summer, to get our master's degrees. You were there both times I waited in the hospital for the results from the biopsies. You opened your spare room to us the night I left Spencer; then you let me and Delaney impose on you for six long months until we could buy this place. You showed me by your strong Christian example how to survive the pain of divorce with class. I thought I had worked my way through all of it. But, dear sweet Lily, I'm telling you, I can't stay here this summer. It's difficult to explain, but it's crushing me. Absolutely crushing me. The bad memories hang as heavy as the humidity. And now, the situation with Delaney. I don't think I can physically, mentally, or spiritually survive if I stay. For the sake of my sanity, and my faith, I have to go west."

Lily plucked a tissue from a square gold box. "What will you do in Wyoming? Do you know someone there?"

Develyn took the tissue, then strolled around the small two-person breakfast table and stood at the window that revealed a six-foot-high spruce tree in the middle of the unfenced back lawn. She held the water glass in her hand in front of her. "No, I don't know a soul in Wyoming. I just have to find some peace of mind and rest for my spirit."

Lily Martin stepped up next to her and gazed outside. She rubbed Develyn's back in a circular motion. "Sweetie, Dee's just going through a twenty-year-old, I-want-to-prove-my-independence stage. She'll work through it. She's a smart girl."

"I pray she will." Dev slipped her free arm across the shorter woman's shoulders. "And I pray I'll live through it."

"What exactly did she say when she called?"

Dev took another sip of ice water, then cleared her throat. "She said, 'Mother, I'm not coming home this summer. I'm not going with you to Maine. I'm not sure when I will see you. I might go live in Charleston and work at the Crab House.'"

"Charleston, South Carolina?"

"Mr. Awesome Corvette lives in Charleston. I believe his father owns the Crab House."

"But, I've listened to you and Delaney giggle and plan this trip to Maine for two years."

Develyn drew the cream-colored curtains closed on the window and turned toward Lily. "Yes, it was to be her graduation present. But, as you know, high school graduation turned out to be a little different than I hoped for. So we had to postpone it until after the divorce settlement. This was the first summer I could afford it."

Lily slipped her arm around Develyn's narrow waist. "Why not just get away for a few days? Or a week? Go up and visit your friends in Michigan. Go out on the lake. You always said how much you enjoyed that. Think things through."

Develyn trailed off to the living room where her buckskin-colored boots and forest-green socks waited by the off-white leather sofa. "I've already thought things through, Lily. I declined to teach summer school with you because of the trip to Maine. But I have no intention of going there alone. I've canceled the cabin." She sucked in her breath. "My dear daughter, my only child, has accused me of being so unforgiving and cold-hearted that I caused her father to have a massive heart attack and die."

"That's not fair."

"In her twenty-year-old mind, it must seem reasonable. She held on to the hope we would get back together."

"Maybe you and I should go down to Nashville again. We enjoyed that long weekend. Remember when we went to that costume place and tried on the Dolly Parton wigs?"

Develyn arched her eyebrows. "I seem to remember we tried on the Dolly Parton everything."

"Only you, Dev. There are some things I need no help with, thank you." Lily studied her eyes. "You see, you can still laugh and giggle, Ms. Worrell."

The sigh was slow, deliberate . . . like a ship departing for a long voyage and none of the crew quite ready to say good-bye. "Dear, sweet Lily, your summer is planned. Six weeks of summer school and a month with the grandchildren in Wisconsin. I'm not sure when I will have grandchildren, nor if my daughter will even tell me. So, I would get to sit at home all summer and feel sorry for myself. I have felt sorry for myself for over ten years. I can't stand that any more."

"Ten years?" Lily questioned.

"That wasn't the only time Spencer did this." Dev handed Lily the glass of ice water, then plopped down on the couch.

"You never told me that."

"I never told anyone that. Not mother. And certainly not Delaney. But like an old wool coat, lies wear thin over the years." Dev tugged on the green socks. "I'm tired, Lily. So tired of having to be strong for everyone but me. Like a runner who has hit the wall, I can't go on. I didn't know I would hit the wall today, but I did. Now, I believe the Lord has put this wild idea in my head. It's my only chance to regain purpose in my life."

"But why, all of a sudden, Wyoming? It's not like you to be impulsive."

"The completely predictable Ms. Worrell does something spontaneous. That will be big news at Riverbend Elementary. It's about time." She pulled on the light tan boots, then smoothed her jeans down over the tops. "Besides, it's not all of a sudden. I've been planning this trip since I was ten years old."

"Ten? You've wanted to go to Wyoming since you were ten?"

Dev strolled over and closed the curtains behind the television. "I was in Wyoming when I was ten. Now, I'm going back."

"But where?"

"A little town."

"What little town?"

Dev stared at the lifeless ashes in the tan brick fireplace. Her voice softened. She no longer sounded like a fifth-grade teacher, but like a child. "I don't know its name. I can't remember."

"Where in Wyoming is it?"

"I'm not sure. The dream is fuzzy, thirty-five years later." Dev meandered to the window on the south side of the sparsely furnished living room.

Carrying the water glass, Lily scooted after her. "You don't know where you are going or where you will stay or what you will do or how long you will be there?"

Develyn closed the floor-to-ceiling curtains. "That's about it."

"I'm worried about you."

She retrieved the water glass and took a sip. "You think I need counseling?"

"It's a thought."

"Perhaps Mr. Thompson?" Develyn grinned.

"I'm afraid our school counselor is busy with community service projects since his last DUI."

"Lily, the most peaceful, wonderful days of my entire life were the two weeks we were stranded in Wyoming with car trouble on our way to Yellowstone. For two weeks a ten-year-old girl lived in a log cabin heated from a big old rock fireplace. I slept in a feather bed that I had to share with my twin brother. We rode horses every morning until I was so sore I could hardly walk. We scouted along the Bridger Trail . . . the real trail where we could still see the ruts of the pioneer wagons. We climbed up on the bluffs once occupied by Shoshone, Crow, Sioux, Arapahoe, and Cheyenne Indians and found arrowheads and artifacts. The air was filled with the aroma of fresh-cut hay, sage, horse sweat, and old oiled leather. Father would give us a quarter, and Dewayne and I would walk barefoot down the middle of that dusty street to the Sweetwater Grocery, which was in Mrs. Tagley's living room. We'd buy an orange Popsicle and sit out on the bench made from a covered wagon seat and pretend we were waiting for Wyatt Earp, or Marshal Dillon, or Stuart Brannon to mosey down the street. In the afternoon, Dewa would go fishing with father. Mother would read her treasured Faulkner, so I lay in that big old hammock in the shade of the cottonwoods and rocked back and forth and wrote stories in the Wyoming blue sky. That was when I decided to become a teacher. Life was too grand to hold it all in. I needed to tell others. In the evening Father roasted hot dogs over the flames of the fireplace and Mother read to us. The only book in the cabin Mother approved for us was Will James's *Smoky the Cow Horse*. Poor Mother, we must have made her read it three times in two weeks. I would go to sleep with horse dreams and wake up with horse dreams then get to start the whole cycle all over again. I remember praying that our old Buick station wagon would never get fixed."

"What a wonderful memory."

"Lily, it just might have been as close to paradise as I will ever get on this earth. We never made it to Yellowstone, yet when we drove out of town, I cried and cried. I promised myself that I would come back the next year. But the years went by. Then I said the summer between high school and college, I would travel west. But I needed to work and save up for

Purdue. So I made it my college graduation present to myself. But Spencer had a summer job with Jacobs Engineering and he said he couldn't live without me." Dev rubbed her chin and bit her lip. "I should have gone that summer. Perhaps things would have been different. No, that's not true. There wouldn't be any Delaney Melinda Worrell. She hates me, but I can't keep from loving her. She's still the joy of my life."

"Release her, Dev. She's twenty. She's a big girl now."

"I know, Mother tells me the same thing. Lily, I'm going to Wyoming. I'm leaving today. I will regret it dearly if I don't try to find paradise one more time. It sounds like John Milton, doesn't it?"

"I was thinking more like Thomas Wolfe. Everything is different now. You aren't ten any more, Dev."

"I can wish, Lily." Dev felt her shoulders tense, then relax. "I can wish. Maybe it won't be paradise. Maybe it will only be 50 percent paradise . . . or 20 percent . . . or 2 percent. It still beats staying here with nothing to do but mow the grass and feed the cats."

Lily shook her head. "I still can't figure what possesses you to do such a thing."

Dev Worrell locked the sliding-glass back door, then strolled to the entryway. "Lingering memories of a dirt-road town."

"Dirt-road town?"

"It must be ten miles off the blacktop before you come to town, and then there are no paved streets, Lily. Can you imagine a town where there is no paved highway, and no paved streets?"

"But that was thirty-five years ago, Dev. How do you know it's the same?"

"I've got to find out. I made a promise to a ten-year-old girl. I got delayed. Now's my chance to keep the promise."

"Doesn't your mother know the name of the town?"

"I don't know. I don't intend to ask her. Father would know, bless his heart. He understood his Devy-girl. He died way too young, Lily. I don't think I ever got over losing Daddy. Mother got over it. Dewayne got over it. I don't think I ever did. Maybe this trip will help that loss too."

"Are those all the shoes you're taking?"

"One pair of boots, one pair of tennies, and I'm taking one blue denim dress."

"The one with fake rhinestones?" Lily pressed.

"Yes, and other than that just jeans, tops, and sweats. One pair of earrings: the diamond studs."

"Now I know you've lost it. You own more earrings than anyone in Montgomery County."

"I want to go some place where it doesn't matter if my earrings coordinate with the rest of my outfit. Somewhere I don't have to fuss with my hair, polish my nails, or wear a fake smile to make everyone think things are fine."

"Are you sure you know what you're doing?" Lily challenged.

"I have no idea what I'm doing."

"You are always in control. Always on top of everything. This is not you, Dev."

She snatched up the duffel bag with one hand and held the

water glass in the other. "I certainly hope not. I'm fed up with the real me."

"Will you phone me every night?" Lily carried the garment bag. "Just call me and say, 'Hey girl, I'm OK.' Then you can hang up if you want to."

Dev felt a tear puddle in the corner of her eye, but her hands were full and she couldn't massage it. "You're serious, aren't you?"

"Yes. You know I worry about you as if you were my sister."

"Lily, I'll phone whenever I can."

"Are you taking your laptop? Can you send me an e-mail from time to time?"

"It's in the Cherokee. I'll try, Lily."

The two women paused in the laundry room, at the door that led to the garage. There was a long pause as their eyes shouted what their hearts couldn't whisper.

Lily cleared her throat. "By the way, Ms. Worrell, where is your other cat?"

"I imagine Smoky's asleep in the big basket on the top shelf of the hutch in the kitchen."

"He sleeps up there?"

"Only when Josephine ticks him off."

"Does that happen much?"

"24/7." Develyn held the garage door open as Lily pushed her way through.

"And you aren't telling your mother, your daughter, or anyone where you are going?"

Dev pressed the button on the automatic garage door opener. "I'm telling you. And I wrote to Dewayne."

Lily opened the back door of the Jeep Cherokee and hung the garment bag on a hook. "Where is your brother?"

"Somewhere in the Persian Gulf, I think. He isn't allowed to disclose his location. He volunteers for long tours of duty since his Audrey died. But he will understand. Dewa always understands me. I wish he was closer."

"If Dewayne were standing here right now, what would he tell you?" Lily challenged.

Develyn shoved the duffel bag in the back seat and slammed the door. She stared down into the glass of ice water. "He'd say, 'Devy-girl, don't yank on the reins and hurt Brownie's mouth. Put only your toes in the stirrups so you won't get hung up, and don't drip orange Popsicle on your white T-shirt.'"

Lily smiled and held the driver's door open. "Your brother is unique."

Develyn slipped in the car and plunked her ice water into the cup holder. "Yes, if there were two men in the world like him, I would have married the other one."

Lily slammed the door and continued to stand in the crowded garage. "How far are you going tonight?"

"I don't know."

"You don't have a reservation anywhere?"

"No."

"Which route are you taking? Or is that a secret?"

Dev glanced in the rearview mirror to check her lipstick. "I'll take 74 across to the Quad Cities, then get on Interstate 80 west."

"You could stay with Ginny McGill tonight," Lily suggested. "She's teaching at a Christian school near Davenport. Do you want me to call her?"

"Lily, I don't even want to see anyone I know, let alone stay with someone. This is way too crazy to have to explain to anyone else."

"So, that leaves out Jack and Sarah Smithwick in Iowa City. They are both full professors now."

"Yes, I know, the psychology department at the University of Iowa. That's not very subtle, Ms. Martin."

"OK, where will you stay tonight?"

"I'll drive until I'm tired."

"You'll pull over if you get sleepy?"

"Of course."

"And you'll find a nice motel before it gets dark?"

"You sound like my mother," Dev scowled.

"You didn't answer me."

"I will be careful, Lily."

"You still didn't answer me."

"I will pull over and get a room when I get tired. That's all I can say."

"Dev, aren't you scared?"

"No, I don't think so. Kind of exciting, actually."

"Well, I'm scared for you," Lily admitted.

"Why?"

"Because there are weirdos out there. This isn't going to be one of those scenes where you disappear off the face of the earth, is it?"

"That is not my plan."

"What is your plan, you know, for returning home? This *is* your home, Dev Worrell."

"I plan on being back by August 14th, so I can lead the teacher's contingent from Riverbend Elementary to welcome the new superintendent."

"Provided he doesn't make a pass at Miss Chambers."

"I hear he's from Idaho," Dev said.

Lily shook her head. "That isn't good."

"Why? Idaho always sounded like a nice place."

"Yes, I agree. So why would a man want to leave such a nice place for central Indiana? He must have been chased out of the state."

"Point well taken, Ms. Martin. You will have to e-mail me and let me know what is waiting for me when I return."

"I like the sound of that. 'When I return.' Sometimes, Dev, this feels like I am saying good-bye forever."

"Don't be silly, Lily. I will be here to see just how Ms. Martin gets along with Dougie Baxter."

"You really requested that he be in my class?"

"No, I requested that he be held back and put in Ken Ainsworth's class. But Mr. and Mrs. Baxter would hear nothing of it. They asked me who the finest sixth-grade teacher was."

"So, naturally you mentioned my name."

"Of course. What else could I say?"

"Perhaps Dougie will mature over the summer," Lily sighed.

"Maybe so, but whatever you do, don't give him a metal ruler or let him near a screwdriver," Develyn cautioned.

"Did they ever get your computer fixed?"

"I don't want to think about it."

"I can't believe you are really doing this."

"It does feel a little strange."

"Aha! You can change your mind. I'll help you unpack."

Develyn handed Lily the house key. "I said it feels strange, not that it feels bad. Actually, it feels good. Very good. And I'm not used to feeling good."

"Is this where we say good-bye?" Lily pressed.

"You'll feed the cats?"

"I'll feed the tormentor and the tormentee."

"OK, then I'm leaving."

Lily motioned toward the street. "Back your Jeep into the driveway, then we'll say good-bye."

Develyn backed the silver Cherokee out onto the white gravel drive, past the Japanese pine, then punched the button to close the garage door.

Lily strolled up to the open window.

"Well, Ms. Martin, you enjoy teaching summer school."

"Ms. Worrell, you have a wonderful summer. I hope that little ten-year-old girl is not disappointed."

"Me too, Lily. Tell me I'm not crazy."

Lily Martin reached into the front seat and hugged Develyn, then kissed her cheek. "I've known you since you graduated from Purdue. You've never done anything crazy . . ."

Develyn reached out and wiped the tear from Lily's cheek. "Thank you."

". . . until now. Go on before I really start sobbing."

Dev took a sip of ice water, then wiped her own eyes. "This is silly. Just think of it as if I'm going away to camp. I'm just going on a summer vacation."

"Yeah, I know." Lily folded her arms and held herself tight. "Bye, Devy-girl."

"Bye, Lily. Thanks for always being here for me. If you were a man, I'd marry you."

"Yeah, the guy who lives next door said the same thing to me," Lily laughed. "Now, go on. Go have an adventure."

Develyn drove the 2002 champagne silver-colored Jeep Cherokee to the end of the gravel driveway. When she looked back, Lily jogged toward her. She rolled the window back down. "What's wrong?"

"Develyn Worrell, don't you go out there to Wyoming and marry yourself a cowboy."

Develyn peered over the top of her sunglasses. "Why did you say that?"

"For the life of me, I can't think of any other good reason for you to go there."

"Lily, I've been depressed for three years. I'll go crazy . . . or worse . . . if I stay here. I promise you, I won't marry a cowboy."

Develyn pulled the Jeep out into Seminole Street.

There was a rap on the window.

She rolled it down. Again.

"If you do find a cowboy, Devy-girl, he has to have a friend who likes graying, plain-looking school teachers."

"Lily, you are not a plain-looking, graying school teacher."

Lily Martin jammed her head in the open window and kissed Develyn's cheek again. "I'm scared for you, Ms. Worrell. You come back to me. I need you in my life. And Riverbend Elementary needs you."

A gravel truck slid to a stop behind the Jeep and honked his air horn.

"That's my signal."

"Good-bye, Dev. May your summer be even better than your horse dreams."

Framed in her rearview mirror, Develyn watched the white brick house, a dark haired sixth-grade teacher, and forty-five years of tightly controlled emotions begin to fade. She reached for the square gold box of tissue.

2

Develyn decided that the tune the highway plucked on the tread of her new Goodyear tires changed with the surface and season, but the rhythm of the road remained always constant. There was one tune for dry blacktop, sort of a "Boston Pops Plays the Best of Frank Sinatra" sound. The smooth concrete interstate came across like the London Philharmonic playing Mozart in a dentist's office. However, concrete highways with rough seal joints every thirty feet beat a constant count like the hearty fellow at Jacobs Field who pounds the drum during Cleveland Indians baseball games.

Gravel roads had an early Creedence Clearwater Revival sound, the kind that wakes you up and keeps your hand tapping on the steering wheel. In the winter time, her studded tires gave the impression of a cheap military march in front of a third-world dictator. And a dirt road? Smooth dirt roads reminded Develyn of the melancholy instrumental prelude to the Eagles's "Hotel California."

But no matter what the tune, the basic rhythm of the road never changed.

"Keep going–keep driving–keep awake–keep running, they are gaining on you."

She kept driving.

And driving.

And driving.

At 10:00 p.m. she bought gas, a stale bran muffin, and a bottle of water in Newton, Iowa.

Develyn concluded that every town in Iowa looked the same, especially from the interstate after dark. DeSoto, Wiscotta, Dexter, Stuart, Menlo . . . she read the names aloud, so she could hear the sound of a voice. It was almost 3:00 a.m. when she took exit 60 into Lorah, Iowa. The only lit building in the tiny town read "Thelma Lou's 24-Hour Café." The gravel parking lot was empty.

The night air chilled her arms as she stepped out of the Cherokee. She retrieved a gray hooded sweatshirt. She ran her fingers through her short hair as she peered into the side mirror on the Jeep, felt in her jeans pocket for her wallet and her keys, then plodded to the front door of the café. The stainless steel door handle felt cold. She glanced down at her short, ringless fingers.

A warm aroma of fried meat, burnt toast, and ammonia greeted her as she pushed her way inside. A woman in a pink apron with a long auburn braid down her back scrubbed the vinyl stools at the counter. She looked about Develyn's age.

"Welcome, honey, sit anywhere you want to. Except the counter here. I'm giving it a disinfectant scrub."

Develyn slipped into the first booth and slid over next to the window.

"Girl, you want coffee? Water?" It was a gentler voice than Develyn expected at that time of the morning. She glanced over at the waitress who wore her white blouse buttoned to the top, and an easy, relaxed smile. "Both, please."

The waitress dried her hands on her apron. "I'll bring you a menu."

"Coffee and water are all I need. Ice water would be nice."

The woman brought the water and two cups of coffee.

"Mind if I join you?" the waitress asked. "I need a break. The cleaning solvent is kind of strong."

"Sit down." Dev motioned to the seat across from her. "Do you work here alone?"

The waitress slid into the booth, then flipped her long auburn bangs off her forehead. She had a small mole, like a jewel, between her eyebrows. "Yeah. Isn't this something? Nine at night to five in the morning, six days a week, with a two-week vacation and a honey-glazed ham for a Christmas bonus. What a life."

Develyn stirred the ice in her water with her finger. "Sounds a bit lonely."

The woman dumped two packets of sweetener into her coffee. "Yeah, that's why I took the job. Sometimes you want to be alone. You know what I mean?"

The coffee steamed Develyn's small, upturned nose as she sipped. "Yes, I do know what you mean. I take it you are not Thelma Lou?"

The woman laughed. "There hasn't been a Thelma Lou in this café since 1954. It's just a name. The present owner is Mildred Muygn. She's Vietnamese."

Dev glanced at the wall above the window at a faded poster of a Sioux City Patsy Cline concert from 1961. "And this is Lorah, Iowa?"

The waitress leaned back in the booth and rested her head on green plastic upholstery. "This is it, honey. It's strictly a halfway town."

"A halfway town?" Dev quizzed.

"Halfway between Omaha and Des Moines, halfway between Clarinda and Carroll. You name it. We aren't anyone's destination. Some even say we're halfway between heaven and hell, but it's closer to one than the other, if you want my opinion."

Develyn sipped the coffee slow and let it trickle down her throat. "Have you worked here long?"

"Eight years. Can you believe that? But I'm not going to stay. As soon as I get things straightened out, I'm going on to Denver."

"Why Denver?"

"Because it's not a halfway town. By the way, my name's

Stef." She stuck a slightly damp, ammonia-tinted hand across the table. She had a very firm grip.

"I'm Develyn, but most call me Dev."

"Dev? I never knew anyone with that name. I like it. It fits you."

"Thank you."

Stef sat up and leaned across the table, head in hand. "Dev, you got me puzzled."

Develyn tugged on the drawstrings of her hooded sweat-shirt. "How's that?"

"You're not local, so you must have come off the interstate. A woman alone on the road at 3:00 a.m. is puzzling, especially a classy looking lady. At this time of the night there are only two types of gals that stop in here alone. College girls trying to hurry back to the university. I don't think that fits you."

"My college days ended twenty-four years ago."

"Twenty-four? You're older than I thought."

"How old did you think I was?" Develyn questioned.

"Mid-thirties."

Develyn grinned. "Stef, you make me feel wonderful for 3:00 a.m. Actually, I'm forty-five."

"No fooling? You are five years older than me."

"Well, if it's any encouragement, you don't look forty."

"Thank you, Dev. I knew we were going to be friends when you walked in. Shoot, we should just sit here all night telling each other lies and feeling good. By the way, your short haircut is totally cute and perfect for your face shape."

"Why thank you, Stef. And your long auburn braid is to die for. I am completely jealous."

Both women laughed.

"Say, this is fun. I like you, Stef. I don't laugh enough. But you said only two types of women stop in here alone in the middle of the night. Who are the other ones?"

"The ones who have black eyes and bruises after leaving the jerk. I didn't see any scars on you."

"Yes, well, no physical wife abuse."

Stef glanced down at Develyn's hands. "Are you married?"

"Divorced . . . well it's a little more complicated than that. My ex had a heart attack and died a few weeks ago."

"That tends to make it final, doesn't it?"

"To say the least," Develyn nodded. "How about you?"

Stef puffed her red bangs back off her forehead then glanced out at the dark night. "Yeah, I'm sort of divorced."

"Sort of?"

"I wasn't actually married. We had been making plans to get married. We even went house shopping once or twice. Anyway, I had this steady guy for three years. He left about eight weeks ago. So it feels like a divorce."

"Sorry about that. It makes the nights lonely, doesn't it?"

"In my case, lonely days. Sometimes they're unbearable. But I need to work. Gives me time to think. Not often anyone but truckers stop by. Hey, is that your Jeep Cherokee out there?"

"Yes." Develyn glanced out at the gravel parking lot, lit by two orange-tinted halogen yard lights.

"How do you like it?"

"I love it. It's the first car I ever bought for myself."

"Ol' hubby always bought the cars?"

"That's about it. I just didn't feel like another minivan, if you know what I mean."

"I drive an old Chevy pickup. What year is it?" Stef pressed.

"2002."

Stef continued to stare out at the cloudless Iowa night. "Oh, it's one of those with a cute butt."

Develyn almost spilled her ice water when she exploded with a laugh. "A what?"

"Truck drivers tell me the newer Jeep Cherokees have the cutest rear ends of any vehicle on the road."

Develyn shook her head. "I've never heard that before."

"I suppose when you don't do anything but drive a truck 24/7, you have time to play games with what you see. Now, what's your story?"

"I'm going west."

"Montana?"

"Wyoming."

"By yourself?"

Develyn stared at the younger woman's green eyes. "Yes."

"Are you running to someone or away from someone?" Stef asked.

Develyn stared out the window. "Not to or from anyone. But it's a good question. I've been mulling that over since I left. I think I'm running from someplace . . . to someplace else. Anyway, I wasn't tired this evening, so I just kept driving."

"Now you are getting sleepy, and you figure it's too late to rent a room. So you'll bulk up on coffee and No-Doz and keep driving?"

"I suppose."

Stef took Develyn's water, purposely spilled a little on the table, then wiped the table with the white paper napkin. "How long ago was the divorce?"

"I left him three years ago. The divorce has been final two years."

"How long were you married to him?"

"Twenty-two years."

"Wow." The waitress stopped cleaning. Her eyes widened. "What happened?"

Develyn hesitated and sipped the coffee.

"Sorry, honey. I know I'm prying. You don't have to answer, really. I'm just sort of hurting myself. Trying to figure how I could have been so stupid with Ray."

"That was your guy?"

"Yeah, I thought he was my guy."

Develyn raised her thin, light brown eyebrows. "Oh?"

"He said he and his wife were finished. I thought that meant he was divorced or getting a divorce."

"He wasn't?"

Stef stared down into her brown coffee cup. "No, as it turns out, he was living with her and dating me."

"You finally caught on?"

The waitress glanced up. "Yeah, the hard way."

"Oh?"

"I live in a singlewide across the street and down a block. About 1:00 a.m. on my night off, me and Ray were . . . ah . . . we were . . ." Stef studied her eyes.

"Dancing?" Develyn blushed.

Stef grinned, then stared down at the table. "Yeah, we were dancing, so to speak, when his wife bursts in screaming and yelling and busting up my place. I was scared that she was going to kill me."

"Oh, my." Develyn leaned forward, resting her chin in the palms of her hands. "Then what happened?"

"She threatened to take the kids to California that night and never return if he didn't leave 'that woman,' come home, and stop seeing me."

"And?" Develyn pressed.

"He put on his clothes and went home. I haven't seen him since." Stef stared back out the window at the dark gravel parking lot. "I hear she's telling a bunch of lies about me now."

"She blames you for it all?"

The waitress yanked out a paper napkin and dabbed her eyes. "Dev, I don't sleep around with every man who comes along. I don't know why she says that. I didn't try to ruin her life. I loved him. I really thought he loved me. He treated me so nice. I didn't want to hurt anyone. I just wanted to feel loved. I just needed a man to really care about me, that's all. I'm not a bad woman. Really."

"I believe you."

The waitress rubbed the creases next to her narrow green eyes and avoided looking at Develyn. "I've been needing to tell someone that for weeks. But there's no one around here for me to talk to. Thanks for listening."

"Stef, I know about needing to talk."

"Max Knowlton," the waitress blurted out.

"Who?"

"See that truck pulling up?"

"I can only see headlights."

"Well, it's Max Knowlton from Tacoma. He had a long haul to Greensboro, North Carolina, and is on his way home. He'll order chicken fried steak and an extra biscuit."

Develyn shook her head. "Stef, you are amazing. How can you know all that from headlights?"

"Like I said, there's not much to do on this shift but clean up and visit with truck drivers." She pointed out to the parking lot to a tall man wearing a denim jacket. "Yep, that's Max. I better go take care of him. Can you stick around so we can visit some more?"

"I suppose. I'm in no hurry." Develyn sat up and jammed her hands into the pockets of her sweatshirt. "But I will need another cup of coffee."

The front door of the café swung open. "Hi, Sweetness!" the deep-voiced driver shouted.

"Max, Honey . . . how was your trip?"

"About as routine as an Iowa corn harvest. Have you been

a good girl?" He strolled up next to their table and hugged her shoulder.

"Now, Max . . . you know I'm always good." He tipped his baseball cap at Develyn. "Now, who's this purdy lady? I ain't used to Thelma Lou's bein' crowded like this."

"This is my younger sis, Dev."

"Dev? Like in Devil?" he hooted.

"Dev, like in Develyn," Stef insisted.

"Mind if I join you two?" he grinned.

"Yes, we do. You go sit over there." Stef pointed to a booth on the far side of the small café. "We've got some girl talk to finish, and I'm not about to let you listen in. Now, go back and wash up and I'll get you the biggest chicken fried steak in Iowa."

"You spoil me, sweetie." His teeth were white, but crooked.

"And you love it."

"I reckon I do." He tipped his hat. "Nice to meet you, little sis. Are you a waitress too?"

"I'm a school teacher," Develyn admitted.

"Shucks, with a teacher as purdy as you, all the little boys must have crushes."

Stef took him by the arm and led him away. "Max, don't you dare start hitting on my sis. And right in front of me too? What's a girl to think?" Stef winked back at Develyn.

With her coffee cup refilled, Develyn Gail Upton Worrell stared out at the black Iowa night.

This is as depressing as my situation. I can't imagine working night shift by myself at some remote diner. When does she sleep? Do you wake up at 3:00 in the afternoon thinking, "Oh boy, I get to go to work today?" It's sort of like teaching the fifth grade in February, I suppose.

Why can't there be contentment with who I am?

Peace with those around me?

Satisfaction in what I do with my life?

I suppose a person can have those anywhere. And that's what I have to have. I don't need fame . . . or fortune . . . or power. Just give me contentment, Lord, some measure of peace and satisfaction.

You are a liar, Ms. Worrell.

You need someone to love you. Someone to care for you. Stef's right. When it's not there, when no man cares, it hurts. It really hurts.

She and I are sisters . . . in pain.

Develyn glanced across the café and watched the friendly waitress chat with the trucker.

Maybe I should learn how to drive a big rig. Dev Worrell: trucker. She grinned and took a sip of ice water. *Then I could run away all the time. Is that what I'm doing? Am I just running away?*

Maybe.

Lord, I don't have a clue what I should do, if I stayed home.

That decision has been made. I'm on the road. Not very relaxed, yet. I should have stopped at a motel. At least I could shower and rest a bit even if I didn't sleep. And I could have called Lily.

Develyn glanced at her watch.

3:30 a.m.? I don't think I've stayed up all night since college days. The night I graduated from Purdue. Spencer had that black '72 Trans Am. We ditched the party and spent most of the night down by Sugar Creek. We snuck into Turkey Run State Park and sat on that bench until the sun came up.

Life had so much potential then.

Love. Marriage. Children. Career.

Everything was fresh, new, vital.

Now it's all worn out, tired, like the blacktop on an abandoned street.

"Hey, Sis . . . how about some company?" Stef slid in next to her until their hips touched.

"What about Max?"

"I got him all fixed up. Even scooped him up some apple pie. I thought if I sat next to you, you could tell me your story without talking too loud."

"My story?"

"Here's all I know so far. You were married twenty-two years, then divorced him and now you are running from home and running to someplace . . . but not to someone. OK, fill me in."

Develyn studied Stef's tired eyes. They seemed to be expecting great wisdom. She took a deep sigh, then sipped the ice water and bit her lip. Her sigh seemed to last for minutes.

Develyn's voice was so low, the waitress leaned closer.

"Stef . . . I was the other woman in your scene."

"You caught him with another woman?"

Develyn bit her lips and nodded.

"Were they . . . eh . . . 'dancing'?"

Develyn nodded again.

"Oh, wow . . . I'm sorry, honey," Stef blurted out. "It just dawned on me the pain I must have given Ray's wife. What happened? Did he divorce you, run off and marry her?"

"No."

"Did he apologize, promise to never do it again, and beg to be taken back?"

"Not until two years after the divorce."

Stef leaned close and whispered, "Who was she, Dev? Tell me she wasn't a waitress."

Develyn let her head sink into her hands. Her eyes closed. "This is hard to talk about."

Stef's arm slipped across Develyn's shoulder and began to rub. "It's all right, honey. I have no business prying. You don't have to tell me."

"No . . . I need to say it to someone. I've practiced these words almost every day for three years. My heart and spirit will explode if I don't tell someone." Develyn sat up, took a sip of water, and swallowed hard. "I have a daughter. Three years ago she graduated from high school. For a number of years, things had not been too good between me and my husband. I could never do things right. I couldn't cook well enough. My clothes were too plain. He hated my short hair. I didn't like doing the things he did. I didn't look young enough."

"Are you kidding me? You might be the youngest-looking forty-five-year-old in the midwest."

"I weighed thirty pounds more than I do now. Anyway, he once told me I was so boring and predictable he hated to come home at night."

"He said that?" Stef groaned. "I can't believe he'd say that."

"He said other things. Often there were comments about the size of my rear end, and lack of size anywhere else. Anyway, we had a graduation party for Delaney. About two dozen of her friends came over. We had food, patio games, all the things we thought would be fun. I was in charge of the kitchen; he headed up the outside activities."

"Delaney is your only child?"

"Yes." Develyn paused and brushed the corners of her eyes. "I bet my mascara looks frightening."

"I should look so good. Shoot, girl, I didn't look that good when I was eighteen."

Develyn leaned against the waitress and shook her head. "You are a natural encourager. Thanks. Anyway, about midnight or so, I had been working the kitchen four straight hours. I've never seen kids eat so much. It was early June and Indiana sticky. I perspired through my blouse and spilled salsa on my khaki shorts, so I snuck up to the bedroom to change." Develyn stared down at the table.

Stef's hand flew to her mouth. "Oh, my . . . no! They were, eh, dancing in your own bedroom?"

"Her name is Heather Raphael. She was one of the high-schoolers. She had been my daughter's best friend since third grade. She practically grew up at our house."

"How old was she? He could be arrested."

"Barely eighteen."

Stef shook her head. "I assume she wasn't boring. What did you do?"

Develyn leaned her shoulder against the waitress. "You mean after I screamed and cried and threw the alarm clock at him?"

Stef glanced over her shoulder at the trucker, then lowered her voice. "Yes, what did you do then?"

"I grabbed my daughter and drove her to a friend's house. We spent the night there."

"Hey, Stefi-babe, I need some more coffee," the trucker called out.

"Max, you know where it is," she shot back without looking at him. Then she whispered, "Did you go back?"

"Two weeks later we snuck back in and grabbed a few of our things. I walked away from everything else. I never went back after that."

Stef's green eyes widened. "You gave him everything?"

"Everything seemed so cheap, fake, tarnished, cruddy. I couldn't take it."

"Are you really a teacher?"

"Yes. I teach the fifth grade. Delaney and I lived with my friend a few months. Then I bought a house, and I've been on my own."

"I'm sorry, honey. Somehow, I feel like it was partly my fault. Isn't that strange?"

"You know, I never blamed Heather. I felt sorry for her. Lots of kids do dumb things on their graduation night from high school."

"I spent most of mine barfing," Stef admitted. "I've never touched alcohol since that night. But all that happened to you three years ago. Why are you now out on the road running from someplace to someplace?"

"It gets worse." Develyn's shoulders slumped. She felt so exhausted she contemplated stretching out on top of the table and taking a nap.

"How can it get worse?"

"My daughter always hoped and prayed that we would work things out and get back together."

"That's natural for a daughter. Does she know what happened?"

"I didn't tell her, but she figured it out. She hasn't spoken to Heather since that night. About a year after the divorce was final, her father sent me an apologetic letter. He said he had no excuse for that night. And that I had done the right thing in divorcing him. But he wanted to straighten his life out, and he knew he had to make peace with me."

"Did he want to get back together?"

"That's what it seemed like." Develyn used her fingertips to massage her temples.

"Was that before or after you lost the thirty pounds?" Stef asked.

"After."

"It figures."

"Anyway, Dee—that's what I call her . . . snuck into my dresser drawer and read her father's letter to me. She decided that he had changed and got excited about us reuniting."

"But you didn't want to?"

Develyn sipped the lukewarm coffee, then picked lint off the sleeve of her sweatshirt. When her throat tightened, she coughed, then sipped the ice water. "Stef, to tell you the truth, I just couldn't stand to be in the same room with him. I didn't believe his words. I didn't trust his motives. I know that's very unchristian. But, there were just so many unresolved things. I didn't think I could handle it again."

"What kind of unresolved things?" Stef whispered.

"I don't even know where to begin. For a while it was rumored that Heather was pregnant."

"Oh, dear."

"And I heard Spencer insisted on driving her to Chicago to pay for her abortion."

"Nice guy."

"I don't know if any of it's true. That's the problem. I don't know what to believe."

For several moments she stared out the window at the scattered lights on the interstate. She shuddered, then rubbed the goose bumps on the back of her neck.

Stef reached over and patted her hand. "It's OK, honey."

"One of the engineers at his office wrote to me after that, to say that there had been other women, and I had done the right thing. I suppose he thought that would make me feel better. It just crushed me all over again. A person can only lie to herself for so long."

"You hadn't known about the others?"

"There are some things I tried not to know. I suppose I thought if I refused to deal with them, they weren't real. Anyway, last Christmas Eve Dee's father showed up, unexpected, at our new house. It was the first time he'd ever come by. He brought presents and asked if he could come in and visit. Dee said yes, and I said no. He left, but Delaney was so mad at me she didn't speak to me all day Christmas."

"Not exactly a holiday to remember."

Develyn leaned back on the cold plastic booth and closed her eyes. "I seem to have had a lot of days I'd like to forget. He sent some roses to both of us on Valentine's Day. I let Dee put them up on top of the television."

"And you began to feel you were too hard on him?"

"I suppose." Develyn sat up straight, brushed the corners of her eyes, and sipped on the cold, bitter coffee. "The first week in March he stopped by and brought us all the old photographs from the house. That was really nice of him. I think I missed those more than anything I had left behind."

"Maybe he really was trying," Stef suggested.

"Yes, well, Dee was convinced things were mending. But I just felt he was using me. Right before Easter I had a teacher's conference up in South Bend. While I was there, I kept arguing with myself and praying about what I should do."

"Do you believe in Jesus, Dev?"

"Yes, I do. But I'm not sure I understand how or why everything turns out the way it does."

"Yeah . . . that's like me."

"Anyway, on the Sunday of the teacher's conference, I went to an early church service by myself. I sat in the back and poured my heart out to God. I just didn't know what I was supposed to do. By the end of the service it seemed to be clearing up. I would go home and invite Dee's father to lunch with us at a restaurant after church on Easter Sunday. I knew Dee would be thrilled."

"Did you get together?"

Develyn chewed on her finger. She took several deep breaths and fought the urge to sob.

"It's OK, honey . . ." Stef whispered.

"No, I have to say it," Develyn whimpered. "I have to tell someone. It's eating me up on the inside. When I got back to my hotel room there was a frantic voice mail to call home. I called and Dee was hysterical. She had been trying to call me for two hours. Her dad had a massive heart attack on a business trip to Atlanta. When I called back she had just learned that he had died."

Stef's hand went to her mouth. "Oh, no. No!"

"My daughter decided that my hardness toward him had precipitated the heart attack, and it was my fault he died."

"Cupcake," Max shouted, "do you want me to scoop my own ice cream on this pie?"

Stef wiped her eyes on a thin white paper napkin. "Honey, I'll be right back. Are you sure you don't want some breakfast?"

Develyn folded her arms on the cold Formica tabletop, then laid her head on them. "No, I think I'll just rest my eyes."

When the trucker left, Stef returned to the table and listened as Develyn told about the change in summer plans, and her memories of a dirt-road town. When another truck driver blustered in, the waitress retreated to the kitchen.

A few minutes later she returned. "Dev, you're welcome to go down to my place and sleep a little. It's isn't much, just an old singlewide. But it's clean and tidy. Really. I am a tidy person. I may not know how to keep a man, but I can keep a house."

"Thanks, Stef. I'm just starting to relax right here. I'm glad I told you all of that. It's been boiling inside of me for way too long. I think it's why I can't sleep at night. Do you mind if I just sit here and rest my head on the table?"

"No, of course not. Let me get you something . . ." Stef disappeared behind the counter and came back with a bright red, heart-shaped pillow, with the words "Sweet Cakes" embroidered on it. "Here, this will be more comfortable."

"Where did you get that?"

"Isn't it atrocious? You wouldn't believe some of the presents I get. Most are unmentionable."

The pillow was soft.

Her eyes felt so heavy.

But there was an unexpected lightness in her heart.

She thought of a wide-rumped brown horse with a white spot on his right shoulder. A smile creased the satin pillow. Blue sky floated above. There was a pleasing aroma of horse sweat and old leather.

Develyn was startled to feel someone rub her shoulder.

"Honey, it's about time for my shift to end."

She sat up. A half-dozen male customers crowded the café. "Was I asleep?"

"For over an hour."

"I need to get back on the road," Develyn insisted.

Stef picked up the empty coffee cup. "You know you can come home with me and take a shower or a nap or both."

Develyn looked over at the men, most of whom glanced her way. "They must have thought I was drunk and passed out."

"Nope. I told them you were my little sis, waiting for me to get off work."

Develyn slipped out of the booth. "I'll just use the ladies' room to wash my face. Then I'll get on my way."

"I'll fix you a couple of egg biscuits and a coffee for the road."

"And a large ice water."

The waitress slipped her arm around Develyn's waist. "Honey, am I ever going to see you again?"

"I was thinking the same thing. You were a special angel for me, Stef. I needed to talk. You are a very good listener."

"Years of practice, Dev. Take care of yourself. If you go back to Indiana this route, please stop by. I needed you tonight too, you know. Remember this halfway waitress in a halfway town."

Develyn hugged Stef and kissed her cheek. "Girl, I'm never going to forget you. Don't you ever for a minute think your job is unimportant. It's not just truckers who need you here. Maybe all of us are somewhere on the road of life . . . halfway."

3

The Pizza Hut delivery girl banged on the door of Room 210 at the Cheyenne, Wyoming, Holiday Inn. Develyn woke up and staggered to the door. She vaguely remembered ordering a small BLT pizza with thin crust right after she got out of the shower, but she didn't recall pulling on her Purdue sweats and sprawling across the bed.

She extracted the smallest piece and nibbled at it while she fumbled with the phone.

The voice that said "Hello" sounded worried.

"Hi, Lily, it's Dev."

"Are you in a hospital?"

"No, of course not."

"Are you in jail?"

"What are you talking about? I'm at the Holiday Inn."

"Are you being kidnapped?"

"Ms. Martin, what are you talking about?"

"Those are the only three acceptable reasons for not phon-ing me until now. I was ready to call the state police."

"I'm sorry, Lily. Please don't worry."

"Sure, that's like telling a sunflower it doesn't have to fol-low the sun."

Develyn jammed her finger in the cheese, then licked it. "I'm OK."

"You sound awful."

"Oh, thank you. That cheers me up. I just woke from a little nap." Develyn glanced around the room at the lifeless impres-sionistic prints that framed the walls. "I totally zonked after my shower."

"Where are you?" Lily asked.

"Cheyenne."

"Wyoming?"

"Yes, is there another?" She peered around at the clock radio. "I got in about an hour ago."

"Where did you end up spending last night?"

In her mind, Develyn could envision the auburn braid and green eyes of the waitress. "On the road, halfway."

"What?"

She picked off a bacon nibble and popped it in her mouth. "I drove most of the night. But I got tired today so I stopped at a rest stop near Grand Island and slept a couple of hours."

"I'm glad you stopped for the night."

"I won't do that again, mama. I'm way too old to stay up all night."

"Speaking of mama, I saw yours in Target today."

"And?"

"She asked if your phone was down. She left a message and you didn't return the call."

Develyn fluffed up the wimpy pillows on the bed, then leaned back against them. "What did you tell her?"

"That I hadn't talked to you for a couple of days. What was I supposed to say?"

"I'll call her."

"When?"

"In the morning before I leave. And when you go feed the cats, write down my messages, then unplug the machine. I forgot all about it."

"Are you having a good time yet?"

"It's interesting, Lily. I really needed this. I've thought through so many scenes in my life. Maybe this summer I'll learn something from my past, instead of just fleeing from it."

"That sounds profound."

Develyn's toes felt cold. She scrunched them under the green and orange flowered bedspread. "It's what happens when I'm sleep-deprived and eating a BLT pizza."

"Oh, I have to go," Lily blustered. "Can I call you back in the morning?"

"Sure, what's up?"

"My date's here."

"What? I've been gone two days and you're chasing around?"

"What can I say, Devy-girl. I met someone."

"Who? Where? What he's like? How does he look in tight Wranglers?" Develyn laughed.

"He's standing right here . . ." Lily murmured.

"You have to call me tonight . . . no, in the morning. You promise?"

"Sure."

"I can't believe it. All these years I've been holding you back."

Lily laughed. "Bye, Devy-girl."

"Bye, sweetie. Have fun and be good."

Develyn finished the slice of pizza, brushed her teeth, turned out the light, and collapsed on top of the thin, slick bedspread of the queen-sized bed.

• • •

By 9:00 a.m. Develyn Worrell drove north through Chugwater, Wyoming, on Interstate 25 and chewed on a cold breakfast burrito. At noon, while the Cherokee was filling with 89 octane gasoline, she spread her road map on top of the hood.

OK, Daddy . . . we drove to Casper . . . and we were heading to Yellowstone. But you took a couple of shortcuts, got us lost, and then the station wagon dropped its muffler on the rocks when we crossed a riverbed, broke a belt, and shot part of the water pump through the radiator. We never made it to Cody, let alone Yellowstone. But that's two hundred miles of wilderness.

Of course, I have all summer.

I just need to watch the gas gauge.

And keep the doors locked.

"Are you lost, ma'am?"

Develyn spun around. A tall man with leather-like tanned face lounged next to a black Dodge pickup that towed a silver-sided horse trailer. "Excuse me?"

His gray and dark brown hair curled out from under the black cowboy hat. He sauntered over toward her. "Don't mean to interfere, ma'am." He tipped his hat. "I just saw you studyin' the map and surmised you might need some help findin' something. You aren't lookin' for that big wild horse auction, are you?"

Develyn studied his creased, steel gray eyes and square jaw. "Oh, no . . . I, eh . . . a horse auction?"

He looped his thumbs in the front pockets of his jeans. "B.L.M. is auctionin' off some wild horses and burros this afternoon."

"B.L.M.?" she stammered.

He glanced at the Indiana license plate on the Cherokee. "The Bureau of Land Management has too many wild horses grazin' some of their land, so they have a program where the prisoners down at Rawlins green break the horses, then they are sold at auction. Well, they call it an adoption. I thought maybe you're looking for the sale."

"Where is the auction?"

He waved his arm toward the west. "Oh, it's in the middle of nowhere, but if you're interested, I'll get you a brochure. I've got a spare."

"I'm not . . ."

"No problem, ma'am, let me grab it for you." He swaggered back to the truck while she folded her map.

OK, you are in the west, Dev Worrell, where cowboys visit with ladies . . . even if the cowboys are older. I wonder how much older?

He shoved back his hat as he approached to reveal a tan line across his forehead. "Here you go, ma'am. They have a cantina for lunch and ever'thin'. It's kind of fun to watch, just in case you wanted to stop by. You don't have to buy one, of course."

"Are the horses broke to ride?"

"That all depends on the rider, I reckon. Do you ride?" he asked.

"Yes, but it's been . . ."

"Yeah, I could tell by lookin' that you rode. Lot of ladies from the midwest are fine horsewomen."

What does he look at to tell that? She shaded her eyes. "Thank you for the invitation, but I probably won't be able to make it to the auction."

He looked straight into her eyes. "That's too bad, ma'am. That disarmin' smile of yours would have perked up the entire auction. I reckon you could light up the arena. It surely cheered up this ol' cowboy. Say, you might like to buy yourself a hat to block that sun. There's a store about a block back down here that has good Bailey straw hats. You'd look good in a cowboy hat, if you don't mind me sayin' so. If I was you, I'd buy one of those ready-made distressed hats so you don't look like some tourist out here on vacation. Now, you have yourself a great day." He pointed to her folded map. "And I hope you find the place you're looking for." He pulled himself into the cab of the truck and started the noisy diesel motor.

Develyn climbed into the Cherokee and pulled her sunglasses down off her head. *I hope I find the place I'm looking for too.* She took a sip of ice water from a tall red plastic cup. *I wonder what it would be like to perk up a whole wild horse auction? I don't think I've perked up a whole anything in my entire life.*

I do believe he was flirting with me. He wasn't wearing a wedding ring. I didn't flirt back. Well, perhaps, just a little. I wonder how old he is? It's been so long. So very long.

* * *

Develyn pushed the new but distressed-looking straw cowboy hat to the back of her head. With the window rolled down, she chewed on a piece of spent spearmint gum as she pulled off Highway 20/26. The battered sign said *Natrona*.

There was no population listed.

Develyn counted eight houses.

Or, perhaps seven houses and a barn.

She couldn't tell which houses were occupied and which were abandoned. Cars and trucks randomly parked in grassless yards where dusty sheets hung on sagging clotheslines. There was no name on the front of the only commercial-looking building, but a hand-painted sign read "Welcome, we're open. Keep the screen door closed." The only other signs on the peeling white paint of the clapboard walls were a little blond-headed boy selling small hourglass shaped bottles of Coca-Cola . . . and a tattered poster of a girl with an umbrella losing salt as she walked along in a rainstorm.

Develyn eased open the door and stepped into the shadows of the store. The building was only twelve feet wide and about thirty feet long. There was one left aisle and one right aisle, with most of the supplies stacked against the walls. At the back counter Develyn could hear someone talking. She strolled slowly, forcing down her boot heels on the worn wooden floor.

As she approached the counter, she spied a large woman with beautiful wavy blonde hair and a smooth complexion.

"Honey, I have a customer. Call me later. Hugs and kisses." The woman blushed, then whispered, "Later."

"I didn't mean to hurry you," Develyn apologized.

The woman's soft, easy smile revealed two dimples. "It's OK. He's a sweetie. He'll call back."

"Your husband?"

"Not yet. Shoot, I haven't even met him yet."

"You haven't met?"

"Not in real time. We were both in the Horses-with-Troubled-Hooves chat room and started to visit. One thing led to another, and now he calls most every day."

"Where does he live?"

"Buffalo, Texas. Can I help you find anything?"

Develyn glanced over her shoulder. The shelves smelled like dirt and vanilla. "All I need is some gum, ice water, and point me to the ladies' room."

"I've got the gum. Bottled water, but no ice. The john's back there." She pointed to the screen door behind her. "It's the one on the right. There's a hammer hanging on a rope outside the door. Bang on the side of the wall with the hammer; if you can't hear any rattle noise, go on in."

Develyn's eyes widened. "What?"

"It's snake season, honey. And you know how they like the shade of an outhouse."

"Outhouse?" Develyn gasped.

The lady chuckled. "You had me fooled. I thought you were from around here. Where are you from?"

"Indiana. The tan is from a tanning booth; the hat I just bought in Casper. The jeans and T-shirt come from 'western dress-up day' at Riverbend Elementary, and the boots? Well, the boots are honest. I bought them in Houston five years ago and love them."

"Pay no mind to what I said about the snakes. There hasn't been a snake out there in over a week."

"I suddenly lost the urge to go."

"I know what you mean. I feel the same way in the winter when it's ten below. I reckon urgency is a state of mind. Do you still want the water?"

"Perhaps I should wait."

"That's what I figured." She reached to the counter behind her and retrieved a pack of gum. "That's forty-nine cents."

"How did you know I wanted sugarless spearmint?"

"Any lady as petite as you wants sugarless, and besides, that's the only kind I have besides watermelon bubblegum."

"Good deduction." Develyn dug down into her jeans pocket for change.

"Are you goin' to or from?" the lady asked.

Develyn shoved the exact change across the worn wooden counter. "Excuse me?"

"Indiana. Are you headed home or leaving it?"

"I'm out here on vacation. Just started it."

"By yourself?"

Develyn hesitated.

"I know, I'm getting personal. I reckon you're headed to Yellowstone, the Tetons and all."

"Actually, perhaps you can help me." Develyn unwrapped the pack of gum. "I'm looking for a little Wyoming town. I just can't remember the name. I wasn't driving at the time and can't recall how to find it. I know we left Casper and were headed up to Cody and . . ."

"Then you had to come right along this road," the woman interrupted.

"That's what I thought." Develyn held the fresh gum between her fingers as she spat the old gum into the wrapper.

"You don't remember any names?"

"I remember a store. It was called the Sweetwater Grocery and it was in Mrs. Tagley's living room. Does that sound familiar to you?" She slipped the new gum in her mouth and milked the mint flavor with her tongue.

"I've never heard of it. How long has it been since you came through?"

"Thirty-five years ago."

"Hah! That was the year I was born. But that was in Cantrell, Montana."

"How long have you been here?" Develyn asked.

"Eighteen months, twenty-one days and . . ." the woman glanced at the antelope horn clock on the wall ". . . and ten minutes."

Develyn studied the woman's pretty round face. "Sounds like a prison term."

"Don't it? Say, do you want to buy a store?"

"You are selling this store?"

"I wouldn't turn down a reasonable offer."

Develyn laughed. "Sorry, I'm not interested in a store."

"Yeah, neither was I."

"How did you decide to buy it?"

"My truck broke down. I was hauling two horses to a show in Torrington, and threw a rod right through the engine.

Ol' Man Alanville offered to trade me this store for the truck, trailer, two horses, and tack. So, I traded him."

"You got a whole store for that?"

"Yeah, what a deal, huh? I'll trade you the store for that Cherokee of yours and a hundred dollars cash."

"Are you kidding me?"

"No, you interested?" The woman painted her lips with a golden orange lip balm.

"Not really."

"Forget the cash. Just a straight trade."

Develyn rocked back on her heels and felt the floor sag. "Thank you, but I don't want to buy a store. But I would like to find the town with the Sweetwater Grocery."

"You need to talk to Ol' Man Alanville. His kin rolled in here with Jim Bridger and that bunch. He's been here so long he knows all the lizards by first name, except some of the younger set."

Develyn caught herself staring. "Eh . . . where does Mr. Alanville live?"

"Head back down the dirt road to the blacktop, but turn right at the mailboxes. That's Garden Gulch Road. It will meander along the wash for a couple of miles, then as soon as you come up out of the dry creek bed, take a right turn. That's Cedar Creek Road, but there are no cedars." She grabbed a halfway clean paper towel and a felt marker. "Here, I'll draw you a map. Ol' Man Alanville has that newer doublewide surrounded by the chicken wire fence. Just honk twice and wait. If he's home, he'll come out and see you."

She handed Develyn the small scrap of paper towel. "Here, just follow this."

"Well, thank you."

"You sure you don't want a store?"

"I'm sure."

"Yeah . . . it figures," the woman mumbled.

Develyn spun rock as she pulled back on to the gravel road that led south toward the highway. She pulled over at the cluster of mailboxes.

There's no way I'm going to wander around out here.

One lone cattle truck rolled east toward Casper. There were distant treeless mountains ahead of her. The rolling prairie had sparsly scattered bunches of pale green short grass. The few buildings were behind her. She could see no houses ahead of her.

She counted the mailboxes.

Twenty-seven? Where do they live? They must drive five miles to get their mail.

"I'm not going down that road," she mumbled out loud. "I'm getting back on the highway and driving to . . ."

Where am I going today?

If this trip followed logic, I wouldn't have begun it in the first place.

Why not go ask Ol' Man Alanville if he ever heard of the Sweetwater Store? I have to ask someone. But why wander off the road? This could be dangerous. I'll stick to the highway. This is only my first day to look. Or is it my second? It's all rather blurry.

She sipped on the remnants of the ice water, then turned down the dirt road to the west. *I can't believe I'm doing this.*

Scattered gray sage and pale green bunch grass dotted the brown Wyoming hills. The dirt road followed the lowest contour.

"Well, Ms. Worrell, you are now the only vehicle on scenic Garden Gulch Road. Do you have any idea what you are doing? Are you trying to self-destruct?"

The ruts, holes, and rocks on the roadway forced her to slow down. She was barely ahead of a self-generated dust cloud. While Creedence Clearwater Revival sang "Proud Mary," Develyn rolled across the dirt road, under a wide blue sky she considered the color of Paul Newman's eyes.

She peeked at herself in the rearview mirror.

Then laughed out loud.

"Ms. Worrell, you are a sight. Dirt on your face. Cowboy hat. Bouncing along some trail to who knows where. No one would believe this. Mother would be shocked. No, maybe not. She doesn't have much hope that I'll ever again make a right decision."

She tapped her foot to the next tune on the CD, then sang, "Just about a year ago, I set out on the road . . ." She hit the power button and rolled down all four windows. She stuck her head out the window and shouted at the top of her voice, "Oh, Lord, stuck in Lodi again!"

Develyn took a deep breath of dusty air. "I feel good, world!" she shouted. "I feel real good, and I have absolutely no explanation for it."

She rolled up the windows and sped up until the Jeep bounced off the roadway and out into the dry creekbed. She left the accelerator jammed down and rebounded back up into the dirt roadway.

I wonder if there is a speed limit out here? I don't know if this is a road.

She slowed down at the top of the dry riverbank. The cloud of dust swirled over her like a frustrated dirt devil, then disappeared.

"OK . . . Develyn Worrell, you are to turn right on something called 'Cedar Creek Road.'" She gazed toward the north, then studied the wiggly lines of the hand-drawn map. "That must be the road, because there aren't any cedars." Develyn giggled. "Of course, there are no cedars for a hundred miles."

As Creedence Clearwater Revival blasted out "Willie and the Poor Boys," Develyn jammed on the brakes, turned up the stereo as far as it would go, and hopped out of the rig, leaving the door open.

With John Fogarty singing lead, Develyn danced around the dust-covered Jeep Cherokee. No matter which direction she looked, there were no houses, no fences, no people, no cars, no trucks, no cows . . . nothing. When she circled the rig once, she reversed her direction and danced back around the Jeep. When the tune began to fade she reached in and hit the repeat button. This time she shuffled as if she formed part of an invisible line of dancers.

As the song ended, she balanced herself atop a wheelbarrow-size granite boulder and shouted, "I've wanted to do that since

I was ten! Did you see that, Mother? What are you going to do with this girl?"

Mother would have scowled, but Father would have gotten out and danced with me. Why, oh why did I wait until I was forty-five to dance around the car? Leaving the door open, she flopped back on the seat. "Dev Worrell, you just might survive after all!"

She watched the odometer. Four miles up Cedar Creek Road, she spotted a structure against a distant foothill.

That must be a house. But how do I know if it belongs to Ol' Man Alanville? I can't even tell if it's a house or a barn from here. I suppose there is only one way to find out.

She spied a lid off a fifty-five-gallon drum, mounted on a T-post alongside the road, that read "No government agents beyond this point."

Is that a joke? Government agents? Back here?

Sagebrush lined the way to the doublewide perched on concrete blocks and jammed against a lone, stubby cottonwood tree. A four-foot-high chicken wire fence surrounded a bare dirt yard. She could not see anyone.

Develyn honked her horn twice.

Then waited.

And waited.

I didn't want to come back here in the first place. This is ridiculous.

She locked the doors of the Cherokee.

Maybe he's not here. Perhaps I should honk twice again. He might not want to see me. Maybe he's pulling on a shirt. Or trying to find his shotgun.

64

Develyn scouted the drive for the best place to turn around when a paper-thin old man wearing a long-sleeve white shirt buttoned at the collar and tattered jeans appeared at the door.

"Don't just stay out there! Come up on the porch and sit a spell!" he hollered.

Develyn turned off the engine and opened the door. "Did the lady at the store phone you?"

He hiked out to the chicken wire gate and swung it open for her. "What store?"

"In Natrona."

"I don't own it any more."

"I know . . ." Develyn parked her gum under her tongue. "The lady there said you might help me."

"Well, come on up to the porch," he motioned. "Would you like some cold tea?"

"Actually, that sounds nice." *What I would really like is a rest room, but I'm not sure I want to ask him. Does he have an outhouse too?*

"Of course, I don't have any ice, but it sat out on the back porch last night. My name's Hugh Alanville. I'm the last of the Alanvilles."

She shook his bony, cold hand. "You acted as though you were expecting me. How did you know I was coming?"

He pointed to the skies. "They told me."

"Who?"

"The aliens. Why do you think I have the chicken wire around the place?"

Develyn eased her way back toward the gate. "Eh, to keep out the aliens?"

"That fence don't even keep out chickens, let alone two-ton aliens. That fence is really a sophisticated antenna that draws in communications from all over the Darlobe."

"The Darlobe?"

"We call it a universe, but they"—he pointed at the sky—"call it the Darlobe."

Develyn took a deep breath, then bit her lip. "Mr. Alanville, have you ever heard of the Sweetwater Grocery store? I'm trying to find it."

"It burnt down."

"It did?"

"Yep, in 1929."

She found herself staring at the old man's narrow eyes. "But I was there in . . ."

"And they rebuilt it in 1933."

"Oh, well, I was wondering . . ."

"A tornado wiped it out in '42," he added. "We haven't had a tornado since then."

"What town was . . ."

"They gave up on the store."

"They did?" Develyn pressed.

"Yep." Alanville rubbed his unshaven chin. "Old lady Tagley kept it open in her living room, but it weren't much of a store."

"Yes, that's the one. Where is it, Mr. Alanville?"

"It's twenty-four miles west of here. In the old days there was a stage stop ever' eight miles, so all the towns and stops are in multiples of eight," he explained.

"What's the name of the town where the store is?"

"It's, ah . . . ah . . . dadgum it . . . it starts with an A." He stared up at the clear blue sky. "I can't remember much since that night."

Develyn cradled her temples with her fingertips. *Please don't tell me the aliens evaporated your memory.*

"Ever since the aliens evaporated my memory," he mumbled.

"Yes, I imagine that can be disheartening. Do I go back out to the blacktop and travel west to get to Mrs. Tagley's store?"

"Nope, there isn't any blacktop in that town."

"Yes. Yes, that's it. It's a dirt-road town. Mr. Alanville, you have made my day. Maybe my summer!"

"Say, you aren't from around here?"

"Oh, no . . . I'm from . . ."

"Sholokka?" he probed.

"Where?"

"Podrihamon?"

"I'm not familiar with those towns."

"Towns? Those are intergalactic mass depository units."

"Mr. Alanville, how do I get to Mrs. Tagley's store?"

"Turn right at the dry riverbed and stay on that road for twenty-four miles. Ain't you goin' to stay for cold tea?"

"I really need to push on." *I expect to see Tommy Lee Jones and Will Smith show up any minute wearing black sunglasses.*

"That's what *they* said." He pointed to the sky. "Good-bye. Naspha habba ooupe."

Develyn was almost at a trot when she reached the Jeep Cherokee. Within seconds, she fogged up dirt as she hurried south.

• • •

The odometer read twenty-six miles when she reached the blacktop on Highway 20. She found no store. No town. No house. Not a car or a mailbox for the entire trip. She parked by the side of the road as two empty cattle trucks rumbled down the highway.

"OK, Ms. Worrell, now what?" she mumbled. *I can't believe that I thought a man convinced of aliens would be able to give me the correct directions. This is empty country, Lord. It's like I'm on the edge of civilization. Or beyond.*

A white '58 Ford pickup smoked and blasted its way northwest on the blacktop. On the southern horizon, oil-field rockers, pumped away like a slow saltz with wealth.

It's like living in a vacuum. Like someone forced people not to live here. Develyn stood beside the rig, drank a big swig of tepid water, and wiped her mouth on her arm. It tasted dusty.

Time for plan number two. I will check on every settlement within twenty-five miles of either side of the highway . . . all the way across Wyoming. It's got to be here somewhere.

68

She pulled her map out of the Jeep. The wild horse sale flyer fluttered to the dirt. She scooped it up and studied the hand-scrawled map.

This sale can't be more than a few miles from here.

Why not, Ms. Worrell? I'm not expected to be anywhere at any time. Let's just see how great your awesome smile really is.

The tiny closed service station had a faded sign that read "Waltman." Following the flyer, she turned north on a gravel road. The road dropped down to a dry creek bed and crossed the rocks to the other side. She shifted into four-wheel drive. The road lost its gravel and turned to dry, yellowish, Wyoming dust. Three miles further, she spotted buildings to the east and a railroad track straight ahead.

At least it is a town. A tiny town. It isn't my town, of course, but it is a town.

As she approached from the southeast, she could see a huge congregation of pickups and horse trailers in a field to the west of the buildings.

That has to be the wild horse sale. Half the people in Wyoming must be here.

When she reached the tracks, she turned west to follow the dirt road to the cluster of two dozen houses.

It's much too small for the one I'm looking for. I remember a larger place. There were a dozen stores . . . well, perhaps a half-dozen.

At the edge of town, a dull green sign slumped at a forty-five-degree angle.

Develyn slowed down. *Argenta? Argenta, Wyoming? No, this isn't it. I'm sure I would have remembered that.*

A one-pump service station stood in front of a washed-out cedar-sided garage with the big door open. A sign hung from the pump that read "Closed Until After the Horse Auction." Several old houses hunkered back in the shade of thick-trunked cottonwoods. She crept along at ten miles an hour past a four-railed corral.

At the sight of a white clapboard house with a sagging front porch, she slammed on the brakes.

With her hands on her cheeks, Develyn started to cry.

Over the porch were the words "Sweetwater Grocery, Mrs. Charles F. Tagley, prop." Under that sign was a newer one: "DVD Rentals and High-Speed Internet Hook-Up."

Develyn Gail Upton Worrell pulled up in front of the store.

She wiped her eyes, blew her nose, and studied her face in the rearview mirror. "You did it, Devy-girl. You found it. I knew you could."

Each board on the porch creaked as she hiked up to the font door. She stepped over to the worn wooden bench made from a covered wagon seat, covered with initials carved in various sizes. When she found DGU, she rubbed the letters with her fingertips.

Dear brother, there you are. Dewayne Gary Upton. I was too scared of being caught to let you carve mine. I can't believe this bench is still here.

Develyn pushed into the house. The living room was stacked with packages and canned goods. The west wall was shelved with videos. At the back a sign pointed to the side room—"Medicines and Sundry Items."

Behind a wooden counter were several cold boxes and a chest-style freezer.

Develyn folded her arms and hugged herself.

"I can't believe I'm actually here."

"I'll be right there," a soft voice called from the back room. "I wasn't expecting anyone until after the auction." A white-haired lady with slumped shoulders dressed in a long faded cotton dress shuffled out to the counter. "I was just watching my soap opera and . . ." She hesitated when she saw Develyn.

"Mrs. Tagley?" Develyn gasped. *She was old thirty-five years ago.*

The lady scooted closer, then leaned so close Develyn could smell peppermints. After a moment she stepped back.

"Hi, honey . . . how's your brother?"

"What?"

"I suppose you want the usual."

"But . . . you can't . . ."

The lady reached into the big chest-style freezer and pulled out an orange Popsicle. "Some kids grow up with the very same face. Yours hasn't changed a bit. This one is on me, but you can't stay away so long next time."

"Mrs. Tagley, this is incredible. You can't possibly remember me."

"I haven't had another Devy-girl in this store for thirty-five years."

Develyn unwrapped the Popsicle. "Dewayne has a career in the Navy. He's out somewhere in the Persian Gulf right now."

71

"So is Lydia's husband."

"Who?"

"Lydia . . . in my soap opera. And if he doesn't get that furlough soon, Lorenzo will run off with Lydia." She motioned to the front door. "I reckon you'll sit on the porch as usual. I'll be in the back room if you need anything. I knew you'd be back."

"How did you know that?"

"Because you promised me. I knew you were the type to keep your promise." The old lady padded into the back room.

The air was dry.

The sky clear.

The Popsicle sweet.

And the wagon seat hard.

You made it, Dev Worrell. You said you were coming back, and you did it.

A red Dodge truck rambled down the road in front of the store. The cowboy-hat-wearing driver slammed on his brakes and jumped out.

"Hey, purdy yella-haired lady! You can't see the world famous Renny Slater ride them wild bucking horses from the store bench."

"Who's Renny Slater?"

He tipped his black cowboy hat. "Pleased to meet you, ma'am. Come on, I'll give you a lift."

She stood up.

This is not the kind of thing you do, Ms. Worrell.

You are not going for a ride with this unknown man.

Or any unknown man.

With dimples pock-marking his smile, he opened the door for her and waited for her to scoot in.

The leather pickup seat felt warm.

Thinning blond hair curled out from under the battered, black beaver felt cowboy hat. Several stitches over his left eye made his dimpled smile seem more like a leer. Brooks and Dunn sang "My Maria" until he jabbed the off knob and slammed his door.

"Ma'am, I'm surprised you got in the truck with me." He peered over the top of his deep orange-lensed sunglasses.

Develyn held her brown leather purse in her lap and stared straight out the bug-blasted windshield as she licked on the orange Popsicle. "So am I."

He rolled down the sleeves of his faded yellow shirt and snapped the cuffs. "I mean, how do you know I ain't some bad man who will drive up toward Hole-in-the-Wall and kidnap you?"

She chewed on the Popsicle stick, clutched her purse with both hands, and refused to glance at him. "How do you know I'm not a bad woman with a .357 Magnum in my purse who's planning on shooting you, stealing your truck, and leaving your carcass for the buzzards?" *I can't believe I said that!*

"Whoa!" he hooted and slapped the steering wheel. "I love it! You've got spunk, and I don't even know your name! You know mine."

"Mr. Slater, I believe." She relaxed her grip on her purse and glanced over at his narrow chin and thick eyebrows. "I'm Dev Worrell."

He tipped his hat. When he smiled, deep tanned creases formed at his eyes. "Pleased to meet you, Miss Worrell. Say, you don't really have a .357 in that purse do you?"

She pushed the straw hat back. *I feel like I'm in a doctor's office for my yearly exam. I should at least check my mascara and lipstick.* "Are you planning on kidnapping me?"

He slipped the truck in gear, and they crept west. "Eh, no ma'am. That ain't my style."

"Then, no, I don't have a gun in my purse. But I do have a cell phone."

"Shoot, so do I, but I can't always get reception out here."

They had barely rolled back to where the main road turned south. "Mr. Slater, do you always drive this slow?"

He tapped his crooked fingers on top of the black steering wheel. "Only when I want to be late."

"Why do you want to be late?"

"They are always happier to see you when they get worried that you ain't goin' to show."

"So you stage being late?"

"Yeah, do you figure that's wrong?"

A blue Dodge pickup honked and sped around them.

"I suppose he doesn't care if everyone's happy to see him show up."

"He's not a mustang breaker. I think he has the spread south of the Big Horn Mountains."

Develyn pulled off the black-framed sunglasses and rubbed the bridge of her nose. "Is Hole-in-the-Wall really north of here?"

"Yep, Devy-girl. It's a nice drive. You and me should go see it some time."

She wrapped her arms across her chest. "Why did you call me that?"

He looked startled. "What?"

"Devy-girl."

He surveyed the field of haphazardly parked pickups. "No offense, Miss Worrell. I reckon I call all young ladies 'girl.' Just a habit. I used to call them all darlin' till Prissy McMahon cured me of that."

"How did she do that?"

He rubbed his right shoulder and shook his head. "I don't want to talk about it. Well, here we are."

A couple of hundred pickups, horse trailers, and a few semi trucks surrounded a large arena with cedar-slatted fencing. He parked between a battered orange Dodge truck and a new white Dodge dually.

Develyn opened the door and slid to the dusty, dry prairie that served as a temporary parking lot. A roar went up from the crowd that hovered around the arena fencing. She smiled. "I'm surprised they started without the famous Renny Slater."

"Well, Devy-girl, I let the boys ride the easy ones, and they save the rank and snuffy ones for ol' Renny." He draped a saddle blanket over his shoulder, then yanked a saddle from the back of his truck. With it balanced on his shoulder, he swaggered around to her.

He was about her height. She saw him glance down at her ringless finger. *Mr. Slater, exactly what is on your mind?*

He stopped strolling and spun around and faced her. "Say, your ol' man ain't goin' to be fumed about me givin' you a lift is he?"

Her neck stiffened. She whipped off her dark sunglasses and waved them at him. "Why do you assume I have a boyfriend?"

He shifted the saddle further back on his shoulder. "Now, Devy-girl, no offense. I didn't mean your boyfriend, I meant your father."

Develyn burst out laughing. "Cowboy, that's about the lamest line I've ever heard. How old do you think I am?"

He pulled his dark glasses off and leaned toward her face. "Eh. . . . well, I reckon when I saw you on the porch with a Popsicle, I figured . . . eh . . . but I can see when I look close at . . . I mean . . . not that you are long at the tooth, but . . . you've got . . . whoa, I'm diggin' myself a hole, now, ain't I?"

Develyn slipped her dark glasses back on. "Yes, you are."

"It's just, back there with the Popsicle, I figured you for one of them barrel racin' angels who's talked her daddy into buyin' her a new horse."

"I take it you are used to hitting on barrel racin' angels?" she prodded.

"Not since Gracie St. John."

"What happened with Gracie?"

He rubbed his left side. "I don't want to talk about it. But you still look like a barrel racer . . . except . . ." His voice trailed off.

"Except I'm too old?" Develyn pressed and wandered through the trucks toward the arena.

"No, Devy-girl. Barrel racers come in all ages. I reckon Martha Josey is older than my mama."

"Thanks, Renny . . . now that you can see me, you know different. How old do I look?"

"I'm not about to go down that trail. Good men have lost their lives answering that one. It don't seem possible, but I'll turn forty-two come July."

"Well, Renny Slater, I was a senior in high school when you were a freshman."

He stared at her from boot to hat. "I don't believe that for a New York minute."

She felt a grin break over her face. "You're good, Renny Slater. You must have been practicing those lines for years. But no matter what you think, I didn't just fall off an Indiana hay wagon."

"Oooooh-wee," he howled as he strutted toward the crowd at the east end of the arena. "I hope them mustangs is easier to break than Ms. Develyn Worrell."

Renny grabbed her arm and pushed his way through the cluster of cowboys of various ages, sizes, and odors. Most tipped their hats her way and stepped aside.

Dirty boots, felt hats, long sleeve shirts, Wranglers with a telltale circle on the back pocket . . . it's like a uniform. Or a different culture. It's like the time I got lost in New York's Chinatown. Lord, I'm not sure what I'm doing here. I just want to hide in the crowd and watch. For the rest of my life. This is a long way from Crawfordsville.

"You just step up on that bottom rail, Devy-girl, and you can see the whole show. Ain't no bleachers here. I'll keep an eye on you, so you don't have to fret."

She jammed the bare Popsicle stick into her back pocket. Her small brown leather purse hung at her side as she climbed up the rail. The afternoon sun peeked under her straw hat, and she pulled it down over her forehead and studied the arena.

Do I look like someone you have to keep an eye on? I've done fifth and sixth grade yard duty during summer school. Two hundred cowboys is a piece of cake.

She guessed the oval arena to be about two hundred feet long and one hundred feet wide. At the east end were dual roping boxes and an empty squeeze chute. On the south side were two faded white-boarded bucking chutes, with gates sagging and open. The entire arena was encircled with dusty men and cowboy hats. Develyn spotted several women, all of whom wore cowboy hats and ponytails or a long braid, no matter what their age.

There was no activity in the arena. Most of the people seemed caught up in animated conversations with those around them, like the rumble at a Friday night high school football game at halftime after the marching band cleared the field.

A draped rope fenced off the west end of the arena. Orange survey-tape flags flapped every few feet. Several dozen haltered but unsaddled horses milled around behind the rope like anxious first-graders waiting for the bell on the first day of school.

The sky was light blue and cloudless. A mild breeze came from the northwest. Sweat, dirt, and cigar smoke drifted across the arena. From somewhere, Develyn smelled the aroma of fried meat. Her stomach growled, and she pulled out the Popsicle stick and chewed on it.

She studied the fence she clutched. The rough-cut cedar rail was mostly worn slick by being polished for years, she supposed, by the backsides of Wranglers. There were several bite-size defects that were rough and splinter-filled. Develyn avoided those with her hands and studied the faces that lined the rail.

I wonder what it would be like to go to a horse sale and buy a horse or two? Is it like buying a new car? "I'd like one that is gentle, pretty, easy maintenance . . . and has cup holders." Or is it like buying blouses? "I want one of those, one of those, and oh, yes . . . one of those brown and white ones."

Parked inside the arena near the bucking chutes, a green Dodge pickup marked "Bureau of Land Management" provided a platform. A gray-haired man in a flat-crowned, wide-brimmed cowboy hat, with jeans tucked inside tall black boots with underslung heels, stood on the pickup bed. Perched next to him was a card table. He hollered into a hand-held loud speaker.

"OK, folks, that's the first fifty. I told you, those are the gentle ones. These others have lots of, eh . . . spunk and potential. We'll run the mares first. Then bring in the stallions. I see Renny Slater finally made it, thank the good Lord for that. 'Course, he was trailerin' some purdy yella-haired barrel-racer, no doubt. We'll take a thirty-minute break and then run the mares. Get out your pocketbook, 'cause there are some beauties in this lot. Don't forget Margaret's portable Cantina parked in the shade of Dyton's cattle truck. She's got green chili burritos, Indian fry bread, and all the fixin's. Those of you that bought this first lot come help us get them out of the arena. You can trailer them up now. That is, you can give it a try."

Develyn watched Renny tote a saddle over his shoulder as he swaggered out toward the green pickup.

"Renny looks like every little girl's image of a cowboy, doesn't he?" The raspy female voice came from somewhere behind her.

She turned to see a dark-haired, brown-complexioned woman with a long braid to her waist and a battered straw cowboy hat standing next to her. It looked like her white-and-blue cowboy shirt had the sleeves ripped out at the shoulders by a dull pocket knife. Develyn stepped off the rail and shoved her Popsicle stick in her back pocket. The woman had a round face, full rounded nose, and two sets of feathered earrings dangling from each ear.

Develyn watched the woman inspect her. "Yes, I suppose the bow legs and dimpled grin kind of fit the stereotype, don't they? Some things are difficult to conceal."

Both women turned and peeked under the top rail back across the arena.

Slater stopped in the middle of the arena and chewed on a wooden match as he visited with a man in a straw panama hat.

"How long have you known Renny?" the dark-haired woman asked.

Develyn glanced at her silver heart-banded bracelet watch. "About nineteen minutes."

The woman grinned and revealed a small gap in her front upper teeth. "No, really."

The woman was the same height as Develyn, and both had cowboy hats pushed back. "It's true. I was sitting on Mrs. Tagley's porch a few minutes ago, and Renny offered me a lift down here."

"I thought you were kidding me." The woman stuck out her hand. "I'm Casey Cree-Ryder."

Returning the tight clasp, Develyn nodded. "I'm Develyn Worrell, but please call me Dev."

"Are you out from Casper?" Cree-Ryder asked. "I hope you aren't offended, but you have kind of a city look."

Develyn tugged off her sunglasses. "I'm afraid I'm even more east than Casper. I'm from Indiana."

The brown-skinned woman whistled between her teeth. "I didn't even know they had cowgirls in Indiana."

"They don't." Develyn dragged the toe of her boot across the dusty yellow dirt. "I teach fifth grade."

Cree-Ryder's dark eyes relaxed. "Are you on vacation?"

Develyn tried to brush dust off the front of her pale blue T-shirt. "Yes. I was actually out here years ago. Thought I'd stop back by."

Casey jammed her hands in the back pockets of her jeans. "So, you aren't here with Renny?"

Develyn felt her neck stiffen. "Not hardly."

The dark-skinned woman surveyed the crowd. "He's a nice guy. Oh, he jokes a lot, but he's one of the good ones. He's born-again, you know."

"Eh, no . . . I didn't know that."

"Yep, I was there at the plunge in Thermopolis when he was baptized. So, he has high marks in my book."

"Thank you for that recommendation. We just met."

"You're not interested in him?"

"I'd enjoy having friends in Wyoming, but I'm not looking for anything else." Develyn studied the woman's round, dark brown eyes. "Are you interested in Renny?"

A wide smile broke across the woman's face. "I might be. Lots of Wyoming cowboys shy away from me . . . must be the color of my skin."

"It's beautiful. Do you see this pathetic tan?" Develyn held out her arms. "It costs me sixty dollars a month at a tanning salon to have fake brown skin. You are born with it. With a name like Cree-Ryder, I suppose that is Native American."

"Well, one granddaddy was Cree, and he married my Mexican grandma. My other grandfather was from Ireland, and he married my African-American granny. So, tell me, what does that make me?"

"That sounds about as American as a person can get," Develyn replied.

"That's the way I figure, but some see it different."

"Small minds can't see beyond the color of their noses."

Cree-Ryder laughed. "Now you sound like a school teacher."

"I take that as a compliment."

Casey Cree-Ryder continued to survey the crowd. "You're not out here by yourself, are you?"

Develyn studied the woman's worn brown lace-up cowboy boots. "As a matter of fact, I am. How about you?"

Cree-Ryder glanced around at the milling men. "Yeah, I'm alone. I live up near Tensleep. Just came down to see if I could buy a couple of prospects cheap."

"Tensleep . . . is that a town?"

"Yeah, the old Indian village was ten days or ten 'sleeps' from Ft. Laramie. I'm living in a twenty-foot gooseneck trailer, but I want to build a log house as soon as my horses pay off."

"Do you show horses?" Develyn noticed the freckles on Cree-Ryder's cheeks were only slightly darker than her skin.

Most of the crowd sauntered toward the parked trucks. The two women now stood alone by the arena fence.

"Show? Honey, you're on the frontier of Wyoming now."
She slipped her arm into Develyn's. "I'm a barrel racer and
break-away roper, and I do some team penning. In my free time
I train horses for little girls from Jackson or Red Lodge."

"You expect to find those kind of horses here?" Develyn
asked.

"You never know about these mustangs. Besides, I can't
afford a rich-girl horse from those big ranches up at Cody or
Sheridan. Hey, you want to go get a chili burrito or something?"

Develyn shifted the strap of her purse and rubbed her nose.
The bright sun warmed her arms, but the slight breeze on her
face felt cool. "Are they any good?"

"Compared to what?" Cree-Ryder laughed. "There's nothing
else to eat out here. They don't taste like a burrito in Nogales or
Juarez or Del Rio, but they aren't bad for central Wyoming."

The horde of men parted as they walked toward the old,
silver Airstream travel trailer, converted to a mobile taco stand.
Many of the men had a long-neck bottle of beer in their hand,
and all seemed to have a cheek full of tobacco.

Casey and Develyn stopped in line behind a tall man with
sweat-stained black hat and broad shoulders.

"Did you see how all of them were looking you over?"
Cree-Ryder whispered.

"Me? They were fascinated with you and that beautiful
braid, I'm sure," Develyn insisted.

Casey Cree-Ryder wrinkled her round nose. "Dev, most everyone in this crowd has seen me since I was three. I've offended them

all by now. Trust me. God gave me the unique ability to make all men angry. And I've been faithfully using that gift most all of my life. They are looking at you, girl. You're like fresh meat at the market, and they are all dreamin' about grillin' you."

Develyn's mouth dropped. Her face flushed. "What did you just say?"

"Whoops," Cree-Ryder gulped. "How about, eh . . . you're like the newest video at the movie rental place?"

"I like that analogy somewhat better."

"I thought you might. If I get too crude, just slug me. I've lived by myself since I was fourteen," Casey added. "I know I'm kind of rough-sounding at times. Shoot, Dev, I am rough. I've been in more fistfights than I can count. But I only got knifed once."

Develyn opened her mouth to speak, but no words came out.

"I've been shot at twice, but they didn't hit me. I think they were just trying to scare me."

Develyn Worrell's hand flew to her chest. She felt her throat tighten. "Are you serious?"

"Crud," Casey laughed. "There I go again. OK . . . you have never been in a fistfight, let alone been knifed or shot at."

"I punched my brother in the nose when I was six and sprained my wrist. That was the end of my fistfighting. But on more than one occasion I've wished I had a gun or a knife and some courage."

"Hmmm." Casey studied her eyes. "I believe you have a story to tell me some time, Ms. Worrell."

"Yes, but not now. Casey, please, just be yourself. You don't have to pretend with me. I've spent most of my life pretending to be someone I'm not. This summer, I want it different."

"Now you're talking, girl. I'll do the same."

Develyn reached over and brushed several straw stems off Cree-Ryder's shoulder.

"I look like I fell off the proverbial hay wagon, don't I?" Casey said.

"No . . . no . . . I'm just so fussy sometimes I alienate my friends."

"Hey, I own a dress. I really do. It's silver and burgundy. It's real classy. I keep it in a sealed box in my horse trailer."

Develyn stared. *I don't relate to this lifestyle. She keeps her one dress in a horse trailer?* Her mind slipped to the walk-in closet at home crammed with dresses.

"Now, what have you decided to order?" Casey pressed.

Develyn strained to read the faded print on the signboard fastened to the side of the trailer. *Lord, I like Casey. But we are so different. She's so out there and unpretentious. I sense her friendship already. It's like one of those dreams, Lord, where I don't know a soul, and yet it seems so familiar. I keep expecting to look up and see my brother swagger up.*

Casey tapped the blue-shirted shoulder of the man in front of her. "Hey, Burdett, did you ever sell that broken-down coyote dun mare that you wanted way too much money for?"

The man spun around and grumbled, "Cree-Ryder, that horse had more stamina than your whole . . ." He glanced at

Develyn and pulled off his black hat. His dark brown and gray hair retained its hat curl. "Howdy, ma'am. I didn't know you were with, eh, Miss Cree-Ryder. I was just trying to figure which of Margaret's tacos would do the least damage to my . . ."

"Quint, this is my good friend, Develyn Worrell. Me and her used to partner down in the Texas circuit. You ain't never seen anyone turn a barrel like Devy. She beat Charmayne James three weeks in a row." Cree-Ryder rocked up on the worn toes of her boots. "Develyn, this is Quint Burdett. He ain't much to look at, but he owns the north half of Natrona County and the south half of Johnson County."

Develyn tried to conceal her gasp.

Burdett shook his head and laughed. "Cree-Ryder, you need to just speak right up and quit being so bashful and shy." He turned to Develyn. "Pleased to meet you, ma'am. Don't believe Cree-Ryder. My place isn't that big. Just thirty sections, more or less. Say, did she say you're from Texas? You look more like Houston than Ft. Worth. Am I right?" He held out his hand.

Develyn shook his calloused hand. "I have been to the livestock show and rodeo in Houston, but, actually I'm . . ."

Casey Cree-Ryder laughed. "I was leadin' you on, Burdett. She's a school teacher from Indiana."

He grinned and jammed his hat back on. "You had me going until I felt that sweet tender hand. That smile of yours and the big eyes reminded me of someone else . . . sorry for the double take. Are you two going to buy some horses?"

"If you and the good ol' boys don't bid them up too high," Cree-Ryder insisted.

"I'm not buying any mares, that's for sure," he said.

"You developed a sudden fear of the ladies, have you, Burdett?" Cree-Ryder chided.

"Not a fear," he said. "But I aim to be careful how I choose. I like the ladies to have credentials."

Develyn again stared at the crude menu on the side of the trailer. "Which one looks good?" she asked.

Quint waved his hand toward the far end of the arena. "Watch that wide-hipped skewbald Tobiano. She has potential if she has the brains. Could be the best of the lot."

Develyn pointed toward the Airstream taco trailer. "No, I meant, what looks good from the cantina?"

"Oh . . ." he grinned. "Eh . . . anything but the Custer's Revenge. I ate one of those in '85 and can still feel the effects."

●　●　●

Toting a grease-dripping burrito called "Alamo & Olives," Develyn followed Cree-Ryder to an older red Ford pickup hooked up to a two-horse, battered, silver horse trailer.

"This is my rig." Cree-Ryder plopped down on the shaded tongue of the trailer and nodded for Develyn to join her. "Actually I have a nice six-horse slant trailer, but mustangs have

90

a rep for kicking the daylights out of a horse trailer so I use this one."

Develyn wanted to brush the dirt off the trailer tongue, but couldn't find a clean place to lay her burrito. "So, you're really going to buy a horse?" She eased herself down next to Casey.

"Maybe. I've got nine hundred bucks. I'm hoping I can buy a couple and have enough left to pay my vet bill."

Develyn studied the burrito as if it were a cup of hemlock. "You can buy two horses for nine hundred dollars?"

"Some of these will go for two hundred dollars, but I wouldn't advise trying to ride one." Casey took a big bite of burrito and wiped her chin on the back of her hand. "Are you goin' to buy a horse?"

"Oh, no . . . I'm just . . ." Develyn nibbled the edge of the burrito and bit into a jalapeno pepper.

"Why are you here?"

Develyn gasped and fanned her mouth with her hand. "Oh . . . oh . . . it's a long story." Tears pooled in the corners of her eyes.

"Are you headed up to Cody tonight?"

Develyn coughed. "No, I'm hoping to find a place to stay here."

Cree-Ryder took a big bite of burrito, then mumbled, "What do you mean here? You mean Casper?"

"No, I mean here." Develyn rolled back the wax paper. "Argenta."

Casey stood and reached into the back of her truck and pulled out a small ice chest. "You got family here, Dev?"

"No. I thought maybe I could rent one of those cabins over by the cedar grove."

"They burned down years ago." Cree-Ryder opened the ice chest. "All I got is one Diet Pepsi left. You want to split it?"

Develyn took a deep sip and felt her mouth cool. "They burned down? There are no more cabins?"

"No, the cedars burned down." Cree-Ryder took a swig of Pepsi, then propped the can on the back bumper of the truck. "The Harkins boy liked to play with dynamite and caught them on fire one New Year's Day."

"And the cabins?" Develyn asked.

"They moved one of them out to Burdett's north ranch. He really does have a large ranch. I hear he stays up in the cabin in the fall. I suppose the home place is a little tough on him since his Miss Emily died."

"His wife?"

"Yep."

Develyn glanced back toward the Cantina, but couldn't see Quint Burdett. "Casey, which cabin burned down?"

"The one next to the cedars. The museum in Casper came out and trailered one of them all the way to town. Only the two with stone fireplaces remain."

"Is anyone living in them?"

92

"I don't think so," Casey said, "but I don't get to town too often."

"Who owns them? I really want to rent the one on the south." *Get to town? Coming to Argenta is coming to town?*

Cree-Ryder picked what looked like a fish bone out of her burrito and tossed it on the ground. "You really goin' to stay in Argenta?"

Develyn inspected the mysterious contents of her burrito. "That's the plan."

"How long?" Cree-Ryder took another swig of Pepsi and passed it to Develyn.

"Just for a few weeks," Develyn explained. "Maybe a couple of months." The shredded meat was so spicy that Develyn needed to gulp down some soda before she swallowed the bite.

"What in the world are you going to do around here?" Casey pressed.

"Ride horses and put my life together."

"Divorce?"

Develyn let out a deep sigh and stared across the parked trucks. "It's much more complicated than that." *Lord, I just can't tell that story again.*

"I've never been married, but it isn't because I didn't try. I proposed to three different guys."

"You did?"

"Yeah, four if you count Harrison Ford. And they all turned me down."

"Harrison Ford?"

"I was in a fire-fighting crew over in the Tetons a few years ago, and Ford helicoptered in some supplies. I hollered at him, 'Will you marry me?'"

"What did he say?"

"Well, either he didn't hear me or he ignored me. So I don't really count that one." Cree-Ryder pulled off her hat and ran her fingers through her hair. "Are you serious about those cabins?"

Develyn folded the rest of her burrito back in the wax paper and put it on the trailer tongue. "Yes, I am. Who owns them?"

"I haven't a clue. Last I heard some guy from Denver owned that place. It's like he comes up every couple of weeks or so. Burdett would know. He grazes off the creek bottom land. I'm not sure the cabins are livable. I think you might want to take a look at them before you rent one." She stood and brushed off her jeans. "Now, come on, the auction is about to start." She held out a brown sack.

Develyn dropped what was left of lunch in the sack. "What kind of meat do you think is in this burrito? It tasted rather strange."

"Don't ever ask what's in Margaret's burritos." Casey clutched Develyn's arm and tugged her through the herd of pickups and the group of cowboys. "It's whatever Gentry shot last winter and is still in the freezer. She doesn't even label the packages. She just calls it burrito meat."

94

By the time they reached the arena, most of the places on the rail had been taken, which made for a line-up of jean-covered backsides.

Casey Cree-Ryder pushed her way forward. "Move your skinny Wrangler butts over for us ladies," she barked.

Develyn's heart raced. She held her breath. *I don't believe I've ever been around anyone so . . . eh, blunt. Maybe she's right. Maybe she has alienated everyone in the county.*

Several men with straw cowboy hats and long-sleeved snapped shirts scooted down, opening up about three feet of space.

Casey waved at the top rail. "You first, honey."

Develyn raised her eyebrows. "Up there?"

Cree-Ryder peered between the rails. "It's the only place to watch the sale. It's about to get bucking again."

Develyn climbed the arena fence one rail at a time, then balanced her backside on the top rail. She scooted over for Cree-Ryder to join her.

An older, unshaved, extremely thin man with a white shirt buttoned at the collar and battered brown felt hat nodded off beside Develyn.

"I think he's asleep," she whispered.

Cree-Ryder glanced over, then shouted, "Uncle Henry, there's your horse!"

The old man sat straight up, waved his hand, and hollered, "Ten dollars!"

The crowd roared.

Rubbing his narrow eyes, the old man glanced around. "Did that half-breed put you up to that?" he mumbled at Develyn.

"I'm insulted, Uncle Henry," Casey laughed. "I figured you recognized my voice even in your sleep. How could you think it was Develyn?"

He rubbed the stubble on his chin as he appraised Worrell. "Her sweet perfume threw me off. Reminded me of one time I was up in Creede at a . . ."

"Don't say it, Uncle Henry. This nice lady is Develyn Worrell, a school teacher from Indiana."

He tipped his sweat-stained cowboy hat. "My grandmother was from Indiana," he replied. "South Bend."

"I'm from Crawfordsville, south and west of there," Develyn explained. "Are you Casey's uncle?"

"I'm everybody's uncle." When the old man grinned, several gold teeth appeared. "My mama named us boys for her uncles."

"You mean, your name is actually Uncle Henry?"

"Yep. Right there on the birth certificate. Uncle Henry Perkins. My oldest brother is Uncle Clarence and my youngest is Uncle Ernest."

"All right, boys . . ." The man at the loudspeaker was back on the truck in the arena. "Uncle Henry has started to bid, so it must be time to get going again. Here come the ladies. Renny will ride the more, eh . . . ambitious mares for us. And this first one is as determined as they come. This is a part of that Owyhee Mountain band that we rounded up just north of Paradise. She's number 73. Must have a little quarterhorse in her, as you can see by those wide hips. A very purdy pinto."

Renny Slater led the horse to the middle of the arena.

"This is the one Burdett mentioned," Cree-Ryder said.

"What a beautiful paint horse. What color is she? Taupe?"

"She's a skewbald. That means white with any color except black. You can call her red roan and white . . . but taupe sounds fine," Cree-Ryder replied. "Just don't tell the men that."

"Oh?"

"Did you ever notice how men only know five colors?" Casey hooted.

A young man with dimples when he smiled sat on the other side of Cree-Ryder and shook his head at her comment.

"What are you staring at?" Casey challenged him.

He stared down at his boots. "Eh, I reckon at the two pur-diest ladies in the arena," he mumbled.

Casey laughed and threw her arm around his shoulder. "Honey, you have great taste . . . for a boy. But you are kind of young for a line like that."

"A fella can enjoy lookin' at a fine thoroughbred even though it's out of his league."

"Oh, honey . . . I do like you!" Cree-Ryder hooted. "You come back and see me in about five years."

"Yes, ma'am . . ." he blushed. "I will."

"Shout your bids out, boys," the man with the loudspeaker boomed.

Develyn nudged Casey, "Are you going to bid on this one?"

Cree-Ryder pulled her arm back from the teen's shoulder and stared into the arena. "No, she's a little wide for a barrel horse. Might make a good roping horse. Just depends on how snuffy she turns out to be."

Develyn could hear Renny Slater talk to the horse as he walked her all the way around the arena to show her off. When he passed by them, he paused, then tipped his hat, "You enjoyin' the show, Devy-girl?"

Develyn sat up straight and folded her hands in her lap. "I haven't seen anything yet, Mr. Slater."

He grinned and nodded at Casey. "Cree-Ryder, them school marms is tough on a cowboy. She probably has a quirt on her desk."

"A what?" Develyn asked.

"A short whip," Cree-Ryder laughed.

Slater led the horse to the middle of the arena, jammed his left foot into the stirrup, and swung up into the saddle. The horse reared straight up, her front legs well off the ground.

"Oh, dear . . ." Develyn gasped.

The audience clapped.

"Dev, that's just Renny's thing," Cree-Ryder explained. "He rears them like that every time he mounts. It's like his signature."

The paint mare bucked twice. Then Slater yanked straight back on the reins. The horse stood still, and he leaned forward and mumbled something in the horse's ear.

"What did you tell her, Renny?" some big cowboy with a long-neck bottle in his hand hollered.

Slater spurred the mare to a trot. "Just one word, Little Pete," Renny shouted. "Dogfood."

Slater loped the horse around the rail of the arena, cut her out into the middle . . . slid her to a stop . . . then backed her up and spun her to the left and to the right.

"Ain't that horse a fine specimen of equine beauty?" the auctioneer called out. "How broke is she, Renny?"

He rode the white and taupe paint horse straight toward the ladies.

"What's he doing?" Develyn said.

Casey held her arm. "You get to go for a ride."

Develyn's eyes widened. "Me?"

"This fine-looking cowgirl here with the short yella hair will demonstrate how broke this horse is." He rode the horse right up against the fence. "Climb on behind me, ma'am."

"What?" Develyn searched Cree-Ryder's eyes. "No, I can't really. I haven't ridden in years," she murmured.

"That's exactly what I was hoping. That will prove what a tame horse she is," Renny declared. "Come on . . . climb on board."

When the old man next to her leaned toward her, there was garlic on his breath. "Say, are you sure you didn't work down in Ely, Nevada, in a . . ."

"Uncle Henry!" Cree-Ryder snarled. "You keep quiet."

Develyn stood on the third rail, handed Cree-Ryder her purse, then swung her leg across the rump of the horse. *Lord, I have no idea in the world what I'm doing, or why I'm doing this.*

"Put your arms around me," Slater called out.

"I'll hold on to the cantle," she replied.

"Boy, you schoolteachers are careful." Slater spurred the horse, and she began to trot around the arena.

Develyn felt the sun-warmed rump of the horse slap up against her backside. Holding the cantle with one hand, she tugged her straw hat down tighter. The wind blew in her face, and she closed her eyes. *Yes, yes, yes . . . this is what I've been wanting. It feels so good.*

"I like this horse," she said.

They continued to circle the arena. "You want to buy her?" he whispered.

"I didn't come out here to buy a horse."

"No one plans on buying a horse. But if you find a good horse, you gotta buy it."

"What do you think she will go for?"

Renny spurred the horse to a gallop. "It depends on whether you want it or not."

Develyn started to slip back and her arms went around his hard, thin waist. "What do you mean by that?"

"Do you want to buy the horse or not?" he called out.

"Perhaps, but I can't pay very much."

Renny glanced back. "How much did you want to spend?"

What did Casey say? "Eh, I have nine hundred dollars, but I want to buy two horses," Develyn proposed.

"She'll go for a thousand, I reckon. But if you want her, I'll see to it you get a discount."

"Really?"

Renny slowed the horse to a trot. "Yeah, but you have to do what I tell you."

Develyn tugged her hat down and glanced at all the eyes in the arena focused on them. "What do you mean?"

"No matter what happens, you bid on this horse."

"What?"

Renny patted her knee. "Promise me you'll bid a hundred dollars on this horse."

"When?"

"You'll know."

Renny stopped the horse in the middle of the arena. "This horse is so broke," he announced. "I'll let this purdy yellow-haired lady ride this paint by herself."

"What are you doing?" Develyn demanded.

"Just ride her around. When I nod at you, slap the right fender hard with the palm of your hand and shout 'giddy-up!'" Renny swung his leg over the saddle horn and the horse's head, then slid to the ground.

Develyn felt her heart race. "Renny!"

He handed her up the reins.

The crowd cheered.

"Now, go on . . . do like I told you . . . when the time comes, bid one hundred dollars."

"We'll start the bidding as this cowgirl rides the paint mare," the auctioneer drawled.

Slater stepped back several feet, then nodded at Develyn. "Slap that saddle fender."

Develyn released the saddle horn and slapped the right flap of the saddle skirt.

The horse dropped her head and kicked up her rear hooves, causing Develyn to lose the stirrups. "No!" she shouted.

When the horse repeated the move, Develyn dropped the reins and clutched the saddle horn with both hands. "Stop. Stop it right now!"

On the third buck, she lost her grip and flew over the horse's head. She landed face first in powdery dry dirt. Like rough sandpaper, it scraped her arms, hands, and face. She spat out dirt and gasped for breath. Every bone ached.

Lord, I'm goin' to die right here in the middle of nowhere. I'll never live through this. Slater and Cree-Ryder ran toward her. She rolled on her back and tried to catch her breath.

"Ten dollars!" Uncle Henry shouted.

"We got a ten-dollar bid," the auctioneer shouted.

I am dying and they are bidding on this horse?

Renny lifted her head and mumbled through clenched teeth, "Bid."

He's got to be kidding.

"Bid," he repeated. "Trust me and bid."

With Cree-Ryder's help she sat up and tried to gasp out, "You're insane."

"Wait a minute!" Renny shouted. "She said she wants to bid."

Develyn could feel the tears dribble down her dirt-covered cheeks. She looked at Cree-Ryder, then Slater winked at her.

I don't have a clue what that wink means.

"How much do you want to bid?" yelled the auctioneer.

"Eh . . . one hundred dollars," Develyn blurted out.

"She said a hundred bucks," Cree-Ryder repeated.

"This brave cowgirl bids a hundred on the contrary mare. Do I hear any more bids? I didn't think so. Goin' once, twice, sold to the young lady with dirt on her face!" he shouted. "Renny, bring us out another."

He helped Develyn to her feet. "Ride this horse out of the arena," he told her.

She tried to wipe the dirt out of her eyes with the sleeve of her T-shirt. "You have to be kidding. I'm never . . ."

"Cowgirl up, Devy-girl. This is the moment of truth." Slater straightened the saddle, then reached his hand out to her. When she opened her hand, he dropped a sticker the size of a large walnut into her hand.

"What is that?"

"A star thistle . . . I wonder how that got under the saddle blanket?"

"You . . . what?" Develyn moaned. "You humiliated me on purpose. Why?"

"You just bought yourself a hundred-dollar horse. I figured I saved you nine hundred bucks. I figure you owe me a . . ."

He caught her hand before it landed on his cheek. "Get on the horse, Devy-girl. Show them you aren't just some Indiana schoolteacher."

Cree-Ryder nodded at her. "You can do it, Devy-girl. Ride with your head up."

Develyn stuck her dirty boot in the stirrup and yanked herself up into the saddle to the applause of the entire crowd.

"Now there goes a real cowgirl!" the announcer shouted. "Bring us out a gentle one this time, Renny . . . a gentle horse, that is."

Cree-Ryder opened the gate, and Develyn rode the paint horse into the crowd of men who parted like the Red Sea as she headed toward the parked trucks.

I can't believe he did that," Develyn fumed as Casey led the horse and her through the scattered trucks and trailers.

Cree-Ryder's belt-length braid swished in time with the horse, but she didn't look back. "Are you mumbling about the nine hundred dollars he saved you or how he got you tossed on your nose?"

Develyn leaned forward in the saddle and stroked the horse's neck. "He purposely tried to bring harm to my body."

"I don't think Renny wants to harm your body, that's for sure." This time Casey glanced back and raised one of her thick, dark eyebrows.

Develyn sat straight up and folded her hands in her lap. "I could press criminal charges . . . that was assault . . . or was it battery? I believe I could sue him."

Cree-Ryder stopped next to her red pickup. She glanced up from under her hat. "Sure, why don't you call the teacher's union?"

"What did you mean by that?" Develyn snapped.

"You aren't in the teacher's lunchroom in Indiana, Devy-girl." Casey Cree-Ryder put her hand on her slumping hip. "This is the frontier of Wyoming. If he did you wrong, punch him or shoot him . . . but don't sue him."

Develyn slipped down off the saddle. Her left leg cramped, and she hobbled around the back of the trailer. "I'm not going to shoot him."

Cree-Ryder yanked off the bridle and fastened a muddy looking red halter to the horse, then tied the lead rope to the horse trailer. "Good. Because I like this horse. I think you got a good deal for a hundred bucks. She's got sweet eyes. She'll do you good." Casey unbuckled the cinch. "I'll tote Renny's saddle back. I reckon he'll need it. Unless you want to."

Develyn glanced over at the noisy crowd of men around the arena. "I'm not going back there."

"Hmmm . . . that's too bad. I think you got those cowboys figured wrong. You think gettin' bucked off lowers your status? Ever'body gets bucked off. Your sand is measured by what you do after you get bucked off. You did good, Develyn. But it's up to you. Brush her down. I'll be right back." Cree-Ryder swaggered back toward the arena, saddle on her shoulder.

Develyn noticed the duct tape that repaired Casey Cree-Ryder's worn boots. *She belongs out here. I'm just visiting.*

Wait until I tell Lily. I could call her right now. Where's my purse? I hope Casey has it. She studied her wristwatch. *An hour and a half ago I was sitting on the porch with a Popsicle, lost in the past. And now . . . I don't even know where I am. Maybe this is another horse dream, and I'll wake up in a big Indiana house with two cats.*

Develyn searched a red plastic bucket in the back of the trailer, pulled out a brush, and stroked the paint mustang. The horse quivered, but didn't yank on the lead rope. "Well, girl, I know you are apprehensive about all of this . . . so am I. You haven't been taken care of much in your life . . . and neither have I. Now, you know, I don't know what I'm doing, but I'll learn. That's my promise to you. Now, I want you to promise to . . ."

"Howdy, ma'am. Am I interruptin' somethin'?"

She spun around to see a suntanned cowboy with hat in hand rocking back and forth on the heels of his worn brown boots. "Oh, I was just talking to this horse," she stammered.

"Yes, ma'am, I understand." He stared down at his feet. "If you two is finished visitin', I just wanted to invite you to the barbecue."

"It was a one-sided conversation." She stepped away from the horse. "What barbecue?"

"The Quarter Circle Diamond has a big barbecue on Sunday evenin' next. It's an annual thing before some of the hands go get summer jobs. Me and the boys would be proud to have a cowgirl like yourself join us. Them that is married bring their wives and kids. It's a family thing."

Develyn studied his brown eyes. *He's not joking? Cowgirl?* "I'm not sure of my plans. Where is the barbecue?"

"At the headquarters, you know, the big house at the head of Spuder Crick. You head up here along Lost Cabin Road, just past Cedar Ridge . . . then go north and cross Badwater Crick . . . then mosey a little to the northwest along the Big Horn Trail until you reach Spuder Crick. You can't miss it."

She watched him watch her. "How far is that?"

He looked down at his boots. "It's just over the hill a ways. Maybe forty miles. Can you make it?"

He needs to be with people more. No one should have to be this embarrassed. "I'm not sure, but thanks for the invitation."

He jammed his hat back on. "Surely hope you can make it. When you bid on that snuffy mare and crawled back in the saddle, me and the boys figured you earned a trip to the barbecue. There ain't one gal in a hundred that would have done that. Is this your rig?" He pointed to the trailer and truck.

Develyn surveyed the battered red Dodge. "No, this belongs to my friend, Casey."

When he rubbed his chin, she noticed a small scar on his neck. "You and Cree-Ryder pals?" he asked.

"Yes, we are." Develyn tugged on her diamond stud earring.

He rubbed his clean-shaven chin. "She can come to the barbecue, too, if she promises not to bring any guns or knives."

"Oh, dear, yes, I will insist on that. But I'm not sure about next week."

"Thanks for ponderin' it, ma'am."

"I'm Dev Worrell." She shoved her hand toward him.

He clutched her hand and grinned. "They just call me Cuban."

"Are you from . . ."

"No. I was born and raised in Dubois, Wyomin'. It's a long story. I didn't quite catch your words. Was that Miss Worrell or Mrs. Worrell?"

"Just an 'm' and an 's' . . . it's Ms. Worrell."

He reached for the Skoal can in his back pocket. "Now don't that beat all?"

"Cuban, you tryin' to hog this purdy lady all to yourself?"

Develyn glanced up to see Quint Burdett meandering toward them.

"No, sir, Mr. Burdett. Me and the boys invited her to the barbecue. We figured she earned it."

"Good," he nodded. "I was planning to do the same thing."

"Is this barbecue on your ranch, Mr. Burdett?" She looked up at the tall, broad-shouldered man.

"You need to call me Quint. I feel old enough. The barbecue was my wife, Emily's, idea years ago. Kind of turned into a big whoop-di-doo. I've been keepin' it goin' since I lost her."

Cuban tipped his hat toward her. "Hope to be seein' you at the barbecue, Miss Dev, ma'am."

"Thank you for the invitation, Cuban. I'm quite flattered."

She watched the gangly young cowboy saunter back toward the roar of the arena.

Quint Burdett rubbed his hand down the paint horse's left front leg until the mare lifted it for him. He studied her trimmed but unshod hoof.

Develyn, with brush still in hand, stood next to the rancher. "Quint, when did your Emily pass away?"

He lowered the hoof, then stared at the railroad tracks that ran over the rolling prairie. "Four years ago on May 15th, but sometimes it seems like only yesterday."

His eyes look so tired. But he would have been quite handsome in his prime. "I'm sorry, Quint."

He looked at her, but it was as if she were invisible. "Thank you, Dev. Miss Emily made ever' day worth gettin' up. After thirty-two years of marriage, a man misses that."

Develyn's eyebrows raised. "That long?"

His eyes cleared. "I know what a lady thinks. OK, I got married when I was nineteen. I was fifty-one when the cancer took her. So that makes me fifty-five. How's that for being honest?"

"Was I that obvious?"

He lifted the horse's rear hooves, then the right front and gently lowered each. "Yep, you were obvious. But I've been missin' that sort of thing."

"OK, Quint, it's only fair for me to do the same. So here goes. I've been divorced for four years. My ex had a heart attack and died about three months ago. And I'm forty-five. I've taught fifth grade for twenty-three years at the same school near Crawfordsville, Indiana, and I suppose I will until I retire." *Why did I tell him all that? I don't even know the man.*

He pulled off his hat. His dark brown and gray hair tumbled out. "Forty-five? No foolin'? I figured you not too much older than Linds."

"Linds?"

"Lindsay. She's a beautiful twenty-five-year-old blonde who lives with me."

Develyn scowled, then looked away, her face flushed.

Quint laughed. "That look, Ms. Worrell, was priceless."

She glanced back at the man's tanned, creased face. "Are you laughing at me?"

"Actually, no. Your glance convicted me to the bone. I just neglected to tell you that the young blonde in question is my daughter."

Develyn ground her teeth. *Relax, Devy-girl.* "What is this? First it's Renny, then you leading me on. Do I have patsy written on my forehead?"

"I'm sorry, Dev. I wasn't teasing. Linds is a beautiful young lady."

"I suppose I'm a little edgy." Develyn rubbed her temples. "I'm sorry for the scolding look. I must have learned that from my mother. Do you have other children?"

"My boy, Ted, died in a truck wreck near Greeley, Colorado, ten years ago on the Fourth of July. It's just Linds and me. How about yourself, Miss Dev? Do you have children?"

Her daughter's sorrowed anger flooded her mind. "A twenty-year-old daughter, Delaney, who is spending the summer in South Carolina, pondering whether to ever speak to me again."

His response was so low, she barely heard it. "She'll outgrow that."

She stepped closer to him. "You promise?"

He stared north, started to speak, then shook his head.

"I'm sorry, Quint. I didn't mean to stir up some hurts."

He sighed and turned toward her. "Well, Miss Dev, the Lord didn't promise us an easy life . . . just an abundant one. Some days it's tougher than others. Sorry for being melancholy. There's something about your smile and big eyes that reminds me of my Miss Emily."

She touched his shirtsleeve. "That's a wonderful compliment, Quint."

He patted her hand, then stepped away. "Miss Dev, hope you make it to the barbecue."

"I'll try to do that."

"Will you be staying with Cree-Ryder?"

"I hope to find myself a place around here to rent for a while."

Quint slipped his hat to the back of his head. "Are you moving to Wyoming?"

"No, I just want to spend a few weeks here, now that I have another mouth to feed." She pointed at the paint horse. "Do you know who owns those cabins where the cedars used to be? I stayed in them years ago and want to rent one again."

He raised his eyebrows. "You stayed there?"

"Thirty-five years ago," she admitted.

112

Casey Cree-Ryder strolled back to the trailer.

"They've been in the Tallon family since statehood," he explained. "The present owner is Cooper Tallon. You're in luck; he's around here today. He's from down Colorado way, but I saw him at the arena earlier. I'll look for him and send him to see you."

"That would be great. Thank you, Quint!"

"I know I said this before." His eyes pierced hers. "I hope you can come to the barbecue."

She replied with a slow nod. "I'll look forward to it."

Casey stood next to her as they watched Quint Burdett disappear into the maze of trucks and horse trailers.

"You got invited to the annual barbecue?" Cree-Ryder gasped. "I can't believe it."

Develyn scratched the back of her sweaty neck. "Is it a big deal?"

"It's only the elite of the cow country that get invited." Casey plucked the horse brush from her hand. "The governor will be there."

"The governor of Wyoming?"

"That's what they tell me. Governor, senators, judges . . . it's a big deal, Devy-girl. 'Course I've never gone."

Develyn slipped her arm into Casey's. "Well, you're going this year, Miss Cree-Ryder. You were invited with me."

Casey's mouth dropped open. "No way!"

"Yes."

"Quint said I could come?"

"Quint was too late. You and I were invited by Cuban and the boys of the Quarter-Circle Diamond. They said you could come if you promised not to bring guns or knives."

Casey rocked back and forth on her boots. "They said that?"

Develyn took both of her hands. "Yes, and I promised you'd come unarmed."

"I'm bringing my brass knuckles," Casey said.

Develyn frowned at the dark-skinned woman.

A smile broke across Casey's full lips. "Oh, Dev, you are so easy to buffalo. I love it."

"Yes, well, it must show. Quint teased me too."

"Quint?" Casey chuckled. "Are you making a move on Burdett too?"

Develyn tried to find her schoolteacher voice. "I don't know what you mean."

"First Renny, then Quint. Wow, and I thought Idaho women were fast. They say Burdett was quite a stud when he was in his prime."

"Casey!"

"Well, anyway, you like him, right?"

"I barely met the man."

"You didn't answer my question."

"I'm not hitting on anyone." Develyn stroked the horse. "She's got one brown eye and one blue eye."

"You just notice that?"

"That's not a problem, is it?"

"Not unless she becomes self-conscious of it. When you

brush her teeth every morning, don't let her near a mirror."

"I'm not falling for that one." Develyn faked a scowl.

"I can't believe I've been invited to the Quarter-Circle Diamond barbecue. I'll have to wash my pair of black Wranglers," she grinned. Casey hugged the horse's neck. "What have you decided to name this girl?"

"My Maria," Develyn blurted out.

"Wow! Like the old Brooks and Dunn song?"

"Yes, Renny was playing it when we drove up."

"She looks like a Maria," Cree-Ryder said. "Hey, I brought back your purse and stuck it in the truck. Uncle Henry was guarding it for you. You might want to check your wallet."

"That old man's not going to take my money."

"Not on purpose," Cree-Ryder replied. "But he forgets what's his and what isn't. He might have thought he was spending his own money."

I can't believe I bought a horse. I don't know the first thing about caring for a horse. "How about you, Casey? Are you going to buy a horse?"

Cree-Ryder thrust her hands in the horse's mouth and yanked it open. "There's more excitement over here than in the arena."

"What are you doing?"

"She's about ten or twelve years old, I'm guessing. I reckon she's had a few foals by now."

"You can tell that by looking in her mouth?"

"The age, but not motherhood," Casey laughed. "But if she's been in the wild, she's been in a band of mares running with a stallion. She had to have some foals by this age."

Develyn tried to peer into My Maria's mouth, but Cree-Ryder snapped it shut as if it contained a secret. "What was all that roar from the crowd? Did Renny get tossed on his ear?" Develyn asked.

Cree-Ryder rubbed the horse's neck. "No, he was just showing off."

"What did he do?"

"Oh, he swings around and rides the horse backward."

"Casey, are you teasing me again?"

"Not this time. Renny likes the applause."

"What do you know about him?"

"Wait a minute, girl . . . you've been sizin' up Burdett and now you are back after Renny?"

"Casey, it's just schoolteacher curiosity."

"Oh? But Ms. Schoolteacher hasn't asked anything about me."

"I figure you are going to tell me all about yourself soon enough, right?"

"I suppose," Casey laughed. "Renny Slater was a pretty good bull and bronc rider on the Rocky Mountain Circuit."

"Was? Tell me more."

"He's in his forties now. That's too old for roughstock riders. He's five feet six inches tall and weighs one hundred and fifty-five pounds. He was married to Kaney Mills for nearly ten years, but he's been divorced for twelve. They didn't have any

STEPHEN BLY

kids. At least, I don't think they did. She lives in Oakdale, California. She has a great big arena where she teaches barrel racing. Renny's getting a little thin on top. Those beautiful teeth are false; his real ones were kicked out by an angry saddle-bronc in Miles City. At one time or another he's broken every bone in his body. He's broken his nose so many times he's lost count. Renny's got a nasty scar from his shoulder clear up to his neck, so he always wears that bandanna. Let's see. Oh, yeah . . . he wears briefs, not boxers."

"What? I . . . I . . . I didn't want to know that much!" Develyn gasped.

"Are you sure you want to stay out here all summer? You could blush yourself into a stroke."

"Yes, well . . . I suppose I've led a relatively sheltered life."

"Howdy, ma'am . . . do you remember me?"

A tall, gray-eyed man wearing a black cowboy hat approached them.

"Eh . . . I eh . . ."

"We met at the service station in Casper. I invited you to the auction."

A grin broke across her face. "Oh, yes! I'm glad you did."

"I didn't know you had plans to head out here anyway. I told you that smile of yours would light up the auction."

"Oh, brother, another one," Casey mumbled, then wandered back toward the arena.

What plans is he talking about? "Thank you, but I'm afraid all I added was a good laugh," Develyn insisted.

117

"That was one special performance." His smile was lop-sided. "You and Slater have your timing down perfect. Do you two ever do contract acts?"

I don't think he's complimenting me. I wonder if he has me confused with someone else? She studied his deep gray eyes. "I'm not sure I understand your question?"

He stepped over to the paint horse. "That fake bucking scene. It was good." He stroked the quivering horse. "Crossed with one of my papered quarter horses, she might make a good brood mare. You interested in selling her?"

"No, I'm not." She pushed herself between the man and My Maria. "What do you mean fake bucking?"

"Slater slipped something under the saddle blanket. That's an old trick. I've seen Mexicans down in the Rio Grande Valley do the same thing."

"Well, I didn't see him. And I resent the insinuation that it was all a charade."

"I didn't say charade. I said it was a show, like a special act at a rodeo. I reckon you and Slater will want to sell the mare and split profits, so I'm offerin' you a deal. I'll give you seven hundred dollars cash for the horse. That gives you six hundred dollars profit, and all you had to do was dive in the dirt."

Develyn became fully conscious of her dirty T-shirt and jeans. "I trust this is just a crude attempt at humor, because the bruises are real."

"OK, you want to do a little horse-hagglin'. I'll give you

nine hundred dollars for the mare. I hope you get half; you did the dirty work."

Cree-Ryder meandered up toting two Cokes. She pushed one into Develyn's trembling hand.

"Mister, in the last hour I've been razzed, conned, and slammed down in the dirt. I'm new here, so that's OK." Develyn took a sip, then a deep breath. "But I do not have to put up with your insults. I faked nothing in that arena. I wouldn't sell My Maria to you for nine thousand dollars. I've spent too many years of my life being put down by better men than you. Do you understand? Now, ride on off into the sunset or something."

"Look, lady, I don't really care whether you are ticked off with me or not. No one has ever been impressed with my sparkling personality."

"That's obvious," she growled.

"I'll give you a thousand cash. Do you want to sell the horse or not?"

"Haven't I made myself clear?"

"Thank you, ma'am." He tipped his hat. "Horse buyin' takes on different forms with different people. There are others more agreeable."

"Yes, I'm sure there are other women you can browbeat and intimidate," Develyn snapped.

The man bristled and stepped toward her. "What in blazes did you mean by that?"

Cree-Ryder flashed a hunting knife in her hand. "She meant it's time for you to mosey back to the arena."

"Where did you get that knife?" Develyn gasped.

The man pulled back. "Good grief, I hope that mare isn't as psycho as you two," he mumbled. "I'm not used to havin' my honor questioned."

"Nor am I," Develyn insisted.

He shook his head. "Good day, then." He turned and stalked away.

"Who in the world was that?" Casey asked.

"I don't have a clue." Develyn held the Coke to her forehead. It felt cool to her temple. "I can't believe you pulled a knife on him."

Cree-Ryder shoved the weapon back into her boot. "I can't believe you didn't."

"This is crazy. I'm a stranger in a foreign land. Maybe I don't belong here," Develyn mumbled. "Perhaps it's a bad dream. Pinch me and see if I wake up."

Cree-Ryder lunged forward.

"Ouch! I didn't mean pinch me there!" Develyn wailed.

"Oh, sorry," Cree-Ryder laughed. "Here, let me pinch you again."

Develyn fought back the grin. "Keep your pinches and your knife to yourself."

"Are you mad at me?"

Develyn shook her head. "No, it's just that everything is happening so fast. I've had more excitement in the past two hours than I've had in twenty years. It's like an emotional bungee jump. I'm losing track of who I am."

Cree-Ryder hugged Develyn's shoulder. "Isn't that why you came out here?"

Develyn felt her whole body relax. "You might be more right than you know."

The dark-skinned lady dropped her hug, then stepped to the battered horse trailer. "Dev, do you have a saddle and tack?"

"No, I'll have to buy everything."

"I'll lend you the gear. I've got plenty of extras. Where are you going to keep her?"

"I really want to rent one of those cabins. Quint said the owner's here, and he'll introduce me. There's pasture right at the cabins. Maybe that will work out. That would be so perfect."

Cree-Ryder rubbed the horse's neck. "You can always come bunk with me in Tensleep."

"But you are living in a travel trailer."

With one continuous move, Casey grabbed a hunk of the horse's mane and swung up on its bare back. "We can share. Do you snore?"

"I have no idea in the world. No one has complained in the past four years, that's for sure. How did you do that? How did you get up there so easy?"

"It's my Indian blood, paleface," she laughed. "Or maybe it's my Mexican blood . . . I forget. Untie her; let me ride her a little."

"Don't you need a, eh . . . a mouth thing?" Develyn asked.

"Oh, wow, a mouth thing? I've got a lot to teach you. No, I don't need a spade bit, a snaffle bit, or even a hackamore. The halter will work fine." Cree-Ryder turned the horse north. "Hey, here he comes."

Develyn scanned the parked rigs. "Who?"

"Quint Burdett."

She looked up to see the tall, square-jawed rancher ambling toward them.

"Greenwald with the B.L.M. asked me to tell you that you still need to pay them for the mare and get the bill of sale," he said.

"Oh, yes. I'll get my wallet." She strolled toward the front of the pickup. "I suppose they need cash."

"They'll take a credit card, too. They'll do just about anything not to have any horses left at the end of the day." Burdett paused by the front fender. "Say, did you get a cabin rented?"

Casey Cree-Ryder kept the nervous horse near the rear of the rig.

Develyn reached through the open window and pulled out her brown purse. "No, I haven't talked to the man yet."

Burdett pushed his sweaty hat back. "What do you mean you haven't talked to him? I sent him over fifteen minutes ago."

Develyn fumbled to find her wallet. "He didn't make it yet."

"But I saw you talking to him," Burdett insisted.

"No, I was talking to some obnoxious guy intent on insulting me and my horse."

His creased eyes narrowed. "Did he have on a blue shirt, rolled up to his elbows, and a black Resistol?"

Develyn felt her heart race. "You mean that jerk is . . ."

"That so-called jerk is Cooper Tallon. He owns those cabins."

"Ohhhh." Develyn dropped her wallet back into her purse. *Lord, I think this day is spinning out of control. Can I rewind it, say back to the porch and Popsicle?* "You told him I wanted to rent a cabin?"

"No, I told him a purdy lady wanted to talk to him."

"Your purdy lady chased ol' Coop off," Casey hooted.

"Me? You're the one who waved a knife at him."

"Yeah, but I didn't mean anything by it."

Quint Burdett folded his arms across his chest. "I reckon it takes some time to get used to the Wyoming mind."

"What am I going to do?" Develyn murmured. "I drove all the way from Indiana to stay in one of those cabins, and I just insulted the owner."

"You want me to go talk to him?" Burdett asked.

"Shoot, I'll go talk to him," Casey chimed in.

"No . . . Casey, you and your knife and your gun and your brass knuckles stay here. Quint, please tell him I'd like another opportunity to explain myself."

"I'll see what I can do, Miss Dev." He ambled back to the arena.

Casey rode up next to her. "I don't really have brass knuckles," she muttered.

"But you have a gun?"

Casey Cree-Ryder flashed a wide grin. "Not on me, right now. It's in the truck."

• • •

The orange sun paused on the western horizon before ooz-
ing its way into evening. The voice echoed skepticism. "Wait a
minute . . . wait a minute . . . give me time for this to sink in."

Develyn leaned back against the outside of the log cabin
wall, her straw cowboy hat perched on her knee, cell phone
pressed to her ear. "It's all true, Lily."

"Are you telling me the town still has dirt roads?"

"Yes."

"And you were able to rent the same cabin?"

"Like I told you . . . it was rather awkward, but Quint han-
dled things."

"So, you've been there six hours and you rented a place,
bought a horse, made friends with a gun totin' cowgirl, and at
least three men are drooling over you?"

Develyn leaned forward. "They aren't drooling."

"Hmmm. I'll bet they are."

"And there aren't three."

"You mentioned dear Quint, and Renny, and one named
Cooper."

"Cooper is the man I rented this place from. You can scratch
him off the list. He rather detests me. Besides, he's older."

"My age?" Lily teased.

"What about that big date the other night? What happened
to him?"

"I had to take him back to the home."

"What?" Develyn watched a black cat saunter up the long dirt driveway toward her cabin.

"I'm teasing. He's nice enough . . . for a Hoosier. But don't you change the subject."

The cat spotted Develyn, spun around, and slunk back toward the road. "What is the subject?"

"All the men who are interested in Ms. Worrell."

"Did I mention Cuban?"

"A Cuban in Wyoming?"

"Never mind. It's all too bizarre."

"Are you having fun, honey?"

Develyn stared at the black cell phone, then put it back to her ear. "Some moments are fun, some are terrifying, Lily. None are boring."

"I can't believe you just drove out there and found that town. It can't be that simple."

"That's what I keep telling myself. But I'm here, and it feels good, Lily. How are my cats?"

"Naughty. They miss mama. One of them shredded your silk date palm by the front door."

"Oh, dear, she does get rather opinionated."

"Do you have indoor plumbing?"

Develyn thought about her tiny bathroom. "Of course."

"Does it work?"

"Sort of. But you don't want to hear about that," Develyn insisted.

"Tell me everything you see," Lily pressed.

"What?"

"Describe where you are right now."

"OK, I'm on the uncovered front porch of a log cabin that is painted a dull red, and I'm sitting on an empty wooden box labeled 'Caution: Dynamite.' The cabin has two rooms: a bed-room-kitchen-living room combo and a bathroom. It's musty, but Casey and I cleaned it up."

"Where's your gun-totin' pal now?"

"She went to Tensleep, but she'll be back tomorrow."

"What else do you see?"

"An identical cabin about one hundred feet to the east."

"Is it for rent?" Lily asked.

"No, Mr. Tallon uses it when he's here. I think he lives in Colorado."

"He's one hundred feet away, and he despises you?"

"I believe so. Anyway, about one hundred yards to the south is the town of Argenta, Wyoming. There's a service station right out of the early fifties on the corner of the road to the highway. A couple of houses sit back in the trees. Mrs. Tagley's store is next with dirt parking out front and covered-wagon-seat benches on the porch. Beside that is a big concrete foundation that had been the Francis B. Saloon, with a dance hall up above, but it burned down on V.E. Day in 1945. After that are three old singlewides, surrounded by a dozen pickups in vary-ing degrees of working order. To the right is a meat market about the size of Gloria Peter's gladiola stand. A half mile fur-ther west are corrals and the arena."

"And what's on your side of the railroad tracks?"

"A half dozen houses set back in the cottonwoods and these two cabins. That's it."

"That's the whole town?"

"Yes, isn't it great?"

"Great? It sounds like a bad dream. So, where is that horse of yours? What's its name?"

"My Maria's in the jacuzzi."

"What?"

"Oh, Lily . . . sorry. It's just that everyone out here is always teasing me. My Maria is about fifty feet from me in a three-acre pasture that came with the cabin."

"Are you in the mountains?"

"It's kind of like a high rolling prairie. Mainly light green grass and sagebrush all around. It was windy most of the day, but it's still, now. The sun just dropped behind the horizon. Now do you get the picture? If I stood on top of my cabin, I would see the Bighorn Mountain to the distant north, and oil wells pumping in the south."

"So, no one is there with you?" Lily quizzed.

Develyn surveyed the bare dirt yard. "Uncle Henry is here."

"Uncle who?"

"Uncle Henry."

"Who is this?"

"There was an old man . . . an old cowboy at the auction. His name is Uncle Henry."

"Ms. Worrell, are you opening a home for old cowboys?"

"He held my purse when I got bucked off. I told you about that. I guess he took ten dollars from my wallet and bid on a donkey."

"A donkey? You don't mean a mule?"

"No, a wild burro. Anyway, he won the bid, but since it was my money, he gave me the burro."

"You call the burro Uncle Henry?"

"Yep."

"Yep? Dev, you're an Indiana schoolteacher. Don't you 'yep' me!"

"Oh, Lily, this is all strange, and yet so nice."

"You sound happy, honey. I'm glad you didn't break your collarbone or something. I would hate to have to fly out there and nurse-maid you."

"Hmmm . . . are you begging?"

"No, Ms. Worrell . . . that's your adventure; I've got mine."

"Oh?"

"I met this man at the steakhouse in Greencastle. One thing led to . . ."

"I can't believe this. You are going wild! Another man already?"

"Me? Honey, may I remind you that I'm still in the same old house tonight. You're the one out there on the edge of . . . who knows where."

"What's he like?"

"He's a lawyer."

"You didn't tell me what he's like."

"He seems nice. We're going to a summer theater play at the college."

"Are you having fun, Lily?"

"Yes, I am. I keep asking the Lord if that's OK."

"What does he tell you?"

"He tells me to call back later; he's on the other line trying to keep Ms. Worrell from doing something dangerous or dumb."

"Yes, Mother."

"Speaking of your mother, did you . . ."

"Yes."

"Did you tell her . . ."

"Sort of."

"Is she . . ."

"Ticked off? I suppose so." Develyn shook her cell phone. "Lil, I think I'm losing my cell. I'll have to charge it up in the Jeep tomorrow."

"Why? I mean, you do have electricity, don't you?"

"No. I have to go down to Mrs. Tagley's to check my e-mail. I've got to go, sweetie . . . Uncle Henry is trying to eat my side-view mirror."

"Dev, am I losing you?"

"Yes, the cell battery's getting weak."

"That's not what I meant, Ms. Worrell."

D evelyn washed her hair in a galvanized bucket of lukewarm water. It had been steaming hot when she used it
for a sponge bath. The shoulders and neck of her white shirt
dripped as she wrapped the olive green and brown plaid towel
around her head. Worn linoleum chilled her bare feet. She
swung open the heavy front door and stepped out on the splintery front porch. A warm, drifting west wind greeted her.

The thin blue clear sky sported an out-of-focus, almost mys-
tical hue. She heard a low crunching sound and surveyed the
surroundings. A distant plume of dust followed a truck speed-
ing south out of Argenta. A red-tailed hawk soared heavenward
on a thermal. She searched for other movement. Then she spotted Uncle Henry down at the gravel road at the end of the
drive, chewing on an abandoned cedar fence post.

The only sound is a munching burro a hundred yards away? I can't believe I even hear him. No motors racing, horns honking, playground shouts, garbage truck clangs, or dog barks. This might be the quietest place in the whole country. Maybe this is the edge of the earth, Lord. But I need it.

"Uncle Henry, why are you eating a fence post?" she called out.

The short burro glanced back at the cabin, then trotted straight toward her.

"No, I didn't mean you had to . . ."

Uncle Henry didn't stop until his front hooves banged on the porch step.

Develyn walked over and scratched his ears. "What am I going to do with you? I don't know anything about horses and even less about burros." His huge brown eyes seemed alert, as though he expected the conversation to continue.

Dust rolled up from the end of the rutted driveway. A red Dodge pickup bounced toward her.

"Renny? I . . . I'm . . ." She yanked the towel off her hair. She looked down at the burro. "Uncle Henry, I'm not ready to receive guests. You entertain him for a while."

She scampered into the cabin and squinted into the small, foggy mirror. It hung crooked above the laundry basin that served as her only sink. With every stroke of the comb, she felt the tangles tug on her short blonde hair.

It's only 7:00 a.m. No one comes to visit at 7:00 a.m. That's rude, Mr. Slater. Very, very rude. Where's my mascara brush? I don't have time for foundation, let alone makeup. Lipstick . . . no man is going to see Develyn Worrell without lipstick. Pale, Puritan lips, Spencer used to call them. I'm not sure he liked anything about me. Forgive me, Lord, I don't want to become a bitter old lady, for Dee's sake as well as my own. She loved her father dearly. He will always be wonderful in her eyes.

She heard the truck stop.

A pickup door slammed.

Uncle Henry brayed.

"Mornin', Devy-girl . . . I saw you out on the porch, so don't go hidin' on me," Renny called from the yard.

She stepped to the front door, but left it closed. "Renny, I'm not decent yet."

"Pull on some clothes and come on out. I want to ask you something."

"I have clothes on," she snapped. "But I'm barefoot and uncombed."

He laughed, then hollered. "So is that mare you bought, but that don't keep her from prancing around in the pasture for all to see."

Develyn pushed the door open a few inches. "I do not intend to prance in the pasture."

His black cowboy hat was pushed back, and he chewed on a blue plastic toothpick. "You ought to be out ridin'. Mornin' is half gone."

"Half gone?" She glanced at her bare wrist as if wearing a watch. "It's 7:00 a.m."

"That's what I said," he said.

"I'll be out in a minute."

Develyn scurried to the mirror and smeared on Coral Silk lips. She glanced at the white bottle labeled "Wander Lust," but left the perfume unopened. She ran her fingers through her wet hair, then sighed. *It really doesn't matter, Lord. Who am I trying to impress now?*

The sun glared as she stepped on to the porch. Develyn shaded her eyes with her hand. "Renny Slater, if you say one word about my ugly toes, I will turn Casey Cree-Ryder loose on you with her brass knuckles and hunting knife."

Twin dimples appeared in his cheeks under his blue eyes. "Hey, you look good fired up. I'll bet every fifth-grade boy in Indiana has a crush on Ms. Worrell."

She shook her head and couldn't suppress her grin. "Slater, you could charm middle-aged parents to give up their only child kindergartener."

"Is that good?"

"Unparalleled."

He started toward the front step, but Uncle Henry cut him off. "Thank you, ma'am. Does this mean you'll forgive me for the burr under the saddle?" Slater scratched the burro behind the ears.

Develyn kept her arms folded across her chest. "Never. I will merely wait until a proper time to respond." *I should have changed my shirt. I'm glad it's only wet on the shoulders.*

"That sounds like revenge. Doesn't the Good Book say don't repay evil for evil?"

She had one light brown eyebrow cocked high. "But it doesn't prohibit repaying a practical joke with a practical joke."

"I see your point." He glanced out at the pasture. "You did get yourself a nice-looking mare."

"Thank you for that." Develyn stepped to the side of the porch, and Uncle Henry moved over with her. "Casey Cree-Ryder's coming to ride with me this morning."

When he cocked his head, deep, tanned creases formed around his eyes. "Dev, I need to go to town and pick up some medicine at the vet's early evenin'. I was wonderin' if you'd like to ride along. It would be a privilege to buy you supper."

She peered at the blond-headed cowboy. *Dimples. Bowlegs. Little boy grin. Worn boots. Sweat-stained hat. There are men all over the world who wish they could be you, Renny Slater.* "Renny . . . I just met you yesterday. So far, all you've done is purposely get me bucked off a horse."

"It's just a trip to the vet's and supper at El Sombrero . . . not like some big, romantic date, Ms. Worrell."

I don't know whether to laugh or cry, Lord. I don't know if I want him to ask me out or not. She hesitated.

Now it was Renny Slater who had his arms folded in front of him. "Dev, do you reckon we need to get to know each other better, before you go out with me?"

"That might be nice." *Dev Worrell, you are forty-five years old and your voice is as shaky as a thirteen-year-old. It's been years since I felt this way.*

"My thoughts exactly. Now, your burro won't let me up on the porch, and I don't go into a woman's home unless there's company around . . . so just exactly how are we going to get to know each other better?"

She stepped to the edge of the porch and stroked Uncle Henry's back. "Come to think of it, I think a trip to town will be nice, Renny."

Once again the dimples punctuated his brown, leathery cheeks. "That's fine. I was plannin' on headin' out about 3:30 or 4:00."

She tried to fluff her damp hair out with her fingers. "Will we be home by dark?"

"If you want to. Are you afraid of the dark, Ms. Worrell?"

"No, Mr. Slater. I'm not afraid of the dark, but I am concerned about what happens after dark."

He tugged his hat down and swaggered to the open door of his red pickup. "Do you like Mexican food?"

Uncle Henry trotted after him with a snort and a bray.

"Yes, I do, Renny. But I'm from Indiana where black pepper is considered spicy and jalapeno peppers are outlawed as lethal weapons."

"I like your wit, Develyn Worrell. Have you ever noticed that most purdy women have a lousy sense of humor?"

"No, I haven't. And thank you for the compliment. I should have returned to Wyoming long ago," she chuckled.

He stared out across the pasture. "Yes, ma'am . . . I wish you would have."

This is getting too serious too quick. "Renny, I'll look forward to the drive."

"That's mighty fine, Devy-girl. I'll see you later." He stood on the running board and glanced at her over the cab of the truck. "You can bring your burro along, but he'll have to ride in back."

She stared at Uncle Henry.

"I was teasin' you, Ms. Worrell."

"I know that, Mr. Slater. I was just pondering what to do with him. He seems to be quite protective of me."

"Think of him as your watch-burro," Renny laughed, then sped out of the dusty drive.

• • •

Casey rode the buckskin down the draw ahead of Develyn. The wash was dry sand and scattered rocks. Clumps of grazed brown grass framed the dry, sandy wash. Cree-Ryder waited on the far side. Develyn scooted her jean-covered backside against the smooth leather saddle and coaxed My Maria forward with a boot heel to the flanks.

Casey twirled her braid like a short rope. "I can't believe you got a big date with Renny already."

"I told you it's not a big date." Develyn prodded the horse through the sand. "I'm just riding to town with him to the vet's."

"That's a big date in Wyomin'," Cree-Ryder hooted. "Shoot, in some counties it's the same as being engaged."

Develyn shook her head at the dark-skinned woman wearing a long-sleeve denim shirt. "Don't you try to con me."

"It must be my Irish blood," Cree-Ryder laughed.

Develyn leaned forward as the paint horse pulled herself up the far slope of the sandy draw. Her stomach rested against the flat top of the wide saddle horn. She sat up straight and waited on top as the short-legged burro trotted to keep up.

Cree-Ryder spurred her horse forward. "Uncle Henry follows you like a dog."

"He is rather loyal for an animal I just met yesterday." Develyn kicked the flanks of her horse to follow.

"Are you ready to see what kind of legs My Maria has?"

"What do you mean?"

Cree-Ryder tugged the front of her battered hat down low. "Let's turn them loose and let them gallop."

Develyn felt her stomach knot. "I don't think I'm ready for that."

"Sure you are. You're a natural in the saddle."

"What if I get tossed off?"

"It won't be the first time." Cree-Ryder leaned forward and stroked the neck of her dark-maned gelding. "Besides, there's nothing out here but sage, dirt, and buffalo grass. Just kick her hard and give her her head. She'll know what to do."

"You stay ahead of me. You know, just to slow her down if I lose control."

"I'll be running alongside you. My Montana Jack is one swift horse. But I'll hold him back. Screw your hat down tight. I'll race you to the barranca."

"The what?"

"That narrow wash up there."

"Where?"

"That green line on the horizon."

"No racing."

"Are you ready?"

Develyn shoved her hat down, scooted deep into the seat of the saddle, and locked her knees against the a-fork. She clutched the leather reins in her left hand and grabbed the saddle horn with her right. Then she kicked her heels into My Maria's sides, and called out, "Giddy-up!"

The paint horse began to trot.

"Oh!" Develyn called out and grabbed her hat.

Cree-Ryder rode over to her. "That's not a gallop, not even in Indiana." She trotted Montana Jack alongside Develyn. Then she leaned over and slapped My Maria's rump with her hat and screamed, "Hey-yaaa!"

The horse bolted forward as if bitten by a rattlesnake. Develyn grabbed for her hat, but it was gone by the time her hand reached her head. She felt herself bounce back up on the rear of the saddle.

I'm going to fall off!

Both feet out of the stirrups, she dove forward and grabbed the horn with both hands and pulled herself back into the saddle. The hard leather spanked her backside like a junior-high principal after a food fight in the cafeteria.

I'm going to die. I just know I'm dead.

The saddle pounded her. She jabbed her feet until she found the stirrups. Develyn stood up just enough to take some of the weight off her bottom. The shock of each stride vibrated through her knees. She leaned forward over the saddle horn as they raced east along the edge of a dry gully.

Where is Cree-Ryder? It's a cinch I'm not turning around. I hope she finds what's left of my body. OK, Lord . . . get my room ready . . . but the wind does feel nice in my face.

The scant vegetation blurred. Brown hills rose on the horizon.

She's got to get tired sooner or later.

Over her shoulder, Develyn spied a cloud of dust.

I can't remember horses being this fast when I was a kid. She can't keep up this pace.

The pound of hooves drummed in unison to her heartbeat for several moments. *There's a little gulch up there . . . must be a runoff stream. Is that the barranca? I'll stop here and say I thought that was our objective. My Maria will have to stop there. Won't she? If we plunge down that embankment I'll end up with a horse on top of me. This is crazy. Dev, go home. Go back to your boring, depressing summer and your two cats.*

She yanked back on the reins and called out, "No!"

My Maria lowered her head, jerking Develyn forward and crushing the saddle horn into the pit of her stomach. The horse picked up speed. Develyn quit yanking back. Both hands and the reins were locked around the saddle horn.

She's going into that gulch. And I can't do one thing about it. Oh, Lord . . . deliver me from a painful death.

My Maria galloped even faster as they advanced on the narrow gulch but instead of dropping off into it, the paint horse raised up.

Jump it?

She can't leap that far.

Develyn closed her eyes until the horse's front hooves crashed into the embankment on the other side. My Maria's rear hooves slipped down the side of the gully, but then caught on something. She lunged to the prairie floor.

Then, My Maria continued to gallop.

I'm alive, so far. This is madness.

Inching her way forward in the saddle, Develyn leaned across the horn and grabbed the leather bridle just above the spade bit. With a hand on each side she jerked straight back on the bit and hollered into My Maria's sweaty ear. "No!"

My Maria tried to jerk the bridle from her hands.

"I said, 'No!'" Develyn screamed.

My Maria violently shook her head back and forth.

What am I doing wrong? What would Renny do?

Develyn sat straight up, pulled back firmly on the reins, and commanded: "Whoa!"

The mare almost sat on her back legs as she slid to a halt.

Yes!

Develyn lost her grip and was thrown over the horse's head.

No! Not again!

She scrambled to keep her feet down and hit the dirt running faster than she had ever run in her life. She couldn't stop, but did manage to hurdle a three-foot-high sage. She slowed to a stop at the base of a steep incline.

Develyn, bent at the waist, hands on her knees, threw up. She wiped her mouth on the tail of her T-shirt as Cree-Ryder trotted toward her, leading My Maria.

Develyn waved her hand and tried to say something, but no words came out.

Casey swung her leg over her horse's head and sat sideways in the saddle. "Hey, that was quite a dismount. I saw Hawkeye Henson do that one time at a rodeo in Douglas when I was a kid."

"Ah . . . ah . . ." Develyn felt her heartbeat pound in her head. "Ah . . . I . . . that was. . . ."

"And I didn't know you knew how to jump."

"I could have . . ."

"You have one fast horse."

". . . been . . ."

"Ol' Montana Jack got outrun."

". . . killed . . ."

"You did good, girl."

"Don't . . . did good . . . girl . . . me!" Develyn cried. "I was . . . I about . . ."

"It was fun, wasn't it?"

"Fun?" Develyn gasped. "Fun?"

"The wind blowing in your hair, thundering hooves, racing heart, on the edge of disaster and a thousand pounds of muscle under you . . . it's fun, isn't it?"

"I could have been seriously injured."

"Come on, admit it. It was fun."

"OK . . . OK . . . it was sort of fun . . . except . . ."

"Except for what?"

Develyn stared down at the prairie dirt. "Vomiting."

"You barfed? All over the horse?"

"No, after I made that graceful dismount, I lost my lunch."

"We didn't eat lunch."

Develyn shuffled over to My Maria. "You know what I mean."

"Mount up, cowgirl, we'll take the horses back at a walk."

"I can't even stand up straight, let alone ride."

"You can do it."

"I think maybe we went a little too far today." Develyn rubbed her backside.

"Nonsense, a little horse liniment will fix things."

Develyn took the reins from Cree-Ryder. "For My Maria?"

"No, for your sweet tushie."

"Are you teasing me again?"

"No, it works. Trust me."

"Trust me? Why would I ever trust you?"

"Did you have fun?"

"OK . . . do I have to mount up?"

"Yes."

"Can I stand in the stirrups?"

"Until your knees get tired."

"I need to find my hat."

Cree-Ryder swung her leg back over her horse. "I think Uncle Henry has it." She pointed her thumb back toward the plodding burro with the straw hat in his mouth.

Develyn led My Maria back toward the small donkey. "This is getting weird," she mumbled.

"You mean having a watch-burro who's a retriever? I think it's kind of cute."

"But it's not right. I mean, I hardly know him."

"What is it with you Indiana schoolteachers? You don't like anyone or anything unless you grew up with them back in Crawfordsville?"

Develyn stared up at Cree-Ryder's brown eyes. "I need to be cautious."

"Have you been cautious all your life?"

"Yes, I have. I have a reputation for being cautious."

"How has it worked out?" Cree-Ryder challenged.

"What do you mean?"

"Do you like the way your life turned out being that cautious?"

Develyn felt the muscles in her neck tighten. "That's not the point. It's Christian prudence to live a careful life."

"Did Jesus live a cautious life?" Cree-Ryder challenged.

"For about thirty years he did."

"And then?"

"He was consumed to fulfill his purpose for being here."

"There you have it."

"Have what?"

"Be consumed with fulfilling God's purpose for your existence."

Develyn gazed at her new friend.

"Hey, I graduated from Bible school at age twenty, and I have known Jesus as Lord and Savior since I was twelve. See, I shocked you. You think just because I'm rough around the edges, I can't have any spiritual depth?"

"No, I'm not shocked . . . well, just a little surprised. My spiritual life feels as pounded as my body right now. Do I really have to get back in the saddle?"

"Yep."

Develyn grabbed the saddle horn on the 14.5-hand paint mare, then jammed her left boot in the stirrup. When she eased down in the saddle, My Maria glanced back at her. "Don't give me that look, young lady," Develyn murmured. "You've never had your backside beat up for three straight hours."

"It hasn't been that long," Cree-Ryder reported.

"Nonsense, I can't even remember when I could sit without hurting." Develyn rode alongside the donkey. She reached and tugged on her hat. "Uncle Henry!"

The burro released the straw hat.

"That's a good boy." She tried to smooth the teeth marks on the brim, then slipped it on her head. "Let's go home."

Uncle Henry took off at a trot ahead of them.

"Where's he going?" Develyn asked.

"Home, I suppose."

"But he doesn't know what I said . . . does he?"

"One way to tell: if he's back at the cabin waiting for you, then he knows what you said."

● ● ●

The sweet nectar of the orange Popsicle dribbled down her throat as Develyn stood on the front porch of the old house converted into a store building. Casey Cree-Ryder stretched out on the bench beside her with nothing but the stick of a Dove Bar lodged like a tongue depressor between her full lips.

Mrs. Tagley, with white starched full apron over her long, faded blue housedress, stood behind the screen door and peered out. "Devy, why don't you sit down?"

"Mrs. Tagley, I won't be sitting down for a long time."

"Did you use some Dr. Bull's?" the elderly lady probed.

"Dr. Bull's?"

Mrs. Tagley peered over the top of her silver-framed glasses. "Dr. Bull's Female Remedy."

Develyn glanced over at Cree-Ryder, who shrugged. "Casey said I should use horse liniment."

"That's for rubbing on the outside. You *drink* Dr. Bull's," Mrs. Tagley explained. "It really works. I've taken a dose ever day since prohibition. I'll go get you a bottle." Mrs. Tagley disappeared into the recesses of the front-room store.

"Have you ever heard of Female Remedy?" Develyn murmured as she continued to lick the Popsicle.

"I've never even heard of Dr. Bull!"

At four-feet-ten, Mrs. Tagley had a pixie-like look when she stepped to the porch and handed Develyn a six-ounce, round

146

amber bottle with the label "Dr. Bull's Female Remedy: used externally and internally for generations." The woman in the picture who held a bottle above her head looked like she had just stepped off a Victorian calendar.

"So, I just drink it?" Develyn asked.

"Oh, just a spoonful at a time, honey. You young girls won't need very much." Mrs. Tagley scooted back into the store.

Develyn handed the bottle to Casey. "It's been a long time since I've been called a 'young girl'."

Casey studied the bottle. "Shoot, I was never called a young girl. Called a young boy a few times. I used to wear my hair short, shorter than yours."

"When was that?"

"When I was about ten. Hey, look at this. This stuff is made by the Mystic Trading Company of Seattle."

"Is that good?" Develyn watched a slumping black and white dog circle, then lie down in the shade of a cottonwood.

"They make a product called Miracle Oil."

Develyn nibbled the last bite off her Popsicle. "What do you do with Miracle Oil? Rub it on like suntan lotion?"

Cree-Ryder waved her ice cream stick like a pointer. "I suppose you could, but it's a fuel additive for chain saw motors." She handed the bottle back to Develyn.

"What am I going to do with this?"

"Rub some on your tushie, and take a snort," Casey laughed. "One of the two ought to help. You ready to promenade back to your place?"

"As long as we go slow."

Uncle Henry waited for them next to the sleeping dog in the shade of a cottonwood tree.

"If you don't want to walk, you could ride your burro."

"That's not even close to being humorous. I hurt all over."

Casey strutted beside her. "That bad, huh?"

"I went skiing one time in Colorado. Spencer, my husband, decided we should go to Colorado for Christmas when Delaney was about ten."

The two women and trailing burro trudged west along the dirt road.

"Did you go to Aspen? Vail? Steamboat?"

"Squaw Ridge."

"Never heard of it."

"Yes, well . . . Spencer was not known for being a big spender. Some flight attendant had convinced him it was a great place to go, but that's a different story. After five minutes of instruction, he had me and Delaney in a chairlift headed to the top of what he claimed was the easiest ski run in Colorado."

"Tough skiing, huh?"

"I wouldn't know. The chair lift broke down. Instead of waiting like everyone else for it to start, good ol' hubby ordered us to jump down and start skiing right there. He leapt off, then got Delaney to do the same. They both urged me to go for it . . . so I did."

"How high up were you?"

"About ten feet off the hard-packed snow, I suppose. When I leapt I caught my coat sleeve in the chair lift, landed on my shoulder, and bounced and rolled two hundred yards down the mountainside."

"Oh, wow, did you break anything?"

"I separated my shoulder. We had to wait a couple of hours for the rescue guys to bring me down off the mountain in a sled behind a snowmobile. That ticked Spencer. I had ruined a perfectly good day of skiing. I spent that Christmas in a tiny, cheap lodge room with my aching shoulder taped up watching an *I Love Lucy* marathon while my husband and daughter skied. But I don't think I hurt as much then as I do now."

"Do you ski much?"

"That was my first and last time. Spencer went almost every year and took Delaney several times. He said there was no reason for me to go and sit around and get fat. I could stay home and do that."

"So that's what you did?"

Develyn felt her thighs tighten with every step. "Mother owned her dress shop then, and I helped her during the Christmas season." She shook the bottle of Female Remedy. "Maybe I should have had some of this back then."

"Are you going to use it?"

"I don't know. It sure would make a conversation piece back in Indiana."

• • •

When Develyn stepped out of the bathroom, Casey stood near the combination desk and dresser in the dimly lit cabin.

"Hey, I got an alarm clock just like this."

"Is it broken?"

"Yeah, Montana Jack stepped on it."

Where does she sleep that a horse can step on her alarm clock?

"Wow, that's a cute outfit!" Casey sorted through the dresser. "Hey, I like this perfume . . . Wander Lust, huh?"

"I like the fragrance better than the title."

"How was your cold shower?"

"I thought I would die. I had to bite the washcloth to keep from screaming."

"You should try a cold shower in the winter."

"I'd rather not bathe than go through that in the winter."

"Now you're sounding like a true Wyomin' girl," Casey said. "Are you going to wear this perfume on your big date?"

"It is not a . . ."

"I know, I know . . . it's not a big date."

"You can come with us if you want to," Develyn blurted out. *Why did I say that? I don't know if I meant that or not.*

"Hah! I'm not goin' to crash your big night with a mustang breaker." Cree-Ryder splashed some perfume on her fingers and rubbed it on her neck and under her ears, then shoved it at Worrell.

"But you are going to stay here tonight?" Develyn put the perfume on the desk without using it.

"Someone has to be here when you come home, so you don't park out in the driveway half the night. Remember, I have a flashlight, and I'm sneaky."

"You sound like my mother."

"What's your mother like?"

"Everyone says she's just like me."

"That's scary. The only thing I remember about my mother is that she liked to fish," Casey murmured.

"Fish?"

"Yes. Every free minute it seems like I was drug to the lake or river or reservoir. She liked to fish."

"I've never known a woman who really liked to fish," Develyn said.

"She'd catch them and cook them right by the river. I can't stand to eat fish even to this day."

"What are you going to do about supper?"

"Hey, I had a Dove Bar."

"Sorry there's nothing here. I thought I'd get some food while I'm in Casper."

Casey slid her hands into the back pockets of her blue jeans. "You're goin' all the way to Casper?"

"Renny said we were going to town."

"Which town?"

"The town that has a vet."

"That could be Riverton, Thermopolis, or Casper, to name a few."

Develyn shrugged. "I guess I don't know."

"Let me get this straight. You've known this buckaroo for about twenty-four hours and now you are getting in his red truck and you don't even know where you're going?"

"It didn't . . . I think . . ." Develyn stammered . . . "You said he was nice."

"He is. And you have nothing to worry about. Still . . ."

"Still what?"

"I want you to find out where you are going and let me know before you go."

"Now you sound like Lily . . ."

"Is she your sister?" Casey asked.

"She should be. She's a good friend. We've taught next door to each other for twenty-three years. She wants me to call her every day and report in."

"That would be nice . . ." Cree-Ryder murmured. "It dawned on me a couple of years ago that I don't have anyone who really cares where I am and what I do."

"Some would call that freedom."

"They are fools. Anyway, being melancholy doesn't wear well on me. I'm not really complaining. I live my life the way I want to." Casey peered out the front window of the cabin. "Only, I'd rather not live it alone." She whipped around. "Dev, what do you think is wrong with me that guys never want to get very close?"

Develyn surveyed the dark-skinned girl. "You mean besides the fact that you scare men spitless?"

"Yeah, besides that?"

"You are asking the wrong woman." Develyn turned back to the little mirror and studied her face. "The only guy I ever attracted turned out to be rather worthless."

"You're doin' OK. Renny's toolin' up the drive."

"That's because he doesn't know me yet. Give him time and I'll bore him to death. I still feel funny about leaving you here."

"Would you feel funny if I had a date and was leaving you?" Cree-Ryder challenged.

"Of course not." Develyn put her hat on, glanced in the mirror, then pulled it off again.

Casey continued to stare out the window. "Then quit worrying about me."

"I was serious about you coming with us."

"And I was serious about not doing that."

"Any food items you want me to bring back? I'm really glad you are going to stay a few days."

"I can't believe you are going grocery shopping on a date."

"It's not a date." Develyn started to the door.

Cree-Ryder grabbed her arm. "What are you doing?"

"Going to meet Renny."

"Make him wait . . . I'll tell him you are just about ready."

"I am ready," Develyn insisted. "I am always ready on time."

"Always?"

"Yes. All my life."

"How boring," Cree-Ryder murmured. "Wait here. Trust me."

Casey slipped out on the uncovered porch.

Develyn stepped over to the mirror and fussed with her hair. Lord, I am not tiresome. Am I? Maybe she's right. I like Casey. She is unlike anyone I know, and yet she reminds me of someone. I just can't figure out who. She is so blunt . . . almost crude . . . yet so sincere. I just know we will be good friends for a long time.

The door to the cabin banged open. Casey ran in and grabbed her hat. "Hey, guess what?"

Develyn started toward the door. "What?"

"Renny asked if I wanted to go to town with you guys and . . ."

"And you told him?"

"Hey, with both of you beggin' me, I figure I'll ride along." Cree-Rider unzipped her jeans and tucked in her bright purple T-shirt, then licked the palm of her hand and mashed down her wild black bangs. "I don't look too sexy, do I?"

The voice sounded like a seasoned sixth-grade teacher. "Where are you right now?"

"On Mrs. Tagley's front porch with an orange Popsicle, talking on the cell phone to Lily-gone-wild," Develyn replied.

"Me?" Lily shouted.

Develyn moved the cell phone away from her ear.

"I didn't move to the edge of the earth to chase cowboys!"

Two dusty cowboys in an old dirt-plastered International pickup sputtered by and waved at Develyn. "I am not chasing cowboys. I'm a forty-five-year-old Indiana schoolteacher on summer vacation." She waved back at the two unknown men.

"Hmmm. Yeah, right. Do you have any more dates lined up?"

"I haven't had a date yet."

"What about last week when you went to supper with the bowlegged and dimpled Renny what's-his-name?"

Develyn paced the worn wooden porch and listened to her heels tap out a tune. "Renny Slater. It was not a date. Casey went with us and did most of the talking."

"Who sat next to the cowboy in his pickup? You or this Casey?"

"I did," Develyn admitted.

"You see?"

"She called 'shotgun' first. What could I do, ride in the back of the pickup with Uncle Henry?"

"You had a burro in the back of the pickup?"

Develyn stopped at the wagon-seat bench and traced her fingers in her brother's initials. "No, but he was invited. What about you? You and that lawyer seem very chummy."

"He's smart and funny . . . you'd like him," Lily admitted. "But you changed the subject."

"What is the subject?"

"The many loves of Develyn Gail Upton Worrell."

"Hah, that would make a very short book."

"You are writing new chapters."

"Not yet."

"Are you complaining?"

"No, I'm having a good time, Lily."

"Are you sitting down?"

"No, I'm standing. I only sit in the saddle nowadays."

Lily lowered her voice to a whisper. "Did you try some of that 'Female Remedy' you mentioned?"

"Yes."

"How did it make you feel?"

"Sleepy."

"How about your buns?"

"They felt sleepy, too."

"Well, you might want to sit down anyway," Lily insisted.

"Don't tell me you're getting married."

"Ms. Worrell, don't get silly on me."

"Why do you want me to sit down? Did the new superintendent turn out to have purple hair and a tattoo?" Develyn perched herself on the edge of the hard wooden bench and felt a sharp pain in her thighs.

"I know nothing about the new superintendent. But I saw Lisa D. at the Steak Haus in Waynetown. She's waiting tables again this summer. Lisa said that Delaney called her."

"How is my wayward daughter? She hasn't called me."

"You aren't at home."

"She has my cell phone number."

Lily cleared her throat. "Delaney wanted to borrow some money from Lisa D."

"Why?"

"Lisa said she thinks things aren't going too well in South Carolina and Delaney wants to come home."

"Home," Develyn choked. "Back home to Purdue at West Lafayette . . . or to Crawfordsville?"

"She didn't say."

"Lily, I don't even know how to contact her."

"Stewart's taking me to the Steak Haus after church on Sunday. Do you want me to ask Lisa D. to tell Delaney to call her mama?"

"Yes, I would. So, he's taking you to church now?"

There was a pause. "He's a Christian man. It's just church, Dev. That doesn't mean anything."

"Hah! I happen to know that's a big date in Indiana for the over-fifty crowd, and in Montgomery County it's considered being engaged."

Lily exploded. "You're sounding weird. You've been gone too long, Dev."

"Yeah . . . about thirty-five years too long."

"You like it out there, don't you?"

"Yes, I do. But I've only been here a couple of weeks."

"When's the big barbecue?" Lily asked.

"Tomorrow night."

"So, are all your admirers going to be there?"

Develyn stood and strolled across the porch. "I have no idea what you are talking about."

"It's at Mr. Burdett's ranch, right?"

"Yes . . ."

"And he said you have a smile like his late wife?"

"Well, yes . . ."

"And dimpled Renny, didn't he say you were a Wyoming version of Meg Ryan?"

"He's a talker, Lily. He said Casey looked a lot like Catherine Zeta-Jones."

"Does she?"

"Not in any conceivable way. The only similarity is their hyphenated last names."

"And then there's your landlord. How are you and Mr. Tallon getting along?"

"Lily, I told you he rather despises me. Anyway, he went back to Colorado, or somewhere, I suppose."

"He won't be at the barbecue?"

"I don't think so. How are my cats doing?"

"Are you changing the subject again?"

"I hope so."

"One of them did something naughty on your sofa."

"On my white couch? She's better trained than that."

"I think she's pouting 'cause Mama deserted her. You know how children try to get attention. Anyway, don't worry. I took the cushion to Busy Bee's, and Betty Harington said it would clean right up."

"Maybe you should put some towels over the cushions."

"I'm way ahead of you, honey," Lily reported. "I have old sheets draped over every piece of furniture, including your bed."

"Oh, my . . ."

"It looks like an abandoned dwelling or something. I just about cry when I look at it."

"Lily, this summer will fly. We'll be decorating our bulletin boards at school before you know it."

"I suppose, Ms. Worrell, yet . . . oh . . . I have to go . . . the man who's going to fix my sliding glass door is here."

"Is it Stewart?"

There was no reply.

"Lily, talk to me."

"He's very handy, Ms. Worrell."

"Yes, I can imagine . . . have fun, honey."

"I am, Dev. I really am. Bye, sweetie."

● ● ●

"If you drove faster, you wouldn't have to stay in this cloud of dust," Casey insisted.

Develyn Worrell steered her silver Jeep Cherokee along the gravel road. "You aren't anxious to get to the barbecue are you?"

Casey peeked in the mirror on the sun visor, then flopped her black bangs to the side. "Are you kidding? I've been waiting my whole life to get an invitation."

"I hope you aren't disappointed."

"I feel weird with my hair down. I'm so used to that braid."

Develyn kept both hands on the steering wheel and glanced over at Casey. "Your hair looks beautiful."

"Some say it looks like that Zorro chick who's married to that old actor. What do you think?"

"I think you have beautiful hair."

"Yeah, you said that." Casey waved her hands. "Turn here."

"Where?"

"Along that dry crick bed."

"That's a road?"

"You didn't expect blacktop, did you?"

"No, but I assumed gravel, at least." Develyn felt the rear tires slide as she turned the corner. "How in the world can a whole crowd travel on a road like this?"

"Some of them come in from the west."

"Why didn't we take that road?"

"It's worse than this. Besides, I think the important ones fly in."

Develyn gazed at the treeless prairie in front of them. "There's an airport?"

"An airstrip. Burdett flies his own plane. So does his daughter."

Develyn gripped the steering wheel. "What's Lindsay like?"

"Linds was Miss Rodeo Wyoming a few years ago. You know what that tells you," Casey said.

Develyn slowed as the dirt road washboarded. "Eh, no. I don't."

"Oh, you know . . . plastic smile, unflappable wavy hair, and that mechanical wave of hers as she races around the arena."

As the roadway smoothed out, Develyn sped up to forty-five miles per hour. "You've known Linds for quite a while?"

"I don't know her at all. I've just seen her around. We don't hang with the same kind of people, if you know what I mean. Actually, I heard she was nice, in a snooty sort of way."

"Who told you that?"

"Carli Myers. She was runner-up the year Linds was queen. They traveled a lot together. Carli's been to the barbecue. The year she went, Harrison Ford flew his helicopter to the ranch."

Develyn stared over at Casey, one eyebrow cocked.

"It's true. I told you this is a big deal."

"But how can something so remote be . . ."

"Stop the rig," Casey shouted. "Pull over."

Develyn slammed on the brakes. "Are you sick?"

Cree-Ryder hurled out of the car and pointed at the blue, clear Wyoming sky. "I told you," she hollered.

Even before Develyn sprang out of the rig, she heard the roar in the sky above. She shaded her eyes with her hand. "Are you telling me that's Harrison Ford in that helicopter?"

"Nope." Casey waved at the helicopter. "That's a State of Wyoming chopper. Probably the governor or someone like that."

"But I thought the barbecue was for cowboys."

"Mostly cowboys . . . and politicians . . . and celebrities . . . and Indiana schoolteachers."

"And bronzed lady horse trainers?"

"Are you alluding to my dark skin?"

"I am totally jealous of your dark skin."

Cree-Ryder nodded. "I've always thought white is a pathetic color for skin. I mean, people turn white when they die."

"Yes, well." Develyn glanced in the rearview mirror at the creases around her eyes. "We are forced to make up for our deficiencies with wit and charm."

Cree-Ryder stared at her for a minute, then chuckled. "Yeah, right."

A roar slung itself over the rise behind them and they jumped in the car and rolled up the windows, waiting for the vehicle to pass.

"It's a Hummer," Casey declared.

Develyn studied the vehicle in the mirror. "I think they are slowing down."

"How do I roll down the window?"

"The button to your right."

Develyn leaned over toward Casey and peered out as the electronic tinted window on the big black vehicle rolled lower. A broad-shouldered, square-jawed man with sunglasses leaned out.

"Do you ladies need some help?" he said with an accent.

Casey's chin dropped. Her eyes widened. "Ugh . . . ugh . . . ugh . . . ugh . . ."

"No, we just stopped to look at something," Develyn called out. "Thank you, anyway."

"I suppose you are going to the barbecue," he replied.

"You . . . you . . . you . . . you . . ." Cree-Ryder stammered.

Develyn nodded. *I think I've seen him somewhere.* "Yes, thank you. Perhaps we'll see you there."

"That would be nice. Does your friend have a speech impediment?"

Casey waved her finger as she choked. "I . . . I . . . I . . . I . . ."

"No, she's usually quite loquacious."

He peered over the frames of his dark glasses. "I know where there are some great speech coaches. They are all in southern California, but they can do wonders. I'll give you a phone number at the barbecue."

"Thank you very much," Develyn replied.

As he rolled up his window, Develyn heard him say, "Maria, write that down, so I don't forget."

The Hummer and a stampede of accompanying dust roared north.

"That was . . . that was . . ." Cree-Ryder stammered. "That was . . ."

Develyn pulled back to the middle of the dirt road. "You are acting so strange."

"That was . . . you know . . . you know . . . you know . . ." Casey gasped.

Develyn felt her eyes widen, and she slapped the steering wheel. "Isn't he the governor of California?"

"Turn around," Casey commanded.

"What?"

"I said, turn around. I want to go back. I'm not going to the barbecue. I acted like an idiot. I can't show up. It's too embarrassing."

"That's absurd. We are not turning back. I'm sure he sees that all the time."

Casey folded her arms across her gold-sequined black T-shirt, and hugged herself. "I don't handle ridicule well."

"You think Arnold is going to get on a loudspeaker and announce that Casey Cree-Ryder is a stammering fool?"

"You aren't going to turn around?" Casey demanded.

"No."

"Then I'll destroy the first cowboy who ridicules me."

Develyn tasted the bitter yellow dust that oozed into the rig. "You were supposed to leave your guns and knives at home."

"You didn't say anything about a half-stick of dynamite."

●　●　●

Cottonwood trees towered along both sides of the mile-long driveway up to the headquarters of the Quarter-Circle Diamond ranch. Red dirt prairie opened to the west. Cedar-lined rimrock framed the north. The distant Bighorn Mountains looked a dull purple. A three-slat wooden fence that covered eighty acres of irrigated pasture on the east had been turned into a temporary parking lot as they neared the structures. A thin cowboy with a flat-crowned hat and tall, stove-top black boots rode a red roan horse and signaled them where to park.

Develyn stepped out of the Jeep as the cowboy shouted back to the long one-story building, "She's here!"

Like an echo off a cliff, they heard the shout repeated. "She's here! She's here! She's here!"

Develyn slipped her arm into Casey's. The two boot-and-jeans-wearing women giggled their way toward the road. "Are they talking about you?" Develyn teased.

"Yeah, right. It's not me. It's you they're interested in."

"Haven't they ever seen an Indiana schoolteacher before?"

"Not one as cute as you."

"Thank you, Miss Cree-Ryder, but I do look in a mirror from time to time. That's not what I see."

"Dev, what do you see when you look in a mirror?"

"Forty-five hard years, crow's feet and dark rings under the eyes that can barely be covered up with foundation cream, and loose skin sagging under my chin. I see three slight pock marks left from a bad case of chicken pox when I was eight, and hair that would be half mousy brown and half gray if it were not for the magic of Clarice at the Hair Port in Crawfordsville . . . shall I go on?"

"No, but if I were you, I wouldn't mention any of that to the cowboys."

"I have no intention of doing so, and if you say a word about any of that, I will rip your lips off," Develyn challenged.

Most of the gathering lounged around fifty eight-foot tables lined out in five long rows between the largest building and the fenced corral.

Develyn pointed at the big house. "I presume that is the Burdett residence."

"That's my guess." Casey swaggered along ahead of Develyn. "I hear they put that screened porch clear around buildings in the old days so you could drag the beds out in the summertime.

The long one-story building must be the bunk house, and that one at the end with three chimney stacks has to be the cook house."

A man on a black horse trotted toward them. "Evenin', Miss Dev." He tipped his black cowboy hat, then nodded at Casey. "Welcome to the Quarter-Circle Diamond annual barbecue."

"Hello, Cuban. Thank you for inviting me," Develyn said.

"Inviting *us*," Cree-Ryder corrected.

"You ain't packin', are you?"

"No, your manhood is safe," Cree-Ryder replied.

"Casey."

"Yes, Mother."

Develyn surveyed the headquarters. "Cuban, how many people live back here? It's like a town."

"During the spring work and the fall gather, they carry two dozen punchers and a cook, plus Mom and Pop Gleason, the Old Man, and Lindsay. But in the off season, only six of us and the Gleasons are on steady. And most take off a couple of weeks at Christmas. Last year it was just me and Tiny here with the old man and Linds. They invited us into the big house, and we ate right off fine china and linen tablecloths. They are nice folks. I wouldn't want to work for anyone else."

"Looks like a big turnout tonight," Develyn remarked.

"Yeah, did you know the Terminator is here?"

Casey waved toward the pasture with the parked rigs. "We saw his Hummer pass us as we came in."

"He and the Old Man are up on the porch discussing politics, no doubt."

Develyn studied the young cowboy's face. "Cuban, Quint Burdett isn't really that old."

His eyes widened. "No, ma'am."

"Then why do you call him the Old Man?"

"Miss Dev, I don't rightly know, but the ranch owner is always called the Old Man, no matter what his age. Would you like me to introduce you around?"

"That would be nice," Develyn replied.

"Climb up here behind me." He motioned.

Develyn glanced over at Casey.

"Don't worry abut me. I'll check out the chow . . . and stay as far away from the front porch as I can."

Cuban reached down and offered his hand.

"I can just walk."

"The ones I want to introduce you to are all on horseback," he insisted.

● ● ●

Thirty minutes later, Develyn had met twenty ranch hands, toured their spotless bunkhouse, and visited the horse barn. She and Cuban rode back toward the crowd when she heard a signal clang. "That sounds like a school bell."

"Almost," Cuban reported. "It's the supper bell. I reckon we can go get in line soon."

"I still can't believe there are this many people back here," Develyn said.

"Sort of like half the state, ain't it? We was expectin' over four hundred people."

Only in Wyoming do four hundred people seem like half the state . . . "Cuban, where can I wash up? I petted too many ponies not to clean up a little."

"The ladies and children use the big house . . . the men use the bunkhouse. Go straight through the screen door, then the door straight behind it. Once inside, take the first door to your left."

Develyn tried to brush horse hair off her jeans as she strolled toward the huge, square two-story house with screen porches on all four sides. People milled toward the south side, and the crowd noise muffled the western background music.

The wide stairs up to the porch were weather-beaten and worn, but the screen porch was more like a sunroom, furnished with beautiful overstuffed chaises and glass-top coffee tables.

The door to the house led to a hall just off the kitchen that gave off a warm sweet aroma like daybreak at a Krispy Kreme. The door to the left had a cold, round, old-fashioned brass doorknob. It was locked.

Hearing running water, Develyn gawked into the kitchen. *There are large restaurants in Indiana that don't have kitchens this size.*

"Hi, there."

Develyn glanced under hanging pans above a huge chopping block and spotted a younger lady, with a bright hot-pink sequined blouse and a white cowboy hat pulled down on her long wavy blonde hair. "Well, hi. I was just waiting to wash up."

"Come over here and use one of the sinks."

Develyn sauntered to the counter that sported three stainless steel sinks side-by-side. "Thank you. I'm going to take a wild guess and say you are Lindsay Burdett."

The lady held out her hand. "How did you know?"

"Your father said you were a beautiful blonde."

"Yes, and he said you had a smile and eyes just like Mama's. I recognized you the moment you rode up with Cuban."

"You know who I am?"

"You are Ms. Develyn Worrell. You teach fifth grade at Riverbend Elementary School in Crawfordsville, Indiana. Your favorite color is green, and your favorite movie is *Gone with the Wind*. You have two cats, named Josephine and Smoky, and like to eat at an Italian restaurant called Carrabbas Italian Grill in Southport."

"How did you know all that?"

"I cheated," Lindsay grinned. "I checked you out on the Internet and found your school Web site."

"You checked me out?"

The blonde leaned her backside against the polished wood counter. "When Daddy came home with a big grin talking about some schoolteacher, I figured it was time to investigate."

"Oh, dear, and that's such an old picture of me."

"You've lost a few pounds since then, I take it."

"Yes . . . I've lost . . . well . . . more than pounds. Anyway, I'm flattered Quint mentioned me."

"I like it when people call him Quint. Around here, he's known as 'Daddy' to me. And 'Mr. Burdett' to everyone else."

Develyn admired the immaculate kitchen. "I've enjoyed getting to visit with him. Where is he?"

Lindsay pointed out the window above the sinks. "Probably out front looking for you."

Develyn dried her wet hands on the starched and pressed tea towel, then turned back toward the screen porch.

"No, no . . . come with me through the front room." Lindsay swooped over and laced her arm into Develyn's.

They promenaded through a polished oak doorway. "Oh, my. What a beautiful room," Develyn said.

"Mama loved to decorate. She was always bringing home another piece of furniture."

Develyn paused near a huge river-rock fireplace and gaped above the mantel. "Is that your mother?"

"Yes. Daddy calls her Miss Emily."

"What a lovely lady."

Lindsay bit her lip, then murmured, "Thank you, and she was a true lady. She was at home while attending the Metropolitan Opera . . . or the calving shed at 2:00 a.m. Absolutely nothing ever upset her. Talk about cool under pressure."

"I wish I could have met her."

"Everyone liked Mama."

"There you two are!" Quint Burdett burst through the door. "Dev, I'm really glad you came tonight."

"So am I. I've had a delightful talk with Linds. And met all your ranch hands."

"They were all anxious to visit with you. But there are other guests to meet, and we need to get this supper started right."

Quint offered his right arm to his daughter and his left to Develyn. They strolled onto the porch and down the stairs. A large gathering waited on the south lawn. Most of the men sported boots and cowboy hats. A few of the women wore prairie skirts, but the majority had on jeans and bright-colored blouses.

Quint led them to a microphone, then released the women.

"I didn't know you'd have a live band," Develyn whispered.

"Daddy brought them down from Calgary," Lindsay reported. "They are quite good."

Quint tapped on the mike, then waited for the feedback to die down. "Folks, can I have your attention?"

He paused for the crowd to grow quiet.

Develyn spotted a waving Casey Cree-Ryder standing next to Tiny, a huge cowboy who looked like he surely must have played nose guard for the Colts. She waved back.

"Ladies and gents, welcome to the annual Quarter-Circle Diamond ranch-hand barbecue. We have lots of special guests tonight. I hope they introduced themselves to you, because I'm not goin' to. It was Miss Emily's idea, and me and Linds are happy to keep it going. There are no introductions, no name tags . . . everyone is on equal ground at the ranch tonight. Among us are three governors, two senators, a congressman, and a niece of a U.S. president, to name a few. So visit with whomever you want, eat next to anyone who will have you, and dance with anyone who keeps from stepping on your toes. But before supper we should take a minute to thank the good Lord."

He dropped his head. "Lord Jesus, there isn't much in this world worth havin' if it doesn't come from you. So we thank you for the spring gather, for healthy calves, nutritious grass. We ask your blessing for all the folks with strong bodies and beautiful smiles who have gathered here. We are sinful, Lord, and deserve none of your blessings, but thanks to the cross of Jesus, we are given a chance. May we use it wisely, give you thanks for all things, including the best ranch food on earth. And all the cowboys said . . ."

There was a thunderous chorus of "Amen!"

"Now, there is another tradition that Miss Emily insisted on. This is a ranch hand barbecue, so all the ranch hands of the Quarter-Circle Diamond . . . and any other hands . . . get to be first in line. Sorry, governors, that's the rules. It's a salute to the men who do the work. So, the ranch hands and their guests go first."

Cuban pushed his way to the front of the crowd, holding his hat in his hand. "Miss Dev, I'd be pleased to escort you to the line."

She glanced up at Quint. "Cuban asked you first, Ms. Worrell. But I intend to occupy some of your time later on."

"I look forward to it, Quint."

Develyn took the arm of the beaming, bowlegged cowboy as they snaked their way through the crowd.

"What about Casey?" she asked.

Cuban paused and turned back. "Tiny, you escort Cree-Ryder!" he hollered.

"Is she packing guns or knives?" Tiny shouted back.

"No," Develyn replied.

"What about scissors or pruning shears?" Tiny said.

The crowd roared as he took Cree-Ryder's arm and led her behind Develyn and Cuban.

● ● ●

The sun dropped over the western horizon about 8:30 p.m., but twilight lingered until after 10:00 p.m.

Develyn lounged in the shadows of the Chinese lanterns near the corral fence and watched the dance. The floor consisted of plywood nailed to wooden pallets that were crushing a very nice lawn.

"Miss Dev, are you up to another dance?" the cowboy drawled.

"Cuban, I'm flattered you asked, but you cowboys have worn me out. These boots are fine in the saddle, but I'm afraid I've blistered my feet with about thirty dances."

"Pull 'em off, Miss Dev."

"I think I will."

"Would you like a hand?"

"Oh, no," Dev blushed. "I can . . ."

"Shoot, Miss Dev, it don't mean nothin' to help pull off boots."

"You're right. Yes, thank you." She lifted her right foot toward the cowboy in the shadows.

Cuban grabbed her heel with one hand and the toe with the other, then slowly tugged off the boot.

"You've done that before, cowboy."

"No, ma'am . . . I mean . . . it's jist sometimes me and the boys need help with our boots and . . . I ain't never . . . it ain't that I . . ." He smoothly tugged off the other boot.

"Cuban, if it were daylight . . . I bet your face is red."

"Shoot, ma'am, I reckon my ever'thin' is red. Did you want to dance barefoot?"

"Not until every cowboy on that dance floor is barefoot."

"Yes, ma'am. I understand." Cuban tipped his cowboy hat and meandered back into the noisy crowd.

Develyn studied the shadows. She thought she saw Renny Slater dancing with Casey, but they were so close together she couldn't tell. *Lord, this is nice. I don't know anyone but Casey and Quint and Renny, oh, and Cuban and Lindsay . . . but the others have made me feel so at home. These are good people whom I never knew existed until a few weeks ago.*

"There you are."

She studied the tall cowboy. "Good evening, Quint."

He swung his long leg over a metal folding chair and sat in it backward to face her. "You're a good dancer, I see."

"I danced more tonight than I have in twenty-five years combined. I enjoyed it until my feet wore out."

"Miss Emily loved to dance."

"Do you miss her tonight?"

"Actually, I've been too busy. The governors decided to do some advance planning for the western governor's conference . . . and in between that and the stopped-up toilets in the ladies' room, I haven't had much time for anything or anyone."

"Oh, dear, are you the plumber?"

"And mechanic and electrician, etc. This far from town, you either fix it or keep it broke." He glanced down at her sock-covered feet. "Your boots too tight?"

"Yes, I do believe I got to dance with every working cowboy in the county."

"You might be close to the truth on that one."

"Excuse the socks, but I'm not used to dancing in boots all evening."

"What size do you wear?" Burdett asked.

"This is embarrassing," Develyn mumbled. "Size ten."

"That's what I figured. Miss Emily wore the same. Say, she has . . . I mean, I have a pair of eel-skin boots that she said were so soft she could dance across Texas in them. She was from Amarillo, you know."

"Did she grow up on a ranch?"

"Yep. Cattle . . . and, well . . . other more profitable interests. Let me get those boots for you."

"Oh, no, Quint . . . don't trouble yourself. I really am too tired to dance anymore."

"I didn't mean just tonight. I want to give them to you."

"Oh, I couldn't . . ."

"It would be a help to have someone enjoy them. Linds has size-six feet, so she will never need them. I insist. It's a waste for them to sit in a closet until they rot."

"Thank you for your generosity."

Quint pointed toward the lights in the big house. "Did you get to meet the governors and their wives?"

"Yes, Linds introduced me."

"I like them," he reported.

"Yes, but I'm afraid I blabbed too much to Mrs. Schwarzenegger when I said I had a horse named Maria. I presume they all left in the helicopter."

"Yes, they all flew to Jackson Hole. He left the Hummer here at the ranch and will pick it up next Wednesday."

"You have a beautiful spread, Quint. Remote, but so peaceful."

"I love it back here, Dev. Always have. My granddaddy bought this place back in 1909."

"Did your Miss Emily enjoy the remoteness of the ranch?"

He pulled off his hat and ran calloused fingers through his hair. "She cried for the first two years, she was so lonesome.

Then one day, she just sucked it up and said, 'I'm through moping, Quintin. This is my home, and I choose to enjoy it.'"

"Good for her!"

"Of course, once we got the airplanes and learned to fly, she didn't feel so isolated."

"Miss Emily was a pilot too?"

"Yes, ma'am, the best of all of us . . . well, our boy, Ted, was probably the best."

"Is there anything she couldn't do? Oh, I didn't mean that in a negative way."

Burdett laughed. "Miss Emily couldn't make a decent potato salad, if her life depended on it."

"What?"

"I like potato salad, and hers was always awful. Other than that, she could do it all."

When the music stopped and the dance floor cleared, Renny and Casey slalomed through scattered chairs and guests.

Cree-Ryder flopped down in a chair next to Develyn. "By daylight, I'll be danced out."

"How about you, Mr. Slater?" Develyn challenged. "Are you worn out?"

"Dancin' with Cree-Ryder is always an adventure," he drawled.

"Don't tell me she steps on your cowboy toes."

"Gettin' my boots crushed is the least of my worries."

"You braggin' or complainin', cowboy?" Casey challenged.

"Just statin' the facts, ma'am. You have dance steps previously unknown by any man on the face of the earth."

"Did you hear that, Dev? Renny likes my moves!"

Slater shook his head and grinned. "It has been a fun evenin'. Mr. Burdett, thanks for the invite. I think I'll call it a night while I'm reasonably healthy."

"See you Wednesday, Slater. It won't be so fun, then," Burdett said.

"I reckon not. How many you got for me?"

"Eighteen. The first dozen you won't break a sweat. Four of them will take some time . . . and those other two . . . well . . . don't get yourself hurt. They aren't worth it. If you don't break them, I'll just shoot them and be done with it."

"Ah, that's what I like . . . a challenge. They aren't as bad as those two you had back in '99 are they?"

"Worse. And those broke your leg and dislocated your shoulder."

"Hmmm . . . well, thanks for the warning." Renny pulled off his hat. "Evenin,' Miss Dev, thanks for the dances." He leaned down and kissed her cheek, then turned to Cree-Ryder. "And thank you, ma'am, for the dances. I'll kiss your cheek, too, if you promise not to maim me."

"I ain't promisin' nothin'."

Renny bent forward, and Cree-Ryder threw her arms around his neck and slammed her lips into his. When she released him, he staggered back.

"I don't kiss cheeks well," she said.

"And I think I'll just shake hands," Quint laughed. "See you in a couple of days, Renny."

"Five o'clock?"

"Come on out at 4:00 and have breakfast. We'll have room in the bunk house, of course."

Renny scooted through the crowd.

"Did you ever notice that roughstock riders only kiss you for eight seconds, then quit as if the event was over?" Casey smirked.

"No," Develyn said, "I don't suppose I ever thought about that."

"Well, it's true." Casey stood up. "I'm going for punch."

"You goin' to throw one or drink one?" Develyn asked.

"Now I'm gettin' it from my best friend!"

I've known Casey a couple of weeks and I'm her best friend? Maybe she's right. "Bring me some punch."

"Which one? The red, the white, or the blue?"

"The white one."

Quint pulled off his hat and twirled it in his hand. "Dev, I was hoping you and me could spend a little more time visiting tonight. It just got crazy. Sorry about that. Maybe you could come back out, and I'll show you around in daylight."

"That would be wonderful. I'd enjoy it."

"Do you have any problem flying in a small plane?"

"I don't think so. But I haven't been in anything smaller than a commuter plane between Indy and Chicago." *And I thought I would die when we hit turbulence.*

"I could land down near Argenta . . . there's a strip out behind Mrs. Tagley's. I could show you the ranch from the air."

"That would be fun." *As long as I remember some Dramamine.*

"In the old days, Miss Emily would tend to party details, and I would circulate and visit with everyone. Now I'm too busy to see them all. I miss that."

"You make a very gracious host, Quint."

"I must say, Dev . . . seeing you here . . . even when you danced with the hired help . . . put a bounce in my step and a smile on my face. That feels so good." He stood up and offered her his hand.

She reached up, and he pulled her to her feet. "Quint, you know how to make a middle-aged schoolteacher feel good about herself." Her hand lingered in his.

He stepped around in front of her, still clutching her hand. His other calloused hand slid across her shoulder and parked on the back of her neck.

"Miss Dev!" a cowboy shouted, and Burdett's hands slid to his side.

She peered through the shadows to see Cuban hurrying toward her. "You promised me one more dance."

"Cuban, I think I said my feet hurt."

"Yes, ma'am, but you also said you wouldn't dance until all the cowboys pulled off their boots."

"Yes, I believe I did."

He pointed down at his wiggling toes. "We are all barefooted, Miss Dev."

M ost nights the tap-tap-tap of a loose piece of tin roofing flapping in the wind drummed Develyn to sleep.

Not this night.

She reached under the feather mattress and extracted a small, steel flashlight and pointed it across the room. The brass alarm clock, with cracked glass, still read 12:20. Then she sat up and surveyed the floor with the light before she pressed her bare toes into the cold, worn linoleum. *I don't see any cockroaches or mice, so I'm not going to light the propane lantern. I need to go back to sleep.*

She fumbled on the dresser for her watch.

Three a.m.? Why did I wake up now? I have been sleeping better for weeks. Go back to bed, Ms. Worrell.

I should fix some coffee, but I don't want to turn on the gas stove. Where's my Wal-Mart eighty-eight-dollar microwave when I need it?

She clutched the black plastic handle of the aluminum coffee pot and emptied its contents in a blue tin cup.

I hate cold coffee.

She grimaced and swallowed.

"But it's not as bad as it used to be." Her voice was barely audible.

She thought she heard voices float outside the cabin. She slid over to the front door, checked the gate latch that served as a lock, then leaned against the door. The raw wood scraped her ear.

No wonder pioneer women left alone would go insane in this wind. It haunts and torments like a classroom of first-graders after a chocolate party.

Develyn grabbed a small, tattered quilt from the bed and dragged it to the worn, overstuffed chair that smelled like the dust of 1969. She pulled her feet under her, covered her lap with the quilt, then turned off the flashlight. She sipped cold coffee and stared out the curtainless window. Stars flashed like galactic turn signals as the scattered clouds raced under them.

I don't know why I can't sleep, Lord. No, that's not true. I do know. Monday will be three weeks since I've left home, and I still don't have a clue why I'm here. I wanted to find my dirt-road town . . . and I did. I wanted to ride every day, and I'm doing that. I wanted to meet new friends, and I have. Casey has gone home to Tensleep for a

*few days, and I miss her even though she is so totally unlike me.
I came out here to find out if I could relate to a man . . . any man . . .
at my age. And I suppose I've succeeded. The cowboys make me feel
special, but perhaps that's because of their isolation. Renny makes me
laugh and relax and forget about being the uptight Ms. Worrell. I like
that a lot.*

*And, Quint . . . well . . . oh, my . . . maybe he's the reason I can't
sleep.*

*He's such a perfect gentleman . . . the hard-working rancher. When
he flew me up to the ranch, I thought my heart would never stop racing.
Casey was right. He owns half the county. He loves what he does. Even
more important, he loves you, Lord. He loves his daughter and the
memory of his son.*

And, he still loves his Miss Emily.

But that's OK. The man knows how to love.

Some men never learn.

She took another sip of cold coffee, then circled her head,
trying to relax her stiff neck. *I didn't mean that, Lord. I truly
hope Spencer is there with you in heaven. He never learned how to
love me . . . or Delaney, really . . . but perhaps he learned how to love
you. I never knew how to really love him, either.*

That's what scares me about Quint. He's such a tender man.

*I'm not sure I'd know how to take care of him. I didn't do so good
the first time around. But Quint . . . he and his Miss Emily were so
wonderful together. As long as I can be Develyn Worrell, nothing more
and nothing less, I'll be OK.*

Quint's stern with naughty horses and lazy hired help, but so gentle with me. It's as if he understands me and my struggles. He is strong in spirit and body . . . and not a bad body for a man that age.

Her hand went to her mouth. *Dev Worrell, don't you start thinking that way!* She took another sip of cold coffee and swallowed it quickly.

I am forty-five years old, and I don't know how to love a man. Yet I want a man to love me.

I really don't know how to do a relationship with a man, especially a man like Quint. I wish Miss Emily had left instructions.

A shout or a dog bark echoed in the stiff wind. She glanced up at the window.

With this wind, a person could shout in Cody and it would blow across the state.

Develyn put the empty tin cup on the floor, then pulled the quilt up to her shoulders and hugged herself.

Lord, I like Wyoming. I do feel better about myself. I don't have to be Ms. Worrell . . . they only want me to be Miss Dev . . . and certainly it's been good for my ego . . . I hope it's been good for my faith. I've prayed and talked to you more than I have in twenty-five years. I know now that you led me, but I'm not sure why.

I like Quint Burdett. Sometimes I think he's a dream. He has to have some hidden vices and flaws, but I can't find them. But if I'm truthful, ranch life scares me. I love the horses . . . for a while . . . but thinking about the isolation . . . the long, frigid winters . . . I'd have to drive two and a half hours to go to a mall. On the other hand, Quint could fly me there.

And to be honest . . . I don't know if I could give up teaching. Some days I want to scream . . . but those fifth-graders have kept me alive for decades because they need me and love me. I'm an Indiana schoolteacher. I suppose I could change.

I wonder if he is really rich . . . or just puts on a show. I know most cattlemen have all their funds tied up in the land and the cows. Would I be so fascinated with him if he lived in a singlewide in Casper and worked in a minimart? There's a sobering thought. Surely, Lord, I'm not swayed by possessions.

Or am I?

How strange. Why am I thinking about him at all? I've gotten along fine for years without thinking of a man. OK, I've sorta survived for several years without thinking of a man. Why now? Why this guy?

The howling wind and the constant tap of the loose tin roof didn't mask the honk of a horn. Develyn stood up. Wearing the quilt like a cape, she scooted across the cold bare floor toward the window.

If Mr. Tallon is back, he is certainly making a lot of noise. I wonder if he's drunk. I can't imagine any other reason to honk a horn in your own driveway. If he comes near this cabin, I'll call the police.

Develyn stood in the dark room and peered across the prairie toward the other cabin. Headlights from a parked truck illuminated the porch. She thought she could see two or three men.

He has company? At this hour? No one has sober company at 3:30 a.m. Where's my cell phone?

Develyn padded her way to the chair, retrieved her flashlight, then found her phone on the dresser. She turned the flashlight off as she stepped in front of the window.

Any of you take one step in this direction and I'll phone the county sheriff . . . or the state troopers . . . or the National Guard . . . or someone.

She thought she heard shouts, and studied the silhouettes as two of the men waved their arms.

This isn't good, but why do I expect the worst? Lord, I don't like Cooper Tallon very much, but I have no real reason for that. He misjudged me once . . . and perhaps I'm misjudging him. I just wish I knew what they were arguing about.

Develyn unlatched the window and shoved it open a couple of inches. A gust caught the window and slammed it against the side of the cabin.

A blast of wind whipped in and she staggered back, then pushed her way to the counter in front of the window. Develyn tried to reach out and pull the multipane window closed, but was unable to grip it.

The whole cabin will be blown into a mess if I don't get it closed.

Still wearing shorts and a T-shirt, she shoved her cell phone in her back pocket and plucked up the flashlight. She scurried barefoot to the front door and flipped the gate-latch lock. Clutching the door tight, she opened it and slipped out into the windy night.

Develyn closed the door, then paused on her porch. She staggered in the wind.

What am I doing? I have to close my window. Then I'm going to bed and pull the covers over my head and not come out for week. This

188

is crazy. I'm freezing. They are one hundred feet away, and I'm running around in my pajamas. Well, what I've been using for pajamas. Lord, look after fools like me.

Her toes now numb, she turned off the flashlight and crept around the cabin to the east. The open window banged against the shutter, and she yanked on it to close it. It slammed closed.

The shouting next door stopped.

Develyn dropped to her bare knees on the rough dirt beside the cabin.

Did they see me? Oh, Lord, this is a bad dream. I want to wake up at home. Where is that rancher? Or Renny? Or even Casey Cree-Ryder when I need them?

The shouting continued and she turned and sat in the dirt, leaning against the cabin and watching the headlight-lit silhouettes at the other cabin.

"You owe me!" someone screamed.

"I owe you nothin'," a deep voice replied.

"Don't give me that crap."

"Go home."

"You'd like that, wouldn't you?"

"Get out of here."

"We could take it, you know."

"You could try."

"You don't scare me. You never scared me."

"Get out of here."

"You're goin' down, old man."

"Not by myself, I'm not."

"Is that a gun?"

Oh, my God . . . oh, no . . . I don't want to be here . . . I don't want to see this. I'm just an Indiana schoolteacher. I want to go home. I want to go home right now, Lord.

Develyn clutched herself to keep from shaking.

"Porter, we have to get out of here!" This time it was a high-pitched scream. "He's crazy!"

"I'm not leavin' until I get what's mine."

"I'm leaving."

"Hendrix, get back here!"

One man sprinted for the truck.

The wind picked up.

The shouts and curses were inaudible.

Tires spun loose dirt. The pickup spun around in the dirt yard.

Then, a loud explosion.

Oh, my God . . . that was a gunshot. Oh, no . . . what do I do . . . what do I do? Who shot whom? What do I do?

On her hands and knees, Develyn crawled around to the porch and to the front door. She pushed her way into the cabin, closed the door behind her, then fumbled to lock the gate latch. She sprawled on the frigid, slick linoleum with her back against the door and shook.

I don't know what to do, Lord. I don't know what to do. This isn't fun. Something horrible has happened.

She laid her cell phone on the floor between her legs, then pointed the flashlight at it.

I have to call someone. I have to tell someone.

She studied the lit key pad of the telephone. She picked it up, sighed a deep breath . . . then punched 9–1–1.

Develyn waited for six long rings.

"Sheriff's office."

"I . . . eh I need to report . . ."

"Speak up, lady."

She cleared her throat. "I need to report . . ."

"Harry . . . turn off that dadgum microwave! I can't even hear the lady on the phone!" he shouted. "How should I know if it's your wife? Go ahead, lady."

Develyn sat straight up.

"I need to report a fight and possible gunfire."

"Is anyone injured?"

"I don't know."

"Did anyone get shot?"

"It's too dark. They were arguing and cussing and then they ran to the truck and there was a gun shot."

"Relax, we'll take care of it. Tell me your name."

"I'm Develyn Worrell from . . ."

"OK, just relax, Evelyn . . . we'll . . ."

"Develyn—with a D. Dev."

"Don't scream into the phone. Are you at home?"

"No, I live in Crawfordsville, Indiana."

"Where are you now?"

"In a cabin where the cedars used to be."

"In Indiana?"

"I'm a quarter of a mile north of Argenta, Wyoming."

"That's in Natrona County."

"I think so."

"Ma'am, this is the sheriff's office in Johnson County. You'll have to call the Natrona County sheriff."

"But I dialed 911."

"Yes, ma'am. You used a cell phone, right?"

"Yes."

"Sometimes the relay tower that picks up the signal is in a different county so your 911 calls are routed through their emergency number. If you'd call 307-577-5577, you can talk to the Natrona County sheriff."

Develyn felt tears trickle down her cheeks. "You mean you can't help me?"

"Just call them. They will take care of it. Did you get that number?"

"Yes, I . . ."

"OK . . . now phone them."

"But . . ."

Develyn leaned against the door and listened to the dial tone.

With slow determination she punched in 307-575-5577.

On the fourth ring, a man answered and mumbled, "Yeah?"

"Is this the Natrona County sheriff's office?"

The man's voice sounded sleepy and irritated. "Is this Natalie?"

"I need the sheriff's office."

"This is a lame joke, Natalie."

"All I want is . . ."

"Every guy in Casper knows what you want," the man snarled. "Sober up."

Develyn heard a woman in the background shout, "Is that her again, Matthew? I told you never to talk to that woman again!"

"Shut up," the man hissed.

"I need the sheriff's office," Develyn whimpered.

A deep female voice came on the line. "You need a psychologist."

Again, Develyn stared at the face of the cell phone. She brushed tears back with the back of her hand.

She punched speed dial #2.

After five rings there was a sleepy, but familiar, "Hello."

"Sorry, Lily, I need some help."

"Dev? What's wrong, honey? What time is it there?"

"I don't know . . . maybe 3:30 a.m."

"Are you OK?"

"I need your help . . ."

"Oh, no . . . oh, honey . . . what is it?"

"I need you to phone the sheriff for me."

"Oh, Lord Jesus, no! Dev, are you hurt?"

"Lily, I'm OK. There's been a fight and a gunshot next door, and I can't seem to get the right county sheriff. Now I'm too rattled to get the right number."

"Just punch in 9-1-1, honey."

"I tried that," Develyn whined. "Lily, call information for the Natrona County sheriff's office in Casper, Wyoming."

"Where are you?"

"On the floor in my cabin."

"I'll have them phone you, OK, honey?"

"OK."

"Dev, tell me you're all right one more time."

"I'm OK . . . I just got scared and frustrated."

"Call me back as soon as you get things taken care of. You promise?" Lily insisted.

● ● ●

Develyn wore jeans, boots, and a Purdue sweatshirt by the time the Natrona County deputy phoned her and listened to her account. She waited by the window until a deputy showed up next door. As daylight broke, she sat on the hard wooden chair and sipped hot coffee. When her phone rang, she plucked it up.

"Hi, Lily. Everything's under control. I was just getting ready to phone."

"How did you know it was me?"

"Mother's in Austria. Who else would phone me at daybreak?"

"It's not daybreak here. I've been worried for two hours. Did the sheriff's office contact you?" Lily asked.

"Deputy Wayne Altamont who looks about eighteen just left. He looks like the Simkins boy."

"Harold or Larry?"

"Harold."

"Well . . . I want to know everything," Lily demanded. "I even checked into emergency air flights to see if I could come help you."

"Oh, Lily . . . you are my special angel. It's OK, really."

"Tell me more."

"It's sort of confusing. On the phone, they said that Tallon was a convicted felon and it was illegal for him to possess a firearm, and if I could prove he had one he would be thrown in jail."

"A felon? You are renting a cabin from a felon? Honey, you have to move."

"Move where? I love this place. Anyway, it gets more bizarre. The deputy talked to Cooper Tallon and then came and told me everything was all right. He said he was mistaken about the felon comment, and that the altercation was just a couple of drunks wanting some gas money. Tallon said he refused, and their pickup backfired going out of the driveway."

"That's it?"

Develyn paced the cabin, the phone pressed to her ear. "That's not what they were arguing about, Lily. I heard them."

"What are you going to do?"

"What can I do?"

"You could move, for one thing."

"No . . . I told you, this is my place. I'll just lock the door every night, take two Aleves, and pull the quilt over my head. They didn't threaten me."

"Dev, don't you think it's time to come home?"

"No, I don't. Not until I understand what I'm doing here."

"I pray to God you know what you are doing."

"Thanks for the prayers. Everything looks better in daylight."

"Is your landlord going to be mad at you for calling the sheriff on him?"

"I suppose . . ." Develyn paused by the window and peered across at the other cabin.

"What are you going to tell him?"

"I'm not sure, but I better come up with something quick."

"Why?"

"He's on his way over here. I'll call you back."

"No!" Lily hollered. "Dev, leave the phone on. Clip it to your jeans pocket or something, but leave it on."

Develyn ran her fingers through her blonde bangs. "OK . . . here goes."

She waited for the knock at the door.

She didn't open it.

"Yes?"

"Ms. Worrell?"

"Yes, Mr. Tallon?"

"Aren't you going to open the door?"

"I'd rather not." She double-checked the interior latch on the door. "What can I do for you?"

"Look, Ms. Worrell, I'm sorry about the scare last night."

She folded her arms. "That story you told the deputy was a lie."

"Yes, it was, Ms. Worrell. I trust that one day soon I can tell you the truth."

"Mr. Tallon, I need the truth right now. Am I in danger by staying here?"

"No, ma'am, you aren't. Would you open the door now?"

"Why?"

"Are you decent?"

"Of course I am."

"I like lookin' a lady in the eyes when I apologize."

Develyn ran her tongue over her thin lips.

She slowly opened the door. The stiff warm breeze swirled dust, and she squinted her eyes.

Peering out from under the brim of his black cowboy hat, Tallon's deep-creased gray eyes locked onto hers. "Ma'am, I'd like you to forgive me for scarin' you like that. I understand why you called the sheriff, and you do that anytime you feel you should. I'd rather you'd come talk to me first, but that's OK. I don't expect that scene to ever be repeated."

"Mr. Tallon, I accept your apology, but I am puzzled at your reluctance to tell the whole story. And I await a further explanation."

"That's all I can expect, Ms. Worrell."

How does such a gray-haired man have such young eyes? "Mr. Tallon, as long as we are neighbors for the summer, and you are my landlord, do you suppose you could call me Dev, and I could call you Cooper?"

"Coop would be fine, Miss Dev." He glanced over his shoulder at the other cabin. "Now, I wonder if I could ask you a favor?"

"As long as it doesn't involve me lying."

He stared at her for a minute, then rubbed his clean-shaven chin. "I reckon I deserve that."

"I'm sorry, Coop. That wasn't very Christian of me."

"The Lord has a lot of things to teach me, Dev. I'm just trying to make sure I don't miss a lesson."

"What is the favor?"

"I was hopin' you could keep your burro over here, or in the pasture. He has a habit of leavin' a deposit next to my truck."

"A deposit?"

"He craps in my yard."

Develyn's hand shot to her mouth. "Oh, dear . . ." She glanced off to see the burro reclined against the tailgate of Fallon's black pickup. "Uncle Henry, you come home right now!"

The burro's ears shot straight up, but he didn't move.

"Dev, burros are stubborn cusses and they don't . . ."

"Well, this one does." Develyn cupped her hands around her mouth. "Uncle Henry, you heard me. You get over here, and get over here right this minute!"

Tallon leaned back.

The burro spun around and trotted straight at them.

Cooper Tallon grinned. "I'm impressed."

"After twenty-three years of yard duty with fifth-graders, one burro is a cinch."

When the burro reached the edge of the uncovered porch, Develyn marched straight at him and grabbed his right ear. "Uncle Henry, you listen to me real close. If you go over to Mr. Tallon's yard once more, I'll lock you in the pasture with My Maria. She's a snotty prima donna who will boss you around until you wish you were a worm. Do you hear me? You stay in this yard."

Uncle Henry hung his head.

Develyn wrestled his ears, hugged his nose, then gave him a slap on the rear. "Now, go on and play. Be nice."

Cooper chuckled.

Develyn leaned into the stiff wind. "And what do you find so funny?"

"You really do treat him like a fifth-grader."

"And your point is?"

"He seems to know exactly what you're saying."

"He hates to be fenced in."

"Do you treat your mare the same way?"

"Oh, no, I treat her like a junior high girl who's pouting because her mother won't let her get her belly button pierced and a tattoo on her butt."

"Whoa!" The word filtered up from Develyn's belt.

"Is that from your phone?" Tallon asked.

"Oh . . ." Develyn's fingers covered her mouth. "I forgot, Lily's on the line."

"Hi, Lily," Tallon called out. "I'll take no more of your time. Again, my apologies, Miss Dev."

Develyn plucked up her cell phone and hiked into the wind toward the pasture and the grazing paint horse.

"Sorry, Lily, I forgot you were down there."

"It's a good thing someone was looking out for you," Lily said.

"What do you mean by that?"

"You and Mr. Felon certainly got chummy in a hurry."

"I was just trying to act civil. Besides, I told you, there is some confusion over whether he or someone else is the felon."

"Civil? 'Oh, Coop . . .' giggle giggle."

"I do not giggle."

"Honey, this is Lily . . . you know, the one who goes to the rodeo with you in Indy when we giggle over every cowboy who gets bucked off at the gate."

"Ms. Martin, I simply have no idea what you're talking about."

"You were giggling."

"I was not. I was trying to act cordial, after a very tense night."

"Ms. Worrell talking about tattoos on the you-know-what- . . . is acting cordial? In the twenty-five years we've known each other, I've never heard you say something like that. Especially to a man."

"I can't believe I said that, either. I think Cree-Ryder is wearing off on me."

"Where is the bronze princess of the prairie?" Lily asked.

"In Tensleep, trimming hooves and shoeing her horses."

"Are you OK now, Ms. Worrell? Can I go down to Turkey Run in peace?"

"Why are you going to Turkey Run State Park? You've been there hundreds of times."

"For a picnic."

"You're taking your summer school class for a picnic?"

"It's Saturday, Devy-girl."

"You and the lawyer?"

"It's just a picnic."

"Prove it."

"What do you mean?"

"Are you going to sit on that bench at Sunset Point?"

"Perhaps."

"Take your cell phone. Call me and clip it to your belt while you and Mr. Legal-Eagle sit on that bench."

"Dream on, Devy-girl."

"Ah-hah!"

"I've got to go, honey."

"Is he there?"

"He will be soon."

"Be good."

"Look who's talking. But I will tell you one thing."

"Oh?"

"He has nice lips."

"What?" Develyn gasped. Then she listened to the shrill of the cellular dial tone. *She hung up on me? He has nice lips and she hung up?*

Develyn leaned against the top rail of the corral and stared out at the grazing mare. "We need to pray for Ms. Martin today, girl. She is getting way too serious about this smooth-talking lawyer guy."

The horse glanced at her, then continued to graze.

"Don't you look at me like that. I am not getting serious about any man. Are you ready to go? Well, that's too bad . . . we're going anyway. Casey won't be back until tomorrow. It's time for a solo ride."

* * *

Develyn tucked two string cheese sticks and a bag of peanuts in her pocket, then rolled up a bottle of water in her sweatshirt and tied it to the rear of the saddle. She led the paint mare behind the cabin.

"We're goin' north into those cedar hills, girl. I've been wanting to ride up there for weeks, but Casey always had a different direction she wanted to explore. When I was ten, Dewayne and I rode that direction one day and saw three antelope."

She walked the horse over to a cottonwood stump, stepped up on it, and threw her foot in the stirrup. She yanked on the reins. "Now, don't you start running off on me."

Uncle Henry peeked around the corner of the cabin.

"If you promise to be good and not run off, you can come," Develyn called.

The short burro trotted up beside them.

The moment Develyn touched her heels to the horse's flanks, the paint mare galloped north. She grabbed her hat and shoved it down tight on her head.

Lord, I have to admit I do love riding this horse. Oh, my . . . how I do love riding.

Develyn sang to the wind . . . "My Maria . . ." The tune rhymed with the rhythm of the stride.

I like the slap of leather . . . the breeze in my face . . . the feel of flight. Oh, how I love the freedom.

She licked her lips, then sang, "Don't you know I've come a long, long way . . ." She tugged on the reins and slowed the horse to a fast trot.

Develyn turned in the saddle after they crossed the first rise in the rolling prairie to appraise the southern horizon. The burro waited beside them.

"Uncle Henry, we've been gone about twenty minutes and we can't see Argenta. We can't see the gravel road or a house or a barn or a telephone wire or even a single fence. This has got to be one of the most undeveloped areas of the entire country. I love it." She leaned forward and stroked the mare's neck and sang, "When she's around, she takes my blues away."

She kicked the horse, and they continued at a walk. Develyn glanced down at the burro. "I know what you're thinking: Does she know how to get back home again? Of course I do. Just turn around and follow this trail south. I don't have to go all that far. I just wanted to explore a little on my own."

The narrow, one-horse trail wound down the coulee, then turned west and slalomed through scrubby cedars no more than five feet tall. By the time they came up on a small creek, the sun was straight above, barely visible through thick clouds. Develyn dismounted and tied off the mare to a short piñon pine tree. Uncle Henry parked all four hooves in the slow-moving water of the small creek.

"Cooling your feet, are you? You're probably ready to head back home. In case you two are wondering, I do have a plan. We are going to veer to the northwest . . . Casey said the Quarter-Circle Diamond headquarters was just twenty miles north of Argenta, but the gravel road was about forty winding miles. So . . . that means we could just 'stumble' into the Quarter-Circle Diamond in an hour or two . . . someone might just ask us to stay for supper . . . or . . ."

She glanced down at the cheese stick she held in her hand. *Or what? What is my real motive, Lord? Am I chasing Quint? Of course I am. Ride twenty miles through the wilderness to just "be in the neighborhood" for a visit. I don't know if I'm anxious to be with Quint . . . or just anxious to find out if he is the one I should be anxious about. I will ride another hour or so. If I don't see anything familiar or cross the road, I'll just turn around. The sun goes down in the west, so south will be easy enough. Sooner or later we'll hit Argenta or the railroad tracks.*

The wind stiffened as she continued to ride to the northwest. She pulled on her sweatshirt when the clouds stacked up above her, blocking the sun. Her trail wound down most of the coulees.

She dismounted and walked the sweaty horse to the top of a ridge, then paused on top to appraise the rolling prairie to the north.

"Look at that, Uncle Henry. There is nothing out here. No ranch, no house, not even a road. Where am I?" She glanced up to find the sun. "OK . . . nothing but clouds. That makes it a little tough to see the sun. I think it's about time to head back. I think I ended up too far west. That must be a spring or creek down by that brush. We're going to ride down there, grab a drink for everyone, then head home. Casey will be coming this evening. I'm glad she doesn't care what we eat. It might be Cheerios and Popsicles."

The ribbon of brush she spotted at a distance turned out to be further away than she imagined. Each crest in the prairie presented a deep, sloping coulee. Like being sucked down into the trough on the rolling sea, the red-dirt prairie towered around her, isolating her from the world. She glanced back up the trail, and spied Uncle Henry at the top of the last rise.

"Are you getting tired, honey?" she shouted. "Why don't you wait there. We'll get a drink in the creek and be back for you."

A wild burro can't get lost, can he? A wild schoolteacher from Indiana can get lost, but not a burro. Did I just call him "honey"? Ms. Worrell, are you still in touch with reality? And if not, do you care?

Develyn tugged back on the reins. "Take it easy, Maria-girl. It's a long ride home, and we'll just walk it. It was a crazy idea . . . I don't know what I would have done, had I found the head-quarters. I'm embarrassed to even think about it."

Lord, I'm a good teacher, but I failed at being a wife. And I'm not having much luck at mothering a twenty-year-old. I don't know squat about horses, except that I love the breeze in my face . . . OK, maybe not quite this much breeze. But I do enjoy learning to be myself and not feeling like a failure in everyone's eyes. Especially yours. Now, I need you to lead us home safely. And let me learn all I need to learn on this day.

As they approached some thick brush at the side of the narrow creek, the paint mare stopped and jerked her head up. Her ears pointed forward as she pawed her hooves and snorted.

"That's just some thunder, girl. We'll ride south out of these clouds."

The mare pranced and shook her head back and forth. "What's the matter, girl? Is there something scary up there? It's OK, baby . . . I just prayed and I'm sure . . ."

Develyn's words faded when a buckskin horse broke out of the brush and galloped past them up the draw. Behind him, eight more horses broke out and galloped straight at them.

The paint mare lunged forward, but Develyn yanked the reins hard to the right. My Maria spun in circles.

"No, girl . . . No! Calm down . . . it's OK . . . let them run."

My Maria stopped, then threw her head back and forth until she jerked the reins out of Develyn's hands.

"No you don't!" Develyn screamed and clutched the saddle horn with both hands. "Stop it right this minute!"

The paint mare bolted after the other horses.

Develyn stuffed her boots into the stirrups and locked her knees against the skirts of the saddle. She leaned so far forward that the brim of her straw cowboy hat pressed against the horse's mane.

I'm not going to get bucked off . . . I'm going to ride this out . . . even if it kills me. That's not quite what I meant, Lord . . . save me!

My Maria caught the band of horses at the top of the draw and showed no sign of slowing down.

Develyn tried to distinguish the thunder in the hooves from the thunder in the clouds. She leaned forward, slowly released her grip with her right hand, and retrieved the reins from near My Maria's ears.

If I try to turn her, she'll stumble and go down for sure. If I yank back, she'll buck me off under forty crashing hooves. I have to ride . . . I have to stay on . . . like running downhill, I have to stay upright until she gets tired.

Like a school of frightened fish in a huge aquarium, the band of galloping horses swirled to the top of one ridge and then back to the bottom, a quarter of a mile east, then back to the west.

They circled and slowed near the crest of a draw, then suddenly stopped as they neared an outcrop of granite boulders that stood out like Stonehenge against the prairie. Develyn leaned forward and patted the panting horse.

"Good girl," she whispered.

At the sound of her voice the buckskin reared up on his hind legs and whinnied like a demon condemned to the abyss. He galloped south with the other panicked horses.

Develyn yanked back on the reins. "No! Not this time, girl . . . no more running!"

My Maria raised up and threw her head left and right. Develyn grabbed for the saddle but only clutched the black tail. When the horse bolted after the others, Develyn lost her grip and landed on her backside in the dirt.

"No!" she screamed.

When she staggered to her feet, she noticed her left boot missing.

"Don't you take my boot!" she shouted.

The band of horses circled south, and she noticed a brown object fall out of the flapping stirrups.

"Thank you!" Develyn hollered.

She limped across the prairie toward the boot. Several drops of water sprayed her face as she staggered around trying to tug on her boot. Develyn stomped her foot down until the boot slipped on, then waved her hand at the sky.

"Don't you dare rain on me. Do you hear me, clouds? I've had enough of this. You stop it right now!"

9

Develyn pulled her hat down as she waded straight into the strong east wind.

I don't have a clue what's the smartest thing I ever did in my life, but this ride has to be one of the dumbest.

The band of horses crested the rise to the west, then disappeared out of sight. "All right, Devy-girl, what is the plan now?" She continued to hike to the west. "If you have a field trip, and upon arrival find the museum is unexpectedly closed, what is the alternative? There is always another option."

I didn't ride way up here for the love of horses or freedom or to find myself. I tried to manipulate a scene so I could burst in on Quint unexpected.

Why did I think that was so important?

She tilted her head into the wind. "What would Renny Slater tell me? If you get bucked off . . . get back on. Of course, dimpled-grinnin' cowboy, that only works with a horse at hand." Her boot heels pressed into the dry red dirt as she stomped west.

Why do I have to control every scene and every relationship? Where is my trust in you, Lord? "At least it's not raining . . . yet." She glanced up at the sky. "Thank you, clouds . . . I'll make sure you have extra time at recess tomorrow."

Lord, I don't know if I've trusted you much for everyday leading. For twenty-five years I've been living in a tightly controlled box. Controlled by me.

Not since the time Dewayne and I were lost right in these same hills did I really cry out for your direction. But we made it home that day. You and Brownie led us home. Well, here I am again in the same wilderness and just as lost. And just as needy. Some things never change.

When she got to the top of the rise, Develyn gazed down a long, sage-dotted slope that opened up on a flat prairie of brown grass. She spied a windmill water pump silhouette about a mile away. The horses circled the water trough, then began to graze.

"OK, I'll catch up with them at the windmill. You are in big trouble, My Maria. You are supposed to take care of me while I take care of you."

I'll make it back today. Of course, that other time, I didn't lose my horse. Brownie would never run off on me. But I was scared and soaked to the bone.

"How do I catch a horse that doesn't want to be caught . . . without a fence for a hundred miles?" She glanced to the north.

"Casey Cree-Ryder," Develyn shouted, "why aren't you here when I need you?"

I don't look good wet. My mascara runs, the makeup sags, the creases around my eyes become more prominent. Develyn began to laugh. *Why in the world would I care about what I look like right now? If Ms. Worrell's perfect hair and makeup got messed up in the wilderness of Wyoming and no one saw it . . . would it really be messed up? Why don't they ever discuss that in an Intro to Philosophy class?*

A quarter of a mile from the windmill, Develyn paused and spied out the grazing horses. Thunder rolled like a second-grader trying to learn the bass drum from somewhere behind her to the east.

The buckskin stallion is watching my every move. If I march up to them he'll break out to the open prairie and lead his harem. Is that a cabin near the well? Or just a pumphouse? . . . or an outhouse? Knowing where a roof is might be an advantage, if it has a roof. I don't think it has a front door.

She smelled sulfur in the heavy air. Develyn kept herself a hundred yards from the windmill. *"If you find yourself in a lightning storm, lie flat on the ground with your head tucked into your arms. Stay away from trees and tall structures." Like windmills. I've repeated that every year for the past twenty-three years.* She circled to the north, and as she did the stallion pushed the others to the south, always keeping himself between Develyn and the band of mares and foals.

Vertical lightning speared the earth to the north where the cedar trees thickened, but she heard no corresponding noise.

Develyn shoved her hands in her back pockets. "OK, Studly . . . I understand why you are doing what you are doing. And I understand the others in your harem, but I don't understand My Maria. After all we've been through together . . . for about three weeks . . . hmm . . . maybe that's not all that long."

Develyn ventured a couple of steps toward the shack next to the windmill. She heard its continuous squeak in the strong wind. "Girl, what do you see in that big muscle-bound stallion . . . I mean, besides the obvious?"

Without taking her eyes off the buckskin, she took two more steps toward the little building. He jerked his head up and snorted, but didn't give ground.

Oh good, at this rate I'll be to the windmill by morning.

Her right hand shoved against something hard in her pocket.

My cell phone! But . . . is there any reception out here, and who do I call? "Hello, sheriff's office? I'm the paranoid ditsy blonde school-teacher from Indiana who phoned you last night . . . listen, I got bucked off somewhere north of Argenta and south of, eh, Tensleep . . . could you send someone out to help me catch my horse?"

She crept forward. The buckskin nonchalantly grazed in the distance. *Or, I could try to call Casey. She said her cell phone only worked half the time at home. I wonder why she bothers with it?*

Develyn eased out her cell phone. She stared at the power rating. *One? They told me it had to read two or higher to even send a signal. So, here goes nothing.* The phone rang once, then stopped. "Casey?" There was no response. "Casey, can you hear me?

That's what I figured. That's OK. I need to do this myself. Of course, I wouldn't mind a little advice. You see, I'm lost out in the wilderness about twenty miles north of Argenta and just got bucked off. I'm not really lost; I just don't know where I am. Anyway, I did get bucked off and My Maria has run off with a wild stallion who has a big harem already. He won't give her back. So, what's your advice?"

The phone was dead.

"Let's see, Trigger always came whenever Roy whistled, but I don't know how to whistle."

The phone was still silent.

"Now I wish I had let you bring those John Lyon horse training videos. Of course, I don't have a VCR or electricity. Oh, well . . . don't worry . . . I'll just improvise like a rookie principal when the special assembly speaker doesn't show up. Bye, Casey. Bring some salsa when you come down tonight; the stuff at Mrs. Tagley's tastes like McDonald's fry-sauce."

Develyn stared at the dead phone, then glanced over at My Maria and the other horses. "I believe I did that rather well, don't you think? I didn't sound terrified a bit, did I?"

She took a step toward the shack. The stallion reared, then chased the others further to the south.

Develyn shoved her hands into the tummy pocket of the hooded sweatshirt. "So that's your limit?"

Develyn backed up several steps. The buckskin moved forward toward the water trough. Several drops of rain pelted her face like spit wads on the last day of school. She glowered at the dark clouds. "I said . . . not now."

The rain stopped.

She rubbed the back of her neck.

I suppose I could call Renny . . . but I don't remember his number. It was 644-mustang . . . or 466-mustang . . . or 464-mustang, but he said he was going to Sheridan after he broke the horses at Quint's.

I do have Quint's number on my speed dial. But what do I tell him? Hmmm . . . I got lost and bucked off trying to sneak up on your ranch to surprise you?

She folded the phone and shoved it in her back pocket.

"Ms. Worrell, you are on your own here. This is like a test, isn't it, Lord? Am I cut out for wilderness ranch life or not?"

She studied the spinning windmill, the tiny one-room shack, and the grazing horses. "Studly, I presume you want to wait out the storm right here. I'll tell you what, you let My Maria go home with me, and I'll promise to leave you here undisturbed."

She took a step forward. The stallion backed up several steps and snorted.

"OK, that doesn't work."

Develyn circled west as thunder rolled behind her. The air was heavy. She noticed she was breathing hard when she reached a spot where the shack blocked her view of the buckskin stallion.

OK . . . if I can't see you, you can't see me. Of course My Maria and a couple of others can see me. I wonder if they will squeal?

She took one step toward the shack, paused, then another. The air felt damp on her face. She pulled the hood of the sweat-shirt up around her neck like a scarf.

There wasn't a cloud in the sky when we left Argenta. But I didn't catch Kathy, the bouncy blonde weather girl with perfect hair, on Channel 6. Perhaps because I don't have any electricity. Do they have propane televisions?

At thirty feet from the shack, she noticed the horses mill toward the south. Most were trying to graze the short brown grass while keeping an eye on her.

Develyn flattened the palms of her hands together and held them to her lips. *Now he'll see me and they'll all run off. This is about as fun as playing "Duck-Duck-Goose" for the first time with two-year-olds.*

She couldn't see him, but she heard the snort, then a flash of lightning to the south.

Develyn dove flat on her stomach in the dirt. Sticky reddish-yellow sticky dirt.

Why did I do that? Wet and muddy. Ms. Worrell . . . you've come a long way since Riverbend Elementary School.

The ground was cold, rough. Lying still, she spied the stallion.

He sees me.

Yet . . . he's . . . he's coming this way? What's he going to do? Run over and stomp on me? This is incredible. Everything I do gets worse. I think I'll go to sleep and wake up in a tanning booth at Shyrleen's.

The sky darkened. Drops of water splashed in the dirt around her face. She ground her teeth. Develyn shot a glance at the heavy, dark clouds. *I am not going to say this again. This is not the time to rain.*

The stallion grazed closer to her.

Oh, sure . . . pretend you don't see me. Who are you fooling, Studly? I could jump up and start screaming. You would panic and race all the way to Idaho. I'd lose my horse, but it might be worth it to show you who's boss. Of course, I'm the one in the dirt, so I guess I already know who's boss.

She watched My Maria meander behind the stallion, coming closer.

Now you decide to come over here? When I'm down on my face. Just like a fickle daughter I know. Oh, Dee . . . how I wish we were close . . . close like . . . well, not me and Mother . . . we were never that close, or we were too close, I can never tell which . . . Lord, give my wayward daughter wisdom to do what is right and good wherever she is right now, whatever she is doing.

She laughed aloud and the buckskin jumped back, then he and the others retreated behind the windmill.

At least they didn't run off completely. I couldn't help it. The thought of me being lost, bucked off, lying in the dirt and mud, without a clue of how this day will end . . . and praying for my daughter . . . well, it was incongruous, to say the least. I hope she is praying for her mother right now.

The minute she noticed the stallion had turned away, Develyn pushed herself to her hands and knees and crawled straight for the doorless entry to the tiny shack. She had just reached the opening, when thunder and lightning struck at the same moment, and the clouds opened up like a stuck zipper that had just broken free. She sprawled on the dirty wooden floor and leaned her back against the unfinished two-by-four framing on the inside of the building. The wind whistled through the cracks in the siding and the openings that at one time contained windows and a door. A breeze muted the putrid odor of the room.

At least I'm dry . . . for now.

She peered around the rancid-smelling shack and waited for her eyes to adjust to the shadows. The only object in the room seemed to be a heavy table with four legs made out of tree trunks. Develyn scooted to the center of the room. Outside the horses still grazed near the adjacent windmill.

I don't think they can see me in here. Of course that doesn't help me catch My Maria. What is this place?

A meat cleaver was stuck in the top of the table. A half-circle scraper and a hacksaw decorated the table.

It's a butcher shop. In the old days, they must have had slaughter houses out where the cattle grazed. These might be antiques.

When the lightning flashed, she spotted blood on the meat clever.

I wonder how long this shack has been abandoned? It's like stepping back in time.

At the next flash of lightening, she drew her finger along the side of the blood-stained clever. She left a clean trail on the fat knife and a patch of red on her finger.

"Oh, my . . . oh . . . no . . . it hasn't even dried," she blurted out. "It's fresh blood."

Her chin began to quiver.

There's got to be an explanation for this. Maybe I'm closer to the head-quarters than I thought, and they slaughter out here to keep the stench from the other buildings.

But Quint Burdett would never use a pitiful building like this for a butcher shop. No one would . . . unless . . . they were hiding out.

But no one would drive to the middle of Wyoming to slaughter cows. Would they? What have they been butchering?

I believe it's time to catch my horse and go back to the cabin. I don't want to know about this. There are some things in life I just don't want to know . . . like what happens to a drug addict hooker in a back alley in New York . . . or what it feels like when you get sucked out of a bro-ken airplane window at thirty-five thousand feet . . . or what happened in this shack during the last twenty-four hours.

I don't want to know, Lord.

She spun around and started for the door, to be greeted by two big eyes.

One blue.

The other brown.

"There you are!" she murmured to the paint horse. "So, you decided to check on Mama, or did you just want to get your nose out of the rain?"

Develyn crept closer.

If I grab the headstall, I'll hold on for dear life. She'll panic and drag me back outside and try to run with the others . . . I'll lose my grip and be trampled to death . . . it will take them months to find traces of my body. Thank goodness for DNA.

She glanced back at the bloody meat cleaver.

On the other hand, what are my choices?

"That's a good girl . . . I'll just touch you, honey . . . it's OK . . . we'll just ride home and be out of this storm soon . . . well, not soon, but eventually."

Develyn kept her eyes on My Maria's. She slowly lifted her hand until her fingers surrounded the chinstrap of the headstall.

Now, don't drag me back into that band of . . .

When the paint mare felt the tug on her headstall, she bolted forward into the shack.

"What are you doing?" Develyn blurted out as she staggered back.

The horse kept shoving forward until she was completely in the cabin.

"Well, isn't this cozy? Do you want to be with me? What happened to Romeo?"

Develyn peered out the window. Wind and rain blasted her face.

"Is he just going to hang around until you come out?"

If I lead her out, she'll bolt with him, and at best I'll be stranded all night in a slaughterhouse. If I got in the saddle, I could run with them for a while, maybe turn her . . . of course, that didn't work last time. Maybe if I run straight north . . . I don't have a clue of what direction is north. Perhaps if I run away from the band, she won't want to follow. What would Robert Redford do? What would Renny Slater do? Tighten the cinch and get back on.

Develyn adjusted the saddle and yanked the latigo until she could buckle it one notch tighter.

OK, the cinch. Now, I'll mount . . . but if she rears inside this shack, I'll bust my head on the rafters and get tossed off on the butcher's block. You're not in the arena, Develyn-girl . . . there are no cowboys to rescue you. No one to applaud your triumph and no one to scrape up your busted body.

Develyn shoved one boot in the left stirrup and bounced up and down on her other foot, then, keeping her head against the horse's mane, pulled herself into the cold, wet saddle.

OK, Lord, there was some reason I came out here this summer, and maybe this was it! I'll make a valiant run, race back to the cabin, and prove that I am a cowgirl at heart. I'll marry Quint . . . start a school for rural ranch kids . . . and live happy all the days of my life.

She kicked My Maria's flanks.

The horse didn't move.

She kicked harder. "Giddy-up!"

The paint mare flinched, but refused to move forward.

"OK, perhaps that was not why the Lord brought me here."

Develyn pulled off her soaked straw hat and ran her fingers through her matted short hair.

"You don't like the rain? What kind of wild horse are you? What if it keeps raining all night?"

Develyn sat in the saddle, her head barely above My Maria's neck, and peeked out at the rain.

I'm not one foot closer to the cabin or town, but it feels so good to be in the saddle. I caught her and got back in the saddle. Renny Slater, did you see this hide-in-the-shack ploy? Hah . . . I bet they don't teach you that one in mustang-breaker school.

Within minutes, she felt her eyelids close.

Just for a moment.

Or two . . . or more . . .

It was too high-pitched for thunder.

Even too high-pitched for a pickup truck.

The whine of a distant engine caused Develyn to blink open her eyes. She stared out the doorless opening.

A shack . . . wild horses . . . it's not raining. How long did I sleep? She peered out the window opening. The sun hung low in the west, breaking through the clouds with bright orange and purple hues.

The hum of several small engines caused My Maria to throw back her ears. Develyn spied the buckskin and his crew stomp and mill around the water trough.

"They're going to bolt and run off . . . we are staying in here, girl." Develyn nudged the mare around the big table to the other side of the shack, facing away from the open doorway. *At least I can try to make it tough to race out of here.* She noticed a wadded denim object in the corner. *I think that's someone's jacket, but I'm not getting down to check on it.*

At the top of a rise to the southwest, Develyn saw the silhouettes of two men riding four-wheelers.

Quarter-Circle Diamond cowboys? Cuban said the "Old Man" wouldn't let them use four-wheelers. Maybe they are search-and-rescue guys, but no one knows I'm out here.

She patted the paint horse's neck. "Whoever they are, girl, they can point us toward Argenta. That's all we need. I hope they race in here and chase off the buckskin and his bunch."

The paint horse paced back and forth, but Develyn held the reins tight to keep her from turning toward the door. In the distance, she heard the engines accelerate. Spraying rooster tails of mud, they raced toward the windmill. The buckskin reared up on his back legs and whinnied, then galloped straight east with all the mares and foals following.

My Maria swung a hoof at the open window frame, but Develyn yanked her back. "You can't go through the window honey. You have to let him go. He wasn't right for you. His interests were too divided. Trust me, I know what I'm talking about."

The thunder of hooves diminished as the whine of the four-wheelers increased. With the band of wild horses out of sight, Develyn rode My Maria to the far side of the shack, pointed at the open doorway.

"I'll wait until they kill those engines. I'm not going to ride out of here, to have you start bucking again. I've had my share of wild rides already."

Finally, she heard the motors shut down.

"Porter, did you see those wild horses?"

Develyn froze. *Porter? One of them at Tallon's cabin last night was called Porter! No . . . no . . . no . . . not them again.*

"How many were there?" the deepest voice asked.

"I counted the stallion and nine," the other one called as he swaggered up to the trough at the windmill and splashed water on his muddy face.

Porter followed him. "If we run out of cows we can sell horse meat."

"Who would buy horse meat?"

"There's a cannery in Douglass."

"Dog food?"

"Yep."

"It don't pay like the butcher in Lander. He gave us two thousand cash dollars. And that Mexican paid a hundred dollars a piece for the hides."

"He was Vietnamese, not Mexican. I told you it would pay."

"Not bad for an early mornin's work."

"It would have been better if you hadn't left your jacket and knives in the shack. Get them and let's get out of here. I want to be in Montana before anyone misses those cows."

"Why don't we gather them wild horses and sell them up at Miles City? At five hundred dollars a head, that's five grand."

"Only the stallion is worth five hundred."

Develyn watched them dry their faces on their shirt tails. The one called Porter had a vertical scar from his belly button to his chest. *They are coming over here.*

Develyn locked her knees against the saddle skirt. *Cooper Tallon, you were dealing with rustlers. Did you cover up for them with the sheriff?*

She leaned forward and whispered. "Easy girl . . . wait . . ."

"I say we head to Nevada," the one with the higher voice sneered. "Women are easier there. I need me a woman."

The sounds got closer to the shack.

"You're goin' to have to find you one in Montana, cause I ain't goin' back to Nevada. Gino and that flat-nosed bunch from the Golden Dream Casino will bust every bone in my body, then bury me alive under some sagebrush. Now get in there and get your coat and knives. I want to get back to the road before it rains any more."

As soon as the first man came into view, Develyn slammed her heels into the horse's flanks and shouted, "Giddyup!"

My Maria flew out of the shack. The two men dove into the mud to escape her pounding hooves.

Shouts and curses faded, but soon there was the whine of small engines.

They must have come in from the west. Surely that's the closest road. I'll turn south and try to get into the brush and trees.

The breeze was cold, but the rain had stopped. The mud flying from My Maria's hooves reminded Develyn of the recent downpour.

Now I'm glad Casey and I raced. I couldn't have done this three weeks ago. The leather pounded her backside, and her knees began to burn as she transferred her weight to her boots. The noise from the four-wheelers grew closer.

I'm just an Indiana schoolteacher. I didn't want this much excitement. If I desired to be attacked, I could have gone to Chicago or Gary or Detroit. This has got to be a dream.

You chose to ride out here alone, Devy-girl . . . deal with it.

The four-wheelers roared closer. She glanced back to see one advancing on the right, the other on the left. She prodded My Maria faster.

I can't keep her at this pace. Just a mile or two, then I have to slow down. I need to find some trees . . . or a creek . . . no, they can cross the creek. Baranca! I've got to find a deep, narrow gulch to jump. I don't think they can jump.

If my class could only see me now. They'd say it was a stunt. That's what I need right now, a stuntwoman.

"Cut! Double! Let's do the jump scene."

Develyn stood in the stirrups and leaned her head next to My Maria. Her legs and knees felt numb. In the broken sunlight she spied a dark ribbon cut across the rolling prairie.

"There it is, girl, we'll jump that!"

Mud splattered her sweatshirt and hat as she kicked My Maria faster. "We can do it, sweetie, don't slow down. You're a good jumper. Pretend that stallion is chasing you and . . . no . . . forget that."

As the gulch approached, she spied the four-wheelers pull even on the right and left of her. *We'll race to the edge, then jump and they will plunge to their painful death on jagged rocks fifty feet below.*

Develyn stared at the approaching gulch.

Her chin dropped. Her neck stiffened. He throat swelled.

That isn't a barranca. It's a canyon! Good grief, we can't jump that! Evil Knievel couldn't jump that. This is where I wake up, Lord . . . help me, now.

She tugged back on the reins, and My Maria pulled her back legs under her, and almost sat down as they slid to the edge of the rough canyon. They were close enough to the edge when they stopped sliding that Develyn could stare down in the shadows at lava rock, at least fifty feet below.

I think, dear Lord, I just had a near-death experience. I want to go home right now . . . take a long, hot bath . . . and have a hot cup of tea.

The four-wheelers spun to a mud-slinging stop beside her.

"Did you see her rein that horse, Porter? Can you do that?"

"That's a good horse," Porter mumbled.

"Shoot, I thought she was goin' to ride it right off the cliff like the ol' boy in *Snowy River!*" the other hollered.

"Hendrix, I figured she was goin' over the edge like *Thelma and Louise.*" Porter waved a black semiautomatic pistol at Develyn. "Get down, lady."

Develyn stayed in the saddle but turned around. The one called Porter wore a muddy black knit ski cap pulled down to his ears. Hendrix sported earrings and a baseball cap turned backwards. Porter wore a denim jacket, Hendrix just a sleeveless black T-shirt.

"I said get down, woman!"

"Look, this is about as much of this as I will put up with," Develyn snapped. "Your behavior is intolerable. Either you back off and let me finish my ride in peace, or you leave me no choice but to contact the proper authorities!"

"Who do you think you are?"

"I'm Develyn Worrell from Crawfordsville, Indiana. Now when I phone the county sheriff, what names do I tell them to come arrest?"

"Poncho and Lefty . . ." Porter growled. "Get down, Evelyn."

"It's Develyn—with a D. I warned you I would phone authorities," she insisted.

"You get down, and I'll let you use the pay phone. Shoot, I'll even give you a quarter for the call!" he hooted.

Develyn tugged out her cell phone.

Hendrix attempted to wipe the mud off his face with his T-shirt. "You can't use that out here!" he chided.

"Put the phone down, woman!" Porter insisted.

Develyn punched 9-1-1.

Porter raised the gun higher. "I said put the phone down!"

She held it to her ear. The line was dead.

Where's that Can-You-Hear-Me-Now nerd when I need him?

She sucked up a deep breath . . . "Sheriff's office? Oh, is that you, Jerry? This is Develyn . . . listen, run a triangulation on this cell phone and send your chopper out here. I've got a couple of cattle rustlers cornered and need you to come pick them up."

"I said toss down the phone, Develyn!" the man screamed.

"One's name is Porter, and the other is Hendrix. Are you going to shoot me while I talk to the sheriff?"

"No, but I'll shoot your horse." He aimed the pistol at My Maria's head.

They butcher steers, and were ready to slaughter the wild horses. He will shoot her.

"Porter, maybe we ought to cut out of here . . . if she done got through."

The man with the gun stiffened his arm. "Say good-bye to the paint," he growled.

He's going to do it. No! No!

Develyn turned and threw the cell phone toward the canyon. Like a fifth-grader's Frisbee on a spring afternoon, it sailed over the edge of the cliff before it dropped deep into the rocks below.

Hendrix stared down at the canyon. "Why did you do that?"

"I wasn't about to have you run up my cell phone bill," she said.

"What difference does that make when you are dead?" Porter replied.

"Are we goin' to kill her? She might be fun if we took her to Montana. I told you I need a woman."

"You like 'em young. She ain't young."

"She ain't old, either."

Develyn tensed. *I don't know whether to laugh or cry.*

Porter took another step closer. "Get down now."

"I'll stay up here until the sheriff shows up."

He dug in his jeans pocket and pulled out a black cell phone. He opened it up and punched a button. "There ain't no power reception out here, woman, so don't give us some crap about talking to the sheriff."

"Maybe she had a better cell phone, Porter."

"That's right, you have an analog phone and mine is digital." Develyn locked her knees to the fender of the saddle and clutched the horn with both hands. *I don't have a clue what that means.*

"If there's no reception, there's no reception. It don't matter what kind of phone. Now get down, or I'll yank you off myself."

"I'm warning you two . . . I've got friends looking for me," Develyn insisted. *That's pathetic sounding Ms. Worrell. Of course, I am pathetic.*

"Isn't that nice? You'll have to introduce us. Get down."

"Cooper Tallon is a friend of mine!" she blurted out. "You know Cooper, right?"

Porter swung the gun around to her chest, his teeth clenched.

"Don't shoot her!" Hendrix shouted. "Lady, if he thought it would cause Cooper any grief, Porter would shoot you on the spot."

"I'm not that good of friends . . ." she murmured. "But I know you were at his place last night."

"Porter, this lady knows too much."

"You might be right, Hendrix."

"You goin' to shoot her? I don't want no part of that."

"We might not have to."

"How's that?"

"She almost had a wreck. What if that pony didn't stop. What if she had kept goin'?"

"The two of them would be dead at the bottom of that canyon."

"Just an unfortunate riding accident."

"Yeah, that's too bad, but accidents do happen."

"This is absurd talk," Develyn blurted out. "I don't know who you are, and I don't even know what you have done or haven't done . . . you ride over the hill and disappear, and it doesn't

229

matter who I talk to . . . which will be hours from now on horse-back. You'll be way down the road by then. You might be guilty of lots of things, but that way you won't be guilty of murder."

I can't believe I said that. I can't believe I'm not in absolute tears.

"Makes sense, Porter. And we won't have Cooper Tallon trackin' us down. She and him might be chummier than she lets on. Maybe she *was* at his place. She said she knew we were there last night."

"Cooper hasn't had a woman at his place in fifty-five years. He's not goin' to start now. Go get your jacket. I'll take care of things here."

He hasn't? I assumed he had been married . . . why did I assume . . .

"You're goin' to do it, ain't ya?"

"Go on . . ." Porter shouted.

"Cooper Tallon isn't the only one who will come after you." Develyn's voice quivered.

Porter swung around. "What do you mean by that?"

"You're right . . . Cooper and I are not going together. Actually, I'm going to marry Quint Burdett. This is his place, and he knows I came out here on a ride."

"Old Man Burdett?" Hendrix quizzed.

"He's not that old."

"You and him is engaged?"

"Eh, yes . . . just about."

Hendrix gaped at her hands. "Did he give you a big dia-mond ring? That would be worth our while."

"I never ride with rings on."

"That's too bad. A ten-thousand-dollar diamond might have ransomed your life."

"Hendrix, you're smarter than you look. We can hold her for ransom. Burdett will pay a whole lot more than ten grand," Porter said.

"She's kinda old for that kind of price ain't she?"

Develyn winced.

"I heard the boys at the Quarter-Circle Diamond once brag that ol' Burdett keeps fifty thousand dollars in cash in his safe on the ranch," Porter said. "He could cough that up without goin' to the bank or anything."

Hendrix rubbed his narrow chin. "On TV they always ask for a million."

"Yeah, and on TV they always get caught. We ask for fifty thousand dollars and make a run for the border."

"What border?"

"We aren't goin' to talk about it in front of her."

"What do we do now?"

"Take her to the shack at the windmill and contact Burdett."

"I thought you said your cell phone don't work."

"It don't. You watch her while I ride west to get a signal."

"Why don't I ride, and you watch her?"

"Because it's my cell phone."

This is where I draw the line. Develyn took a deep breath and let it out slow. "I have no intention of going to that shack with either of you."

Porter swaggered up to the horse, grabbed the curb strap, and shoved the pistol barrel into the horse's mouth. "Get down, lady, or you'll have this mare's brains plastered all over your purdy face."

10

N o!" Develyn shouted. "No!"
At the sound of Develyn's scream, My Maria shook her head left and right.

The gun jerked out of Porter's hand. The force of the mare's shake flung the semiautomatic pistol over the edge of the canyon.

Develyn kicked the paint mare's flanks.

Porter cursed.

Hendrix dove for the gun.

And My Maria galloped forward like a barrel racing horse that's just spied the first barrel.

"Go, honey!" Develyn yelled. "Run for your life! Run for our lives!"

The setting sun broke orange and red through the now-scattered clouds. The shadows of sage and boulders stretched east like dark beacons casting a black light.

"Go, baby . . . run . . . run . . . run! I'll promise not to fall off, if you promise not to slow down."

When her hat started to blow off, she didn't bother reaching up and grabbing it. Under the half-wet sweatshirt, Develyn fought to keep from shaking. She ground her teeth to keep them from chattering. Her skin felt raw when her wet and muddy jeans ground into the saddle.

"Run, girl . . . run!" she shouted.

Develyn turned the paint toward the setting sun.

If there's a road to the west . . . I'll find it. There must be other people left on the face of the earth, even in central Wyoming.

Develyn felt her body warm from the heat of the galloping mare. When they hit the flat prairie, she glanced over her shoulder and spotted the four-wheelers a mile behind her.

"Here they come, baby. I don't know if they have a gun this time or not, but let's just keep running until they shoot us or give up the chase." When they reached a dry gully, My Maria plunged down the sandy embankment.

"Oh!" Develyn cried out. She grabbed a handful of dark mane and the saddle horn, but managed to keep her seat. My Maria struggled up the other side, slipping back, finally making it to the top of the embankment.

Develyn patted her neck. "Good girl, Maria . . . good girl." She glanced across to the gully to see the four-wheelers approach. "They'll make it across, but it will take them a lot longer. Come on, girl . . . giddy-up!"

My Maria raced west.

I may never be able to sit down the rest of my life . . . at least the rest of the summer. At what point does the escape kill me?

Develyn sighed and felt the tension in her shoulders and legs relax.

That's the point of my summer, isn't it, Lord? I came out here to escape. Escape school. Escape Spencer's death. Escape Delaney. Escape Mother. Escape my failed life.

But will I survive?

At what point does the escape kill me?

As the prairie sloped, Develyn saw a dirt road in the distance.

I want resolution, Lord, not escape.

I want something to be settled, so I won't keep being chased across the prairies of my mind.

What am I doing out here? It's like all my fears chasing me at once. Is this really why I came? For this ride?

"Let's go north, girl. I think Quint's headquarters is on this road. Unless we've passed it already, in which case we'll race them all the way to Big Horns."

My Maria stumbled on the ruts in the dirt road, and Develyn yanked her off to the prairie and galloped parallel, still slinging mud. She heard the whine of the four-wheelers still in pursuit.

"If we break away from the road, we might lose them. But we didn't before. Sooner or later they will run out of gas, right? If we stay near the road, someone may come along."

Develyn continued to thunder along next to the one-lane dirt road.

"Where are you, Terminator, when I need you?" she shouted. "I'd love to hear that Austrian accent say, 'I'm back!'"

Shadows began to fade into night as they raced north.

"When we get to that rise, maybe we can see the head-quarters . . . or something."

●　●　●

At the top of the low hill, Develyn could see nothing but more shadowy prairie. The road dropped out of sight to the east. She reined up on My Maria and glanced back at the approaching four-wheelers. Both had their headlights turned on.

"I'm tired of running, baby. I know this sounds crazy, but I think I've been running my whole life, and I'm just tired. You're tired. So, let's make a stand right here. Let's do the thing they least expect . . . let's run them down."

She galloped the paint mare back to the south, down the long slope. Giant granite boulders guarded the bottom of the long draw. The road narrowed to one lane. As she drew closer to the four-wheelers, she watched them spin sideways at the narrowest spot in rocks.

"A roadblock, Maria-girl, but we're not stopping. You can jump them, girl!"

I have no idea what I'm doing, Lord, but I know I'm not running.

As My Maria charged the pair, Develyn stood in the stirrups and stretched out over the mare's neck. "OK, baby . . . don't falter . . . don't slow down . . . don't change your mind . . . right over the top."

She was no more than fifty feet away when both four-wheelers spun mud, and bolted south along the road, then swerved to the west back out on to the prairie.

"Yes!" Develyn shouted as she reined up and slowed the mare to a walk. She rubbed the white, foamy sweat from My Maria's neck.

"Yes! Did you see that honey? We did it! We faced our demons and they fled. We didn't even have to jump. I can't believe they ran away. It was divine intervention. The Lord delivered us."

She climbed to the ground, her chest still heaving, when she heard a dull roar to the north and spotted a flash of headlights.

"A truck?" she mumbled. "Someone's coming? Is that why they ran off?"

Develyn led the horse over to the side of the road and waited as two pickups and a horse trailer rumbled her way. The headlights from the rigs kept her from identifying the occupants.

The rigs braked to a halt.

Pickup doors slammed.

Develyn squinted her eyes.

"You are a mess, Devy-girl," a woman shouted. Casey Cree-Ryder sprinted toward her in the headlights. "But you're cute even when you are a mess." She threw her arms around Develyn. The two spun round and round.

"I got bucked off," Develyn admitted.

"Yes, I can see that."

"Dev, are you all right?" The voice was very deep and sincere. She glanced up to see Quint Burdett with Cuban and Tiny.

"Oh, Quint!" Develyn fought back the tears. She threw her arms around his neck. His warm, narrow lips were pressed into hers.

Did I run up and kiss him first thing? Is this why I left home this morning? I think it just might have been worth it.

She released the startled rancher and stepped back.

"Shoot, Tiny," Cuban laughed. "Do you reckon Miss Dev will greet you and me like that?"

"Eh, I'm happy to see you . . . all of you," Develyn stammered.

"I see you caught your horse," Cree-Ryder said.

"How do you know I lost her?"

"You told me."

"I did?"

"On the phone."

"You heard that call? I didn't think I got through."

"Let's see, you said you met up with a band of wild horses and My Maria chased her dream like Julie Andrews on the Austrian Alps, and you couldn't whistle, so you'd improvise like a rookie principal . . . and I should bring some salsa."

Develyn shook her head. "You heard all of that?"

"Yeah, I was on the road, driving south from Tensleep, so I pulled into the Quarter-Circle Diamond to see if they had heard from you."

Burdett slipped his arm in hers.

"I didn't bother calling Quint. I didn't think I had a signal. Besides, I needed to catch my own horse."

"What are you doing this far from Argenta by yourself?" Quint challenged.

"Shoot, Burdett," Casey snorted, "she came to see you!"

"But . . . but . . . that's a twenty-five-mile ride."

"And you gave her a twenty-five-mile kiss," Casey hooted.

"Did you see any cattle rustlers out here, Miss Dev?" Cuban asked.

Quint pushed his hat back and looked her in the eyes. "The Johnson County sheriff called to say someone phoned from around here on a cell phone to report cattle rustlers in the area. We were goin' to wait until daylight, but when Cree-Ryder showed up . . ."

"Didn't you see them?" Develyn asked.

"Who?" Casey asked.

"The rustlers." Develyn waved her hands toward the granite rocks. "They were right here on four-wheelers until you drove up."

"They were?" Tiny said.

Quint scratched the back of his neck. "Where did they head?"

"West . . . no, I mean east. That way," Develyn pointed.

Cuban surveyed the dark prairie. "We won't catch them out there at night."

"Did you talk to them?" Quint asked.

"Oh, yes. I talked to them, ran from them, ran at them . . . it's been quite a day."

"How about we go back to the house?" Quint suggested. "I'll phone the sheriff . . . supper is being fixed . . . you and Casey can bunk at the ranch tonight . . . and you can tell all of us the adventures of Ms. Develyn Worrell."

"You mean, you're just going to let the rustlers go?" Develyn said.

"That prairie plays tricks on you after dark, Miss Dev," Cuban replied.

"But they threatened to kill me," she added.

"That's why we need to get back and get a hold of the sheriff," Quint explained.

Develyn looked at her sweating horse. "What about My Maria?"

"Me, Cuban, and Tiny will rub her down, then load her in my trailer," Cree-Ryder said. "The boys can ride with me."

"We was ridin' with Mr. Burdett," Cuban insisted.

Cree-Ryder waved her long black braid like a lecture stick. "Well, you aren't now. Miss Dev is ridin' with the Old Man."

"I'm ridin' shotgun," Tiny called out.

"Casey, you ain't got no guns or knives, do you?" Cuban asked.

• • •

Wrapped in a terry-cloth bathrobe, Develyn strolled out of the white-tiled bathroom. She tugged a big purple comb through her wet, tangled, frosted blonde hair.

Casey shoved a steaming mug at her. "Latte breve, decaffeinated."

"Where did you get that?" Develyn smelled the milky-coffee aroma before taking a sip.

"Lindsay has her own espresso machine in the kitchen. This is a fully equipped house."

"This is a fully equipped bedroom." Develyn surveyed the four-poster bed, white leather couch, and huge oak desk.

"Devy-girl," Casey said as she took a swig of Pepsi, "this is the honest truth. I have never in my life lived in a house as big as this one room. She lives like royalty."

"Quint apologized for the size of the room. He said when their son, Ted, died, the sight of his room drove them all to tears, so they took out the wall and made one big room for Lindsay. She bought all of these things with money she won from barrel racing and rodeo queen prizes and all of that. He said she gets room and board and gasoline for her truck, but everything else she has to earn."

"No wonder she doesn't want to leave home." Casey strolled around the room. "Dev, when did you go out on your own?"

"Totally on my own? About a month ago."

"No, I mean . . ."

"Casey, I lived at home on weekends during college days so I could work in Mother's dress shop. Then I got married a few days after graduation. When I left my husband, it was me and a sixteen-year-old daughter trying to survive. So, in a lot of ways, these last few weeks have been the first time I've been 'on my own.'"

Cree-Ryder laughed. "You are doin' quite good, sweetie. Look at this blouse."

"Whoa . . . red and blue sequins . . ."

Casey turned it over. "And a white-sequin star on the back."

"Is that yours?"

"Are you kidding?" Cree-Ryder examined the tag inside the blouse. "This store is one of those in Dallas where you have to buzz them at the door and show them your credit rating before they let you in."

Develyn plucked up the blouse, then paused in front of the mirror, holding it in front of her. "Lindsay wants me to wear it? I can't wear something like . . ."

"Quint picked it out. He wants you to wear it."

"Quint?"

"He came to the door when you were in the shower, shoved these things in my hand, and said, 'I reckon Miss Dev will need a change of clothes.'"

Develyn stared at the blouse. "I've never worn anything like this. It's way too . . . I mean . . . eh . . ."

"Dramatic?"

"Yes, that's a good word. Way too dramatic for a central Indiana schoolteacher."

"I reckon good ol' Burdett doesn't see it that way. He picked out the whole outfit."

Develyn surveyed the clothes on top of the blue-and-white quilted bedspread. "White jeans, white boots, sequined blouse . . . and jewelry." Develyn held the jewelry up to her ears. "Heart-shaped stars and stripes?"

Cree-Ryder stood behind her. "I think he likes dressing you up, Dev. Kinda makes you feel like a full-sized Barbie doll, doesn't it?"

"Well, I certainly couldn't wear that muddy sweatshirt to supper."

"Nope. Did you two have a nice ride back to the ranch? You looked real chummy when you got out of the truck."

"Yes, it was nice and warm."

"The conversation or the truck?"

"The truck," Develyn scowled. "In all the excitement, I didn't realize how cold I had become."

"You are not cold, Miss Dev. The boys think you are hot."

"Casey!"

"It's true. Do you need any help? If not, I'll just mosey on down to the billiard room and shoot some pool. I've never been in a house with a separate room for a pool table."

Develyn stared at the clothes on the bed.

Lord, I think I'm getting over my head in a hurry. These aren't my kind of clothes. I'm conservative. I never like to stand out in a crowd.

If I dressed like this, I'd stand out at the Superbowl. What I'd really like is my old shorts and a T-shirt and to be back at my cabin with a bowl of Cheerios and twenty-year-old copies of Western Horseman.

The blouse and boots fit fine, but the white jeans were tight in the back. She fussed with the zipper, then laced the blue and black horsehair belt through the loops. She glanced at the big silver buckle.

This must be one of Lindsay's rodeo buckles. "QUEEN—Houston Livestock Show & Rodeo . . . 1974." '74? I was only fourteen. Lindsay wasn't born until . . . Miss Emily? This was Emily's.

Develyn opened a polished wooden case on Lindsay's dresser that cascaded open like a tackle box. The entire contents were color-coded tubes of lipstick.

Oh my, when Lindsay said she had some lipstick I would like, she wasn't kidding. Must be one of every shade and hue ever made.

She strolled by the floor-to-ceiling mirror.

I can't believe I'm wearing this . . . I haven't drawn this much attention to myself since I wore the gorilla costume five years ago during dress-up day.

There was a light knock on the bedroom door.

"Can I peek?"

"Come in, Linds . . . this is your room."

Lindsay Burdett bounced into the room. "Supper's ready and everyone's waiting for Miss Dev, the . . ." She stopped. "Where did you get that blouse?"

"Your father picked it out for me . . . is it OK?"

"Well, I'll be, you are amazing, Ms. Develyn Worrell."

"What do you mean?"

"Those belonged to my mother."

"I was guessing that. If you'd rather me not wear them, I'd . . ."

"Oh no, he picked them out for you. You need to wear them. Daddy doesn't do well when people don't mind him."

"Are you sure it's OK with you?" Develyn pressed.

Lindsay's shoulders sagged. "Oh . . . yes. I just . . . it takes some getting used to."

"Seeing someone else in your mother's clothes?"

"Especially those clothes."

Develyn put her hand on top of Lindsay's. "Honey, if I'm doing something wrong, please tell me."

"The Christmas before Mama died, she knew she only had a couple of months left. She battled cancer for ten years, and she knew she wasn't going to whip it. Daddy believed she would get well. Right up to the day she died in his arms, he just knew the Lord would heal her. Anyway, that Christmas Mama wanted to have a picture taken with me and Daddy. She made us promise that we would not allow another picture to be taken after that. She didn't want us to have any photos of her with a weak, emaciated body and no hair."

"I can understand the feeling. Is this the outfit she wore?"

"Yes, she knew it was Daddy's favorite. About six months after Mama died, I asked him about her clothing. He said to go through it and take anything I wanted, except that outfit.

He said some day he would be able to release it. I never brought up the subject again. I suppose today is the day he released it."

Develyn stared at herself in the mirror. "Now, I do feel awkward."

Lindsay sashshayed over and hugged Develyn's shoulders. "Oh no, I didn't mean it that way. Actually, I'm happy for you. If you help Daddy get over his grief, that is good. He has been suffering for a long time."

"I must admit, I've never worn anything this . . . eh, . . ."

"Ostentatious?"

Develyn nodded.

"Then come on, Miss Dev, there are a bunch of men waiting for your entrance."

"I doubt that. You are the beautiful one, Linds. I was never as pretty as you, even in my wildest dreams."

"I'm afraid I'm still a little girl to most . . . and a snotty college girl to the rest. But you, Miss Dev, you're fresh, different, and have those big wide eyes of wonder."

"I never heard them called that before."

"That's what Mama used to say about her eyes. She said she had horse eyes . . . eyes of wonder."

● ● ●

The long, rectangular table could seat sixteen. Develyn counted only ten, but seldom were they all seated at once. Mom and Pop Gleason served the ranch as housekeepers, groundskeepers, cooks, and caretakers. Most of the evening they scurried between the kitchen and the dining room. Cuban, Tiny, Juan, and Kidd seldom ate in the big house. They spent most of the evening watching Quint Burdett to make sure they didn't do anything ill-mannered.

Develyn sat between Quint and Casey Cree-Ryder. Lindsay Burdett parked for the evening on the other side of her father.

Develyn spent most the meal time retelling the story of stalking My Maria . . . and escaping the clutches of Porter and Hendrix. Mrs. Gleason had just brought out the peach cobbler when Mr. Gleason answered a knock at the back door.

Renny Slater, hat in hand, swaggered in. He plopped down in a chair next to Cree-Ryder. "I'm happy to see the Indiana schoolteacher ain't still wanderin' around out on the prairie trying to find her horse."

"How did you know about that?"

"I called Renny and told him to come down and help us find you," Cree-Ryder admitted.

"I see your pony's out in the corral, so I reckon you caught her all right," Renny said.

"You won't believe what Miss Dev went through today," Cuban blustered.

"I believe it," Renny winked at her. "From the first moment I saw her on Mrs. Tagley's porch with that orange Popsicle,

I said, 'Cowboy, there's a young lady who plans on living life to the fullest.'"

"Young lady?" Cree-Ryder hooted.

"Well," he grinned, "the sun was in my eyes, come to think of it."

"I know what you mean," Cuban said. "Cree-Ryder looks good at a distance too."

"Yeah," Tiny blustered. "Twenty miles or more."

• • •

The boys meandered back to the bunkhouse after supper, and the Gleasons whizzed around the kitchen cleaning dishes. Casey, Lindsay, and Renny Slater joined Develyn and Quint in the den, which served as the ranch office. Huge, overstuffed brown leather chairs were scattered in front of a floor-to-ceiling river-rock fireplace.

Lindsay and Casey studied a glass case of horse show trophies. Quint had begun an explanation of a portrait of a black stallion on the south wall when the ringing phone tugged him to the massive oak desk.

Renny and Develyn stayed close to the fireplace.

"I almost wish it was cold enough for a fire," she mused. "This is a beautiful hearth."

"Yep, I heard they hauled these rocks all the way up here from west Texas."

"Really? Aren't there enough rocks in Wyoming?"

"Quint's wife insisted on Texas rock. What Miss Emily wanted, Miss Emily got."

"Did you know her, Renny?" Develyn asked.

"Miss Emily? Everyone in Wyomin' knew Miss Emily."

"What was she like?"

"A saint."

"That's the impression I get."

"A rich saint," Renny added.

"Did she come from a wealthy family?"

"You might say that. Rumor has it that her family owned most ever' oil well in the Texas panhandle. That's exaggerated a tad, no doubt. But that Texas money made the Quarter-Circle Diamond what it is. Cattle business is a good deal, if you have a steady income from some other source."

"So, Quint has some Texas oil money?"

"Miss Dev . . . that's what I hear. But I don't push. I can't believe I'm standing here next to a purdy lady and talkin' about some other man."

Develyn grinned and laid her hand on Renny's arm. "Now, Mr. Slater, don't tell me you're jealous."

Twin dimples blossomed from his suntanned cheeks. "Yes, ma'am, I do believe I am."

"I'm flattered."

"You are?"

"Yes, I was married for twenty-two years, most of which were miserable. I've been divorced for over three years. During that time I have not gone out on a single date. So, I would guess it's been twenty-six years since anyone's been jealous over me. And even though you are joshing, it feels nice and I thank you for it."

Renny's voice lowered. "Would you thank me, even if I said I wasn't teasin'?"

Her hand dropped from his arm. "Yes, I would."

His voice was barely above a whisper. "I was just south of Buffalo when Cree-Ryder phoned me. That's about 150 miles from here . . . half of it a dirt road. I made it in a little over two hours. Some of that time I figure all four tires were off the ground."

"Oh dear, that doesn't sound very safe."

"I was worried about you."

"I need to learn to chase down my own horse."

"Yes, but my mind got to playin' tricks on me."

"Oh?"

"I said to myself . . . what if Devy really was in trouble? I've got a lot of regrets in my life already. I've been foolish, stubborn, and proud to the extent that it ruined my life and others. But, since I gave my heart to Jesus I've tried to overcome all of that. Somethin' keeps pushin' at me that I need to get to know you better. I know, I know . . . this is the wrong time and the wrong place to sound serious. I truly apologize for that. But when I'm with you, I like myself. And I don't feel like such a failure."

"Oh, my . . ." she murmured. "Renny, I'm a bit taken back by . . ."

"I know, I'm out of line. It's just that . . ."

"No, no . . . it's all right. I'm glad you can talk to me. But everything's accelerated in my mind lately. I need to figure out where the Lord is leading me."

"I believe he led you to Wyomin'."

"I agree with that."

"Did the Lord lead you to wear that sequined blouse?"

"I wondered when you'd mention it. It's a little . . ."

"Texas proud," Renny declared.

"I was going to say dramatic or ostentatious."

"Nope. It's pure ol' Texas pride. They do like showin' off that lone star."

"You've seen blouses like this one before?"

"Not like this. But Texas pride is an amazin' thing to watch. I reckon that was Miss Emily's."

"Yes, that's what Lindsay told me. My sweatshirt got muddy, with all of today's activity. So they loaned me an outfit."

"Miss Emily was the embodiment of Texas pride. Every time she used that soft west-Texas drawl to say 'Renny, darlin' . . .' you could hear that panhandle pride."

"She called you darling?"

"No, she called me darlin' . . . she called ever'one, includin' the dog, darlin'. I reckon she had fancier shirts than that one."

"Do you think it's too loud for me?"

"Maybe a little loud in a small room, but in an arena, I'd vote for you to be roundup queen any day."

"Renny Slater, you keep telling me I'm better to look at from a distance. I suppose close up I tend to look like a middle-aged Indiana schoolteacher."

He shoved his hand in his back pockets. "Dadgum it, Dev, what I'd like to say is you look good close up. Real good."

Develyn felt relief when Casey and Linds strolled over to them.

"Wow, you ought to see the trophies Lindsay's mom won! She won grand champion at Houston four years in a row showing four different horses. Is that awesome, or what?"

Develyn glanced at Renny.

He shook his head. "That's awesome, all right."

"That's before she married Daddy," Linds added. "She didn't show much after she moved up here. I think that disappointed Grandma and Grandpa. Grandma was forever pulling me aside and saying, 'Child, I will never understand why your mama wanted to move to the end of the earth.'"

"Oh, dear," Develyn murmured. "Are your grandparents still alive?"

"Grandfather passed away in '99, but Grandmother still lives on the home place."

"I thought this was the home place," Cree-Ryder said.

"Not to Mama. Anyway, Grandma is eighty-three and still rides every day. She says the ranch would fall apart if she didn't look over it. I tell her those oil wells keep pumping whether she watches them or not."

Quint finished the phone conversation and strolled up behind Develyn.

"Are you talking about Grandma?" he said. "Now, there is a real horse woman," Quint added. "But, listen . . . that was Bufe Telford . . . the sheriff of Johnson County. Quite a saga going on here."

"Is it about the men who were chasing Dev?" Lindsay asked.

"That's what the sheriff thinks. There's been some sign of rustling down near Lander for a few months. Then last week a couple of tough-looking guys from Reno showed up looking for two cowboys who stole some money from a casino. They stayed in town a week, then went home, but the rustling stopped."

"You think they settled up with the cowboys?" Renny asked.

"Sheriff thinks the cowboys just took off. The big boys from Reno didn't go home happy."

"Are you talking, like, mafia?" Cree-Ryder asked.

"Sheriff just said he was glad when they left town. Anyway . . . the sheriff over in Converse County was tracking down some illegal beef, and found some Circle-Diamond branded partial hides in a dumpster. So he was putting it all together, and thinks maybe that the Lander duo moved over here. Their method seems to be to slaughter and quarter the animals and find a butcher who's not particular what he sells."

"You told him they called themselves Porter and Hendrix?" Develyn said.

"Oh, yeah, I told him," Quint said. "They got the report back from Nevada. Seems both of them are convicted felons. They were in the Nevada State Prison until last December."

Develyn started to quiver. "Now I'm really getting scared."

Quint slipped his arm around her shoulder. "It's all right Miss Dev. You proved that you can handle the situation. You passed the test."

253

"The Lord takes care of the foolish . . ." she muttered. *Exactly what was the test a qualification for?*

"And the righteous," Quint added as he released her. "Anyway, they found the truck and trailer and are going to wait and see if those two show up. If they don't, he's going to mount a posse and look for them at daybreak. They are watching the highway between Casper and Thermopolis."

"Mount a posse? Do they still do that?" Develyn said.

"Figure of speech, Miss Dev. They'll use four-wheel-drive vehicles, four-wheelers and helicopters."

"Hey, Harrison Ford can help," Cree-Ryder remarked.

"Harry's in London doing some studio work," Quint replied.

Develyn stared at Quint Burdett. *He actually knows Harrison Ford?*

"Anyway, the sheriff says we should keep an eye out. Could be they'll come north to look for gas, or even try to steal a rig. I'm going to go out and warn the boys. Would you like to go for a walk under the Wyoming moonlight, Miss Dev?"

She glanced at Casey Cree-Ryder, who grabbed onto Renny Slater's arm and tugged him across the room. "Come on, mustang breaker, let me show you somethin' you've never seen before."

"That's a scary thought," Renny mumbled.

* * *

Though it was dark, some clouds hung in the sky, and the millions of stars that swarmed behind them seemed like Indiana fireflies. Quint Burdett took long strides, and Develyn scurried to keep up. He reached down toward her hand, and she was surprised how quickly her fingers laced into his calloused ones.

It feels like we've held hands for years. I haven't held hands with anyone since . . .

With her free hand she brushed back a tear.

Lord, this is part of what I've been missing. Not just hand holding, but feeling like a woman. I've felt like a teacher . . . and a mother . . . and a friend . . . but it has been so long since I felt like a woman. I'm truly glad I'm a woman tonight, and he's a man . . . and I'm strolling under a Wyoming night sky.

Develyn and Quint strolled to the bunkhouse.

Visited with the hired hands.

And strolled some more.

They paused in the shadows of the screened porch. He tugged her close. Develyn felt his hand slip to the back of her neck and tug her forward. She felt her thin chapped lips melt with the warmth of his when he pressed them tight. His other hand slipped to the small of her back as he pressed the Lone Star sequins against her.

Later, in the bright light of the study, among company, Develyn decided it had been a dozen kisses, but at the time she thought of it as one long, heart-stopping kiss.

• • •

Lindsay played the piano while Renny Slater accompanied with a guitar. Casey Cree-Ryder held an unlit, skinny candle like a microphone while she sang everything from Faith Hill to the Dixie Chicks to Patsy Cline.

Develyn and Quint sat in side-by-side brown leather chairs and held hands while serving as the audience.

"Casey, you sing really well," Develyn said.

"I've had years of karaoke experience. Why, I'm the 'Queen of the Silver Dollar.'"

"Are you going to sing Emmylou Harris songs now?" Quint chided.

"Take no offense," Renny said as he put the guitar down. "But I'm bushed, and I still need to ride a couple of snuffy broncs before breakfast. Think I'll head to the bunkhouse before Cuban locks the door."

A heavy knock on the front door brought them all to their feet.

Then a shout. "Mr. Burdett? You'd better come out here and see this!"

Quint led the procession. "I'm guessin' the boys must have caught your rustlers."

Wide-eyed and biting her lip, Develyn refused to follow.

Renny sided up to her. "It's OK, Devy-girl . . . me and Cree-Ryder have your flank protected."

Develyn spoke between clenched teeth. "I just don't know if I want to see them again."

Quint reached back and grabbed her arm. "Come on, Miss Dev . . . this might be fun."

She jogged to keep up. *How can cattle rustlers be "fun"?*

When they rounded the bunkhouse, she spotted Tiny, Cuban, and the other Quarter-Circle Diamond cowboys crowded around a man on a horse.

Cooper Tallon? This is like a scene from an old western movie. Is this real? Cowboy hat . . . chaps . . . canvas coat buttoned only at the neck. A gun across his lap.

"Look!" Cree-Ryder shouted. "Cooper's brought them in."

Develyn glanced behind Cooper to see a burro loaded down with two roped and tied bodies. "Uncle Henry, you've been a busy boy!"

"You ought to hear Cooper's story, Mr. Burdett," Tiny said.

"Cooper looks sort of like a mature Clint Eastwood in *Fistful of Dollars*, doesn't he?" Cree-Ryder whispered to Develyn.

"What's the story, Coop?" Burdett asked.

Tallon shoved his battered felt hat back and leaned on his horse's rump. "Uncle Henry came across the prairie toward the cabins by himself. He never wants to be out of sight of Ms. Worrell, so I waited for her to follow. I had seen them pull out for the north earlier in the day."

Develyn studied the leathery lines around Tallon's gray-green eyes. *He was watching me? Of course, the cabins are only a hundred yards apart. I certainly could watch him.*

"So I saddled up and headed north just in case she had trouble."

"Uncle Henry led you to where she was?" Casey pressed.

"The burro doesn't lead . . . but he tagged along. Her tracks were easy enough to read until the rain hit. Most had washed away by the time I got to the windmill. I did see where she got bucked off."

258

"How could you tell that?" Develyn asked.

"Your tracks. You made a heavy imprint like someone thrown from a horse. Anyway, I saw signs of a band of wild horses, so I figured the mare got excited and ran. I surmised you might be sittin' it out in the well house."

"I was there for a while," she admitted.

"Yeah, I know. I could smell your perfume."

She tried to study his eyes but they remained in the shadow. *My perfume? He knows the smell of my perfume? How could he smell that? I trust he doesn't know the name of the perfume.*

"I circled the place and found four-wheeler tracks in the mud after the rain, and signs of a running horse that led over to Little Dead Horse Canyon."

"That's what it's called?" Develyn gasped.

"That's where I found this." Cooper reached behind the saddle and tugged loose a straw cowboy hat.

"My hat . . ."

He handed it to her.

"Thank you, Mr. Tallon."

He tipped his cowboy hat. "You're welcome, ma'am. Anyway, you can imagine how worried I was. There were tracks of the horse running away, but the four-wheelers could have been chasing a loose horse while a worse fate happened to Ms. Worrell. So I climbed down into the canyon to look around."

Develyn felt her chin drop. "You went down in there?"

"Yep, and I tell you I just about panicked when I found this . . ." He pulled a cell phone out of his shirt pocket and handed it to her. "That's when I got really worried. I couldn't imagine any simple way of losin' your cell phone half-way down that canyon."

"I'm amazed you found it."

"It was still on and beeping when I found it. I turned it off, but I reckon the battery was nearly played out. I knew you'd been there fairly recent. To tell you the truth, I was expectin' to find . . ." Tallon paused and glanced out across the dark Wyoming prairie. Then he took a deep breath. "When I didn't find you in the canyon, I started to follow the tracks north, but it was getting too dark. I was about ready to head out to the road, when I heard the cussing."

"By these two?" Develyn asked.

Tallon nodded. "Both of their four-wheelers ran out of gas. They were hiking to the road."

"Did you kill them?" Cree-Ryder asked.

"No, just had to lay them out with the barrel of my carbine. I didn't want a hassle out of them."

Cuban lifted up the head of one of the unconscious men. "We heard they were wanted for rustling and selling stolen property."

"And harassing me," Develyn murmured.

Cooper's tone changed. "Did they hurt you?"

Even in the shadows, Develyn spotted the apprehension in his eyes. "I was scared, but they didn't touch me. They talked about holding me for ransom."

Cree-Ryder raised her dark eyebrows. "A schoolteacher?"

"I figured the Quarter-Circle Diamond was the closest ranch. Uncle Henry's a tough little guy, but I reckon he's plum worn out."

"Boys, pull those two down," Quint ordered. "Stick them in the pumphouse and leave them tied. Take turns standin' guard."

"I'll put up the horse and burro," Renny suggested. "You goin' to turn Uncle Henry in with the horses?"

"Yep, I'm sure not goin' to let him run around the yard like a dog," Quint replied. "Linds, go warm up some supper for Mr. Tallon."

Tallon climbed down, then slipped his Winchester 1894 half-mag carbine into the leather scabbard. "I'd appreciate it. Is there a place I can wash up? The two of them put up a little scuffle." He rubbed his jaw.

"Did you get hurt?" Develyn asked.

"Nothin' that won't heal."

"I'll go phone the sheriff," Quint announced. "I reckon he'll be happy to hear we caught these two."

Develyn glanced at Cree-Ryder, who mouthed the word: *We?*

"I'll take care of Uncle Henry," Cree-Ryder offered. "He will need some talkin' to if he is to stay with the horses. He hates corrals."

"Miss Dev, show Tallon where to wash up," Quint ordered.

Develyn strolled with Cooper toward the back porch of the big house. "I didn't want to say anything in front of the others, but . . ." she began.

"You're wonderin' if these are the same two men who were yellin' and screamin' at me last night?"

"Yes. Who are they?" she asked.

"A couple of no accounts from Nevada, Servan Hendrix and Porter Tallon."

"Tallon?"

"He's my brother, Dev."

"Oh, no, I didn't know that."

"When Mama and Daddy died, Porter started making some bad choices. It just got worse and worse. I hadn't seen him in almost ten years when he showed up on my doorstep, demanding his share of the inheritance."

She caught herself licking her chapped lips and stopped. "You wouldn't give it to him?"

"He got his share years ago. Most of it went to lawyers tryin' to keep him out of prison. To give him more money wouldn't help him at all."

"But how could you . . ."

"Cold-cock him and turn him over to the sheriff?"

"Yes, that must have been difficult."

"It was fairly easy. I told him last night I'd turn him in if he didn't leave the state. Besides, at the time I whipped the barrel down on their heads, I wasn't sure about your safety."

"I appreciate your concern, but I'm amazed you'd head out on a hunch looking for me."

"I reckon I have to do the things I'd regret not doin'. It wasn't much of a hunch. Uncle Henry was missin' his mama."

She leaned against the cold pipe railing that framed the

steps to the porch. "Now I'm even more sorry I called the sheriff last night."

"It's OK, Dev. I just didn't want to be the one to turn him in. But it's obvious that the Lord had something else in mind."

She stared into his eyes.

"We don't know each other very well," he remarked.

"No, we don't."

"Maybe some evenin' we can sit out on the porch of the cabins, just you and me and Uncle Henry, and visit. We could start all over again . . . and lick on orange Popsicles, of course."

A smile broke across Develyn's face. "That sounds nice."

"Just promise me one thing." His voice sounded soft.

Oh, dear . . . "What?"

"Don't wear that blouse."

"You don't like this?"

"It looks as out-of-place on you as an alligator in Alaska. It's horrible," Tallon blurted out. "It's not your style."

She felt herself stiffen. "That's being blunt."

"Here's my Wyomin' advice for you, Ms. Worrell. It is all right for you to look like an Indiana schoolteacher. I don't mean any disrespect."

Develyn tried not to laugh. "That's all right, Coop. I do enjoy someone telling me the truth. It is certainly not a blouse I'd pick for myself."

"That's just what I figured. You're just tryin' to please someone else."

"What did you mean by that?"

"Dev, just point me toward the washroom before my simple brain gets me into worse trouble."

"First door on the left."

"I'm lookin' forward to our visit."

"Me too, Cooper, and I'm buyin' the popsicles to thank you for coming after me."

For the first time since she met him, there was a shy grin. He tipped his hat. "Thank you, ma'am."

● ● ●

Alone on the screen porch, Develyn plopped down in an oversized swing built for two.

Lord, I don't know all you are telling me. I think it will take me days, or weeks, to sort out all I've gone through in the past few hours. I was so tired of the simple, boring routine in Indiana. Now it's beginning to sound peaceful. For a few minutes today, I think I missed home . . . I missed teaching . . . I missed my naughty cats. I don't think I'm any closer to understanding this summer.

Quint Burdett strolled out the front door.

Well, perhaps a little closer. He turns my head every time I see him.

"You look beautiful out here, Dev. You look right at home. It's a perfect fit." Quint slid in next to her.

"The swing?"

"No, the blouse. From the first day I saw you at the auction, I knew you and Miss Emily were the same size." His arm slid around her shoulders. "Sheriff's on the way. He said Porter and Hendrix were wanted in Nevada, Idaho, and Wyoming. They are bad hombres."

She bit her lip when she considered telling Quint that one of them was Cooper's brother.

For several moments they listened to the squeak of the swing.

"You look relaxed. You must be tired after such a day," he said.

"I'm raw from way too much riding . . . my elbow hurts from being bucked off . . . my lips are almost chapped raw . . . but just trying to remember all that's happened in the past few hours is tiring enough. I feel like a kindergartener on the first day of class. There's so much I want to remember."

"I reckon I can't solve every problem, but we can work on them one at a time." She could see his wink even in the porch shadows.

"Oh?"

"Let's see what we can do about those sore lips."

The first kiss was tentative, but warm.

The second was soft, yet enthusiastic. His right arm held her shoulders tight. His left hand rested on her knee.

When he pulled his lips back, she sighed.

"Are you all right?" he asked.

"Oh yes, it's been so long since I was treated this tenderly."

He leaned over, kissed her ear, and whispered, "From now on, Miss Dev, I'll take tender care of you."

At the sound of a buzzer, they both sat straight up.

"Is that your cell phone?" he mumbled.

Develyn fumbled for her jeans pocket. "I'm sorry, Quint. I thought Cooper said the battery was dead."

"I put a relay station in for Miss Emily," he replied. "It doesn't take much power to receive it here at the ranch."

Develyn walked across the porch as she opened her phone. She gazed across a shadowy prairie covered by a star-filled sky.

"Hello?"

"Mom?"

"Dee? Hi, honey, it's good to hear your voice. Where are you? What time is it?"

"It's 3:00 a.m. here. I'm at the airport in Atlanta. I'm catching a red-eye to Indiana. Can I come home?"

"Of course, baby. Do you need some money?"

"I borrowed some from Lisa D."

"You did get my message about me being in Wyoming? I called the Crab House several times. I thought maybe you'd call me sooner."

"I had to think some things through, Mom. Sometimes a person needs to run away in order to find out what they are running from. You are coming home sometime, aren't you?"

"Yes, but I'll have to figure the timing. I was going to stay all summer. I thought you would be in South Carolina until August."

"Oh, I know, Mom. You don't have to come home now. Lily said you were busy chasing cowboys."

Develyn lowered her voice and glanced over her shoulder at the square-jawed man in the porch swing. "Dee, I am not chasing cowboys. When are you due into Crawfordsville?"

"Lisa D. is going to meet me at the Indy airport, and we'll have some breakfast. I'll be home by 10:00 a.m. or so."

"I should be back to my place by then, too. I'll phone you tomorrow, and we'll figure it out."

"Where are you now, Mom?"

"At the headquarters of the Quarter-Circle Diamond ranch."

"Where's that?"

"In central Wyoming, eh . . . Natrona and Johnson counties."

"Like the Johnson County War?"

"Well, there's no war here now." *Only in my heart and mind.*

"Are you with a cowboy?"

"Delaney, I'll talk to you tomorrow."

"He's right there, isn't he? That's so cool. Have fun, Mom. Did Lisa D. tell you about my tattoo?"

"What tattoo?"

"Mom, I'm sorry I have been so snotty. I have a lot I need to talk to you about."

Develyn tried to press the tension out of her temples with her fingertips. "I know, Dee. Listen, call Lily and tell her what you are doing. She's been coming out to the house and feeding the cats."

"Eh, Mom?"

"Yes, Dee?"

"I love you."

Develyn could feel the tears stream down her cheeks. "I love you too baby. Delaney, tell me the truth. Are you really OK?"

"Don't worry, I'm not pregnant." Delaney's voice softened. "At least, I don't think so."

● ● ●

Wearing a hunter-green velvet bathrobe she'd borrowed from Lindsay Burdett, Develyn lay across the top of the covers and listened to the deep snores of Casey Cree-Ryder in the twin bed on the other side of the large guest room. She felt the tears trickle down her cheeks.

I'm a pathetic mess, Lord. I suppose you've known that for years. It's just hard to admit. I like it when I can blame others for all my troubles. I came here to clear my head, think things through, find some peace and joy.

But it all got so serious so quick.

Too quick.

Fast horses.

Attentive cowboys.

Menacing rustlers.

Soft kisses.

Very soft kisses.

And then there's Miss Emily.

If I go home now, I'll take more complications than when I came. Maybe when I wake up, things will seem clear. I'm tired . . . too tired. I feel like I could sleep for days.

● ● ●

"Hey, Devy-girl." A pointed finger jabbed her thin ribs. "Are you goin' to sleep all day?"

Develyn sat up in the lower bunk. "Stop it, Dewayne!" she whined.

"Whoa, talk about a bad hair day," the ten-year-old laughed.

Develyn licked her sticky fingers and tried to press down her long brown hair. She scowled at her brother. "Where's Mama and Daddy?"

"Mama walked down to the store to get some eggs, and Daddy rode to Casper with Mr. Tagley to take the radiator to the repair shop."

The slick linoleum felt ice cold. Her "Barbie" flannel nightgown hung past her knees. "You have to go outside," she commanded.

"Why?"

"Because there is only one room in the cabin, and I need to get dressed. Boys can't be in the same room as girls when they get dressed. It's a rule."

"Yeah, well, I got dressed in here an hour ago, and both you and Mama were here."

"That's different. I was asleep and mamas don't count as girls. Now, go on."

"Can't you dress in the bathroom?" he demanded.

"There are spiders! I'm not going in there."

"You'll have to go sometime."

"No, I won't," she snapped.

Dewayne sauntered to the door. "Well, hurry it up. Mr. Homer has got his horses in a pen, and we get to pick out which ones to ride."

Her wide eyes sparkled. "Really? We get to choose? Oh, I want a pretty paint. Will you let me pick first? Please, Dewayne!"

"Yeah, OK, but I don't know if he has a paint horse."

"He just has to. I prayed last night for a paint horse to ride, and I know he will have one."

"Well, hurry up."

Develyn reached down and grabbed the hem of her flannel nightgown.

"Wait!" Dewayne shouted as he flung open the front door. "Don't you know boys aren't supposed to be in the room when girls change their clothes?"

She stuck out her tongue . . . and waited for the door to slam.

● ● ●

Mr. Homer was the most wrinkled man Develyn Upton had ever seen. She and Dewayne bantered that he could hide a pencil in the creases of his face and not find it for days. Mrs. Tagley said he was a Shoshone Indian, but other than his permanent tan he looked just like any old man.

A very old man.

Two dozen horses milled in the corrals near the arena on the west side of town. Develyn had been in such a hurry that she left the cabin barefoot. That was fine in the soft loose dirt on the road, but when they reached the scattered gravel on the parking lot next to the corrals, she made her brother carry her on his back. He plopped her down next to the old man, who wore a long-sleeve white shirt buttoned at the neck and a crisp, narrow-brimmed Stetson.

"Do we really get to choose our own horses?" she squealed.

Mr. Homer leaned against the weathered fence railing and appraised the horses. "I will leave two in the corrals and take the others up north to pasture."

"Do we get to pick any one we want?" Develyn asked.

"Just about any one. Who goes first?"

"I do!" Develyn's hand shot up. "I'm the girl, and I always get to be first."

"I take it you are the youngest, also," the old man mused.

"I'm just six minutes younger than Dewayne. We're twins. Not identical twins, of course."

"Yes, that much I could see. Well, which horse will it be?"

Develyn's smile made her cheeks hurt. "I want that brown and white paint horse. He is the most beautiful horse in the world."

"The paint, huh?"

She bounced up and down on her bare toes. "Oh, yes, please."

The old man shrugged. "Sorry, you can't have him."

"But why?" Develyn cried. "You said I could have any one I wanted."

"Almost any one. Pick another. The paint has some bad habits from his previous owner."

"But I'll treat him nice."

"I'm sure you will, little darlin', but you could also get hurt by what you don't know. I will not let you ride that horse."

Develyn felt her lower lip quiver. "This isn't fair," she whimpered.

"Can I pick first?" Dewayne asked.

"No, it's still my turn. I want that black horse. He looks very fast," she announced.

"You can't have him, either," Mr. Homer reported.

"But . . . but . . . but you promised that . . ."

"Pick another horse. The black horse has a wild streak. He goes along fine for several days, then he's liable to take off running across the prairie. When he does, no one can turn him. Not even the good Lord up above knows where that horse will run."

"This isn't very fun," Develyn pouted. "I don't get to pick a horse at all."

"Pick the brown one," Mr. Homer suggested.

She climbed up on the splintery rail and stared in at the horses. "The one with the black tail?"

"No, that's a bay mare." He waved a gnarly hand at the band of horses. "Pick the one with brown all over."

"But . . . but . . ." Develyn whimpered. "He's so boring. He looks old. I don't want an old horse."

"Brownie will be a good horse for you."

"Brownie? Even his name is boring!" she wailed.

The old man leaned down and whispered in her ear. "Pick Brownie. He'll take care of you. He'll get you to where you want to go. And no matter where you are, he will always bring you back home. You can't find a better horse than that."

"But I don't want a boring horse."

"He is the smartest horse here. He knows more than the rest of the horses put together. I was afraid your brother would pick him. It's only for a couple of days, right?"

She wiped the tears on her dusty cheeks. "He really is the smartest?"

"If horses went to school, Brownie would be the teacher."

"I want to be a teacher, too."

"Well . . . which one do you choose?" Mr. Homer prodded.

Develyn glanced over at her brother who stood on the rail studying the circling horses. She bit her lip. "I pick Brownie," she murmured.

Dewayne mumbled something.

● ● ●

"What did you say?" Develyn demanded.

"I said, 'Wake up, Devy-girl.'"

Sunlight streamed through the open curtains of the guest room. Develyn found herself sitting up in bed staring at a fully dressed Casey Cree-Ryder.

"I've got My Maria and Uncle Henry loaded in my trailer. We'll head home after we eat. Most of the rest are waiting downstairs for you so they can have breakfast."

"Everyone is still here?"

"The sheriff came in about 3:00 a.m. and took the prisoners. Cuban gave Tallon a ride home about daybreak. Renny's been out ridin' a bronc. But I think he'll come in for breakfast with you at the table. Lindsay's in the kitchen, and your Quint is pinin' for his Miss Dev."

"He is?"

"Of course. Now, what was Ms. Worrell dreaming about?"

"Was I dreaming?"

Cree-Ryder scooted over next to the bed. "You sat up and were mumbling something. I just assumed it was a dream."

"It's all kind of vague."

"Were you dreaming about cowboys?"

"No, that wasn't it. I was dreaming about horses."

"Did you learn anything?"

"I think maybe I got some things resolved."

Casey Cree-Ryder raised her thick, black eyebrows. "Are you sure you were dreaming about horses?"

Develyn flopped back down and stared at the ceiling. It felt like every muscle and nerve in her body relaxed at the same moment. "Maybe I wasn't dreaming about horses. Maybe I was dreaming about dreams."

ABOUT THE AUTHOR

STEPHEN BLY has authored ninety-two books, hundreds of articles, and has over one million books in print. His book *The Long Trail Home* (Broadman & Holman) won the 2002 Christy Award for excellence in fiction. His most recent book *Paperback Writer* (Broadman & Holman) has received strong national reviews (*Publisher's Weekly, July 14, 2003, et. al.*). He speaks at colleges, schools, churches, seminars, and conferences across the U.S. and Canada. He has spoken on numerous television and radio programs, including Dr. James Dobson's *Focus On the Family*. He is the pastor of the only church in town, Winchester Community Church. He also serves as the town's mayor. He is an active member of the *Western Writers of America*.

He and his wife, Janet (who is also a writer), live at 4,000 feet elevation in the mountains of north-central Idaho, in the pine trees, next to a lake on the Nez Perce Indian Reservation. The Blys have three sons: Russ, Mike, and Aaron, two daughters-in-law, Lois and Michelle, and two grandchildren, Zachary and Miranda.

He is seldom, if ever, seen without his cowboy boots, hat, and jeans.

He owns two horses . . . Carlos and Sage (the horse formerly known as Prince.)

In 1963 he married the girl who sat behind him in his freshman English class.

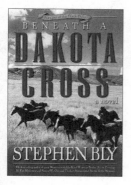
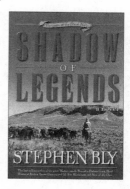
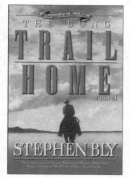
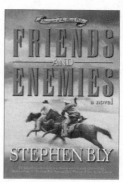

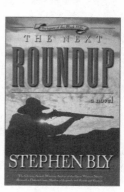

New Contemporary Fiction from Stephen Bly!

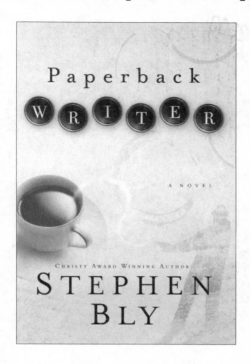

Paperback Writer takes readers into the mind of Paul James Watson, a mildly successful novelist caught between reality and fantasy. After a decade of writing the Distracted Detective series, main character Toby McKenna seems real to Watson—so real that he has imaginary conversations with him! When Watson realizes he has spent too much of his life living through his characters, he embarks on a journey of self-discovery and spiritual re-awakening.

". . . an amusing parody of the proverbial dime-store paperback novel . . . this book is a funny, enjoyable romp . . ." —*Publishers Weekly*

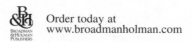

Order today at
www.broadmanholman.com